This book should be retu
Lancashire County Library on or before the date shown

FAMOUS
IN LOVE

Lancashire County Library

30118129783910

FAMOUS
IN LOVE

REBECCA SERLE

MACMILLAN

First published 2014 by Macmillan Children's Books
a division of Macmillan Publishers Limited
20 New Wharf Road, London N1 9RR
Basingstoke and Oxford
Associated companies throughout the world
www.panmacmillan.com

ISBN 978-1-4472-5035-7

Copyright © Rebecca Serle 2014

The right of Rebecca Serle to be identified as the
author of this work has been asserted by her in accordance with the
Copyright, Designs and Patents Act 1988.

All righ
reproduced
transmitted,   l,
photocopyir   1
permission of   ed
act in rel

A CIP

Lancashire Library Services

30118129783910

PETERS	JF
£6.99	28-Nov-2014
CIN	

Printed and bound by CPI Group (UK) Ltd, Croydon CR0 4YY

This book is sold subject to the condition that it shall not,
by way of trade or otherwise, be lent, resold, hired out,
or otherwise circulated without the publisher's prior consent
in any form of binding or cover other than that in which
it is published and without a similar condition including this
condition being imposed on the subsequent purchaser.

This book is a work of fiction. Names, characters, places, and incidents are the
product of the author's imagination or are used fictitiously. Any resemblance
to actual events, locales, or persons, living or dead, is coincidental.

For HBG, who first said I could,

believed it possible,

and never let me go it alone.

In dreams begin responsibilities.

—Delmore Schwartz

PROLOGUE

Listen.

I'll tell you what it's like to be with him. How he kisses me. How he touches my cheek. I'll tell you what he whispers to me before we go out and meet those screaming crowds. How he holds my pinkie, just slightly, so the cameras won't catch us touching. I'll tell you our signals. How blinking once means *it's okay; I'm here*, and how blinking twice means *don't answer that*. I'll tell you everything, but you have to promise never to write it down or repeat it. You have to promise it will be our secret.

Sometimes, during an interview, I'm caught with this intense desire to tell the truth. We'll be right there in the middle of talking about my favorite brand of jeans or something, and I'll want to slip out of my chair onto the floor, sit cross-legged, and just spill. It's my nature. I've always been someone who's quick to trust. I told Holly Anderson freshman year that my sister was pregnant, and by lunchtime the entire class knew. I don't know why I expected her to keep that secret for me, since we weren't even friends, but something inside me was compelled to let her in. I like to let people in. Which is why it's so ridiculous that it's the one thing I absolutely, positively cannot do anymore. These questions have already been answered. The publicist stands by with a clipboard, toeing the carpet and checking her watch manically, like the minute hand is a slow toddler she's trying to hurry up.

"Seven," I say, nodding, because we're working on an endorsement deal with them. I haven't been allowed to wear a single other brand of jeans for the last six months.

"I like them, too," the interviewer says. She winks at me, like we're in on something together, and I suddenly realize I've forgotten her name. I'm not sure I've ever learned it, actually. The only name that matters is mine.

We leave and I round the corner, and then he's there, walking toward me. He's flanked on either side by people—Wyatt and Sandy and two girls I don't recognize—but he sees me, and our eyes lock for a moment. I can't touch him. The only thing I want to do is run to him and have him put his arms around me, to take me someplace that isn't here. Someplace it's just the two of us and none of this matters. But I can't do that because no one knows. Not Wyatt and not Sandy, not even Cassandra. They think we're just friends—that I belong to someone else. They don't know that I've made a huge mistake. They don't know that, like August, I chose wrong.

CHAPTER 1

"You're famous, Patrick." Jake winks at me, and I roll my eyes. It's this running joke we've had since fifth grade, when I was in a production of *The Three Stooges* our school put on. I played the little boy, and for the rest of the year everyone referred to me as Patrick, which honestly isn't even that close to Paige, but whatever. Most people in my class weren't that creative.

I follow it up the same way I always have: "Hey, at least I'm known for something."

The truth is I've always been a little bit different. Like the button on a coat that doesn't line up with its hole. The youngest of four children, a native Portlander with serious seasonal affective disorder, I just...don't fit. Not in my family and not with my hometown. Sometimes not even with Jake, who for the last twenty minutes has been lecturing me about the serious health ramifications of consuming dairy. He's stopped only because there is a poster for my latest stage play up in the entryway of Powell's. We put it there last month. I'm surprised they haven't taken it down yet.

Jake and I have been superclose since we were in diapers, but we're polar opposites. He's quiet and intellectual and a real wizard—he's going to change the world someday. I am pretty talkative and do well in school, but I have to work hard at it. I've never had the natural talent Jake has for biology or chemistry. Or, to be fair, any other subject.

Except theater.

"Why do you still not have a proper head shot?" Cassandra says. She pulls on one of her pigtails and raises her eyebrows at me. She's tiny, but her personality is massive, as is her hair—a gigantic mess of blond curls that never seems to stay just on her head. It makes no sense that she's not the actress of our dynamic trio. She acts like she's constantly onstage. She did even when we were five years old, which is how long I've known her. But she wants to be a marine biologist.

"Jake said he'd take them," I say, staring at the flyer. There is no photo by my name, only a blank space. Paige Who. I asked Jake to take the pictures at least a month ago, but he's had sit-ins almost every weekend.

Jake is always protesting stuff. Plastic, buildings, the cutting down of trees, popcorn. The stuff at the movie theater is genetically engineered. We lost a week of our lives to those kernels.

Cassandra gives Jake a pitying look and turns to me. "If your career is in his hands, you're going to end up in waste management." Jake tries to interrupt, but Cassandra keeps talking. "The point is, I'll do them." She swings her purse around and takes something out. "I got a new camera."

"No way." Jake bounces it out of her hands, and Cassandra squeals. "How did you pull this off?" he asks.

"Babysitting," she says proudly.

"Nice. We should take some shots at the rally next week. I bet if we get good ones we could submit them to the paper."

"Another rally?" I ask. I try to keep the disappointment out of my voice, but I'm not working that hard.

Jake looks at me with that somber expression I know too well. "They will stop when pollution stops, when animals are treated kindly. When human beings start taking responsibility for themselves and this planet."

"Sorry," I mumble.

I always feel bad about not supporting Jake in his latest quest. I mean, I want the world to be a better place, too. It's just that sometimes I also want to go to the movies.

Cassandra slides her arm around my shoulder and turns me back to the board. "Maybe the Aladdin is playing something good this weekend."

We scan the flyers, but I'm only halfheartedly looking. I'm watching Jake fiddle with Cassandra's camera. I haven't seen him this excited about anything since Starbucks started using biodegradable materials.

"Oh my God!" Cassandra shrieks, and my hands fly to my ears. Jake almost drops the camera.

"What is with you?" he asks her.

"Look look look!" She's pointing at the board. "Are you seeing this?"

I follow her finger. It's a flyer for *Locked*, the book Cassandra is obsessed with. Well, three books, actually. It's a trilogy, but only two have been released so far. They're huge. Crazy, international best sellers. They're written by a woman named Parker Witter, about this girl who lands on a magical deserted island after a plane crash. The boy who survives with her (who happens to be her boyfriend's best friend) has some kind of supernatural connection to the island, and they fall in love. But she's also still in love with her boyfriend, who she thinks is dead, since all three of them were on the plane together. I haven't read the books yet, but I did do a little Googling after Cassandra wouldn't shut up about them. The stuff that exists online is intense. Hundreds of thousands of videos on YouTube, community boards, endless fan fiction. Noah and August are the new Romeo and Juliet, apparently. Cassandra waited in line at Barnes & Noble at midnight the day the second one went on sale. The third and final book is supposed to come out in November.

"They're holding auditions *here*!" Cassandra squeals. She dances around on her tiptoes in a semicircle.

I squint at the flyer.

"Auditions for what?" Jake says, handing her back the camera.

"The movie."

My stomach does a little flip, in time with Cassandra's feet, and I look up to see her smirking at me. "Interested now?"

Even though we're in Portland, a city that draws a big artistic crowd, movies are rarely shot here, and casting directors never come looking for talent. Movie auditions are for people who live in Los Angeles—and I've never even been there.

I've begged my parents to let me go to California, but they always say it's a distraction from my studies. What they really mean is that I'm the youngest of four and as far as they're concerned a plane ticket without a direct link to a wedding or funeral just isn't practical.

That doesn't mean I don't go on auditions here; I do, but it's mostly for community theater stuff, like the non-head-shot poster we were looking at. But a real film? I've never had that opportunity before.

When I do get things—a play or a local commercial or something—I'm pretty much always cast as a child, even though I'm seventeen. I feel like I've been playing the same role for a decade. I'm barely five feet tall, which is short even for twelve-year-olds. I have long, true-red hair that is just a little bit wavy—not totally curly, not straight—and my face is spotted with freckles, which doesn't exactly scream leading lady. But the rug rat younger sister? I have that one down. I wonder if there's a sibling in *Locked*.

"Where is it?" I ask. I glance down to show that I don't really care, but since it's Jake and Cassandra, no one is buying the attempted nonchalance.

"Saturday at the Aladdin." Jake rips the flyer down and hands it to me.

"Someone else might want to see that," I say.

"So consider it lessening the competition." Cassandra loops her arm through mine. "Promise you'll think about it."

She smiles at me, and I know she knows I'll be there. But she's also aware of my golden rule about auditions: I never tell anyone I'm going.

Maybe it's something about being the youngest in a big family, but I expect disappointment. The unspoken motto of our house: If you stay closer to the ground, you have less distance to fall. It worked for my parents, I guess. They're both elementary school teachers, which is a great thing in and of itself, but I don't think it's what either of them actually wanted. My mom wanted to be an actress. She was in a few regional productions when she was younger, but nothing since my oldest brother was born. She never talks about it, but I know she has regrets. One time I was looking for a necklace in her jewelry box and came across this envelope filled with theater tickets. Plays and shows my mom had gone to. There were even ones from the seventies in there, back when my parents weren't together yet. Maybe from things she was in. I'm not sure you would hold on to that stuff if you didn't wish your life had turned out a little differently. And me? I don't want a bunch of theater tickets stuffed into an envelope at the bottom of my jewelry box. I want framed posters with my name on them. Those are the kinds of reminders I want. The ones other people can see.

Jake slings his arm over my shoulder. "You'd be an amazing August," he tells me.

"August?" I cock one eyebrow at him.

"What?" he says, his droopy smile growing. "I like to stay informed of pop culture."

"You can't even believe how good it is," Cassandra says, threading her fingers through one of her looped curls. "I have no idea how I'm waiting until November to find out how it all ends."

Jake nods.

"Seriously?" I say. "You two need to start a support group."

"I'm already in one," Cassandra says. "We meet on Sundays. Tuesdays if it's been a particularly bad week of withdrawal."

Jake laughs; I roll my eyes. "You're crazy."

"But you love me," she coos, her nose pressed up against my cheek.

"In spite of," I say.

"Hey," she says, pulling back. "These are great pieces of literature."

"That's what you said about *From Heaven*. And those books were just about horny angels."

"*Guardian* angels," Cassandra corrects, tossing a pigtail over her shoulder. "It's not my fault you don't appreciate great novels."

"I appreciate them," I say.

"Just because you've read *The Glass Menagerie* seventy-two times doesn't make it a book. Sorry." Cassandra wrinkles her nose at me.

"Yeah, but it's still a great work of literature," I snap back.

It's not that I don't read novels. I do, just not in the

same way I read screenplays. I mean, I love Jane Austen and I've probably read *The Catcher in the Rye* about seven times since eighth grade, but most of what I read are scripts. I've read pretty much every one Powell's has ever stocked, which is a lot. They have everything from *Rosemary's Baby* to *Pitch Perfect*, and I like to sit there on rainy Sundays and pick up whatever shooting scripts they've just got in. Some of them I even know by heart, and folding the first page back is kind of like hearing the first few notes of your favorite song on the radio. The one you know all the words to. When I was younger I used to recite lines in front of my bedroom mirror. Scarlett O'Hara, Holly Golightly. I'd pretend I was Audrey Hepburn or Meryl Streep and I was making a movie the world would see.

Sometimes I still do.

"What do you guys want to do this afternoon?" Cassandra asks.

I glance at my watch, a gift from Jake for my fifteenth birthday. It has Mickey Mouse on the face, and his gloved hands mark the hour and minute. Jake had it engraved: *From the cat to the mouse*. They used to be our Halloween costumes every year. He'd dress up as a cat and I'd be a mouse, and he'd chase me all over the streets when we went out trick-or-treating. Sometimes I imagine us getting together, later, and it taking on a new meaning. Him saying something like, "I chased you for years, and now you're finally mine." Silly, I know, but it would be a great story.

For the record, we've kissed twice but not since freshman year. Jake was my first kiss, actually, and the only guy I've ever touched lips to except for this one kid at summer camp. We're not together, though. We never have been. I don't think either one of us is willing to risk our friendship over it—and besides, the thought of actually making him my boyfriend feels like an equation that just doesn't add up.

"I have to get to work," I say. I've spent every summer since seventh grade working at Trinkets n' Things, a boutique that sells all kinds of knickknacks and, like the rest of Portland, smells like patchouli. I come home reeking of incense, but it's a good gig. The pay is decent, and it never gets too crowded.

"Any interest in seeing a movie?" Cassandra nudges Jake, and he drops his arm from around my shoulder.

"Just not that documentary about Buddhism again, okay? We've seen it three times now."

"Whatever. You're the one who wanted to see it the third time." She blinks at me, and I know it's supposed to be a wink. She can never figure out how to close one eye at a time. It's one of the things I love most about her.

I mean, there are a lot of things I love. Like that she doesn't know how to hopscotch and her favorite colors are always ones she makes up: honeyberry, cricket green, clown-nose red. I love that she always used to tell me when I had something stuck in my braces. She's honest. We have no secrets. We never have.

"Have fun, kids," I say.

Jake gives me a little salute, Cassandra plants a wet kiss on my cheek, and the two of them dart toward the exit. I stare at the crumpled poster in my hand and then shove it into my pocket, following their trail outside and down to Trinkets n' Things. I don't need to look at the audition details; I've already memorized them. I also know I'll make up an excuse to my boss, Laurie, and go on Saturday. The flyer says the auditions begin at three, but I'm certain people will be lining up hours before.

I know there's no chance. I know that the odds of actually landing a role like this are one in a number I can't even count to, but the same thing happens every time I go out for a part. I feel a little...hopeful. Like this time might be the time things change. Like after this weekend, everything might be different.

CHAPTER 2

I can hear my niece, Annabelle, crying as soon as I walk in the door. I don't know what it is about that kid, but she's always bawling. Her sheer unwillingness to be ignored is actually kind of impressive. She's not even two yet, but it's like she already knows that in order to make it in this house she's going to have to announce herself, and if she knows that much, she's way ahead of the game.

"Anyone home?" I drop my bookbag down on a stool in our kitchen.

"Paye!" Annabelle yells.

My sister, Joanna, comes running down the stairs, Annabelle tucked underneath her arm like a football. "Have you seen Mom?" Joanna asks. Her face is red, and her hair looks damp.

"No, just got home." I turn my head upside down and look at Annabelle. "Hey, you."

Annabelle puts on this goofy grin and reaches out her tiny, chubby arms. I swing her out of Joanna's arms and into mine.

My sister seems to crumble as soon as I take Annabelle, her shoulders sagging down by her collapsed sides.

"What's up, Jo? You okay?"

"Okay!" Annabelle parrots.

My sister and I are the two siblings left in the house. Both of our older brothers have moved out. There is talk of Bill, my sister's boyfriend and Annabelle's father, moving in, but he recently started community college and his parents' house is closer to school. His family won't let Joanna move in with them, so for now he visits her and Annabelle on the weekends. Here's a fun fact: When you're nineteen and have a kid and no money, your parents control a lot more than you'd like them to.

My sister ignores the question and looks me up and down. "Where have you been?"

Ever since she got pregnant, Joanna has considered herself to be totally grown up. She had this huge belly at her high school graduation, and yet she was instructing me on how to clean my room and how not to come home after curfew. As if becoming a mom made her my mom, too.

I shrug. "Trinkets n' Things."

She eyes me. "What were you doing?"

"Selling drugs out the back door."

Joanna rolls her eyes and flops onto the couch. "Mom was supposed to come home an hour ago."

"I'm not sure what to tell you." I rub my hand in small circles over Annabelle's back, but she just blinks a few times and then starts crying again. Joanna picks herself up off the couch and snatches Annabelle out of my hands.

Joanna sighs. "Look, just tell Mom I left."

She hooks her bag over her arm, shifts Annabelle, and heads out the door. Annabelle waves as they go, her hand like a duck beak, a tear rolling down her cheek.

After they leave, the house is dead silent. The quiet feels strange to me. When I was growing up, our house was filled with kids, and the older I got, the more people were around. My brothers always had friends over, and by the time I got to fifth grade, Joanna was already attached to Bill.

I hoist my bag on my shoulder and plod my way upstairs. Once I'm in my room, I take the flyer out of my pocket, smooth the edges down flat on the carpet, and look at it.

There is a black-and-white picture of a girl on the front, but she's in silhouette, so it's hard to make out any details about who she is or what she looks like. Printed across the top of the page are the words OPEN CASTING CALL FOR

LOCKED. They give me goose bumps. It's the same feeling I get in an auditorium or a movie theater right when the lights go down. Like maybe that could be me up there. That someday people might know my name, even recognize me. That I wouldn't be little Paige, the runt of the Townsen litter. I'd just be Paige Townsen: the one and only. That feeling of possibility. Of the fact that right here and right now, everything could change.

The odds of my getting this part are practically nonexistent, I know that, but still, someone has to. Why not me?

My cell phone lights up. It's Cassandra. She's talking even before I say hello.

"... I think I fell asleep halfway through."

"The movie?"

She huffs, like *duh*. "What are you doing tonight?"

I fold the flyer over in my hands, embarrassed to even be holding it. What I'm doing is practicing. What I'm doing is reading that book cover to cover.

"I'm kind of tired," I say.

"Laurie make you stock shelves?"

"Yes," I lie. The truth is I did nothing but play thumb war with myself behind the register. We had only two customers come in today, and neither one bought anything.

"Jake is here," Cassandra says. I hear some rustling and whispering, and then she comes back on the phone. "Maybe we'll stop by later?"

I picture Jake turning down the cell. He's petrified of radiation and refuses to even carry one, which makes meeting up kind of difficult. Luckily he's usually with one of us already.

"Sounds good," I say.

Jake shouts good-bye—Cassandra must have held the phone out—and then it clicks off.

I hear my dad's car pull into the driveway. I don't have to look out my window to know he's opening the car door, walking around the back to get his briefcase, checking both car mirrors, then the tires, then clicking the lock twice, and walking in the door. He does the same routine every day and has been probably since he could drive. I imagine my dad going through the whole thing when they pulled into the hospital on the nights my siblings and I were born. Did my mom yell? In all my years of seeing my dad's parking regimen, I've never once heard her try to hurry him up.

I walk out onto the landing and see him come in. My dad wears a bow tie every day. He even has some of those tweed jackets with the elbow patches on them.

"You look like a teacher," I tell him.

He looks up and smiles. "Funny you should say that. I just came from school."

"It's summer vacation," I say, making my way downstairs, "haven't you heard?"

"Curriculums rest for no man."

My dad is the only member of my family who gets me. He's also the quietest person I know. I never realized he was a morning person until I joined the swim team sophomore year and had to wake up early for practice. I came downstairs one morning at five AM to find him sipping from a coffee cup. He was so still the air around him could have been water and he wouldn't even have made a ripple.

He smiles at me when I reach the last step. "Where's your sister?"

I try to remember where she said she was going. I shrug and follow him into the kitchen. "Dunno."

Unlike the rest of my family, my dad doesn't discourage my acting ambitions. My sister thinks I'm too self-involved; my brothers don't understand it because it's not a team sport. My mom thinks acting is best reserved for daydreams and the occasional community production, not for "real life."

My dad, though. My dad has never told me outright what he thinks, but I feel his support. I've often heard him say that parenting is like a building. One person has to be the height; the other, the foundation. My dad isn't a tall man, but he's a solid one. With four children, if you're the base, you're pretty well cemented in there.

He gives me a little nod and heads into his bedroom. He'll spend the afternoon fixing whatever is broken around the house. He does all the upkeep himself, always has.

I crane my neck to make sure my sister isn't pulling into the driveway, and then go to her bookshelf and run my hand across the spines until I find her copy of *Locked*. I don't know why I'm being so sneaky about it. It's not like she wouldn't let me borrow it or anything. It's just that I feel like if she saw me she'd somehow know. She'd put it together and then when I didn't get the part it would be further confirmation that my dreams are stupid and shallow and totally unrealistic. I don't really need any more of that in our house. And yet—

What would you sacrifice for love?

The one line, printed across the top of the back cover, makes my heart speed up to a sprint. I take it to my room and close the door. I pull the flyer out from underneath my bed and hold them both in my hands. The girl on the book cover has her back turned, but unlike on the flyer, you can tell her hair is red. It tumbles down her back and looks like it runs right into the waves of the ocean. They surround her, about to swallow her whole.

I open to the first page, and then I start to read.

CHAPTER 3

Saturday goes by absurdly slowly. There are even fewer people in Trinkets n' Things than there were during the week, and Laurie has decided to take the day to lead an aromatherapy workshop in the back room. I wonder if anyone has ever died from a sandalwood overdose.

I finished the first book yesterday morning—read it straight through in one sitting. And the truth is I get why Cassandra hasn't been able to stop talking about the romance, and why it seems the entire world hasn't put the books down. They're phenomenal. And the love story is just so, so good. It's the ultimate fantasy. August and Noah, her longtime crush and boyfriend's best friend, are the only surviving members of a plane crash that had her boyfriend and younger sister on board. They learn

Noah is a descendant of the island and its people—a position that comes with power. The power to heal August after she's almost killed by the crash and—I won't ruin it for you. Let's just say love isn't easy, even when you're the sole survivors of a plane crash and you have the hots for each other.

I jump back in and make it halfway through the second book before asking Laurie if I can head out a little early. She says yes, of course. Actually what she says is, "It's Saturday. No one comes in on Saturday."

I close the door to the back room behind me and loop the keys around the hook by the tarot card shelf. I grab my bag from behind the counter, and as I'm leaning down I catch a reflection of myself in the mirror—my hair whipped around my face, my cheeks flushed and red. For just a moment, I don't recognize myself. I could be anyone. Even August.

Droves of girls are wandering around when I get there. It's not surprising, but the sight is pretty spectacular. There must be a thousand people outside the Aladdin. The last time I saw this many people in one place was when my brother took me to a Muse concert freshman year. We don't really spend a lot of time together. My brothers and I, I mean. There was a period when my sister was kind of close with them, but I think by the time I came around the novelty of having a sister had long worn off. I remember being really surprised Jeff would want me to go. It turned out, once we got there, that he just wanted me to watch the car, because free parking was really hard to come by. "You can sit here and listen to the music," he said. I didn't even say anything, totally afraid I'd burst right into tears, and afterward, when he dropped me off at home and my mom asked me how it was, I lied and said great. Telling her the truth somehow seemed too humiliating.

I work my way inside the audition space. There seem to be two lines. One for people who have registered and one for people who haven't. The nonregistered line is way, way shorter. The majority of people, unlike myself, have prepared for this. Everyone else already has their forms, and they are filling them out on clipboards. They're sitting in chairs, lining the floor, leaning against the walls.

Most of the girls are with their mothers, and for a slight second I feel a wave of familiar sadness. My mom and I have gone to exactly two auditions together. The first was for a cereal commercial when I was seven. I remember I saw the flyer in the grocery store and begged her to take me. She didn't want to, but eventually my father convinced her it wasn't a terrible idea, and maybe I'd make a little money in the process. I got all dressed up in my best dress and the shoes my mom had bought me for Christmas that year, and we went, hand in hand.

We didn't even make it into the audition, though. My mom took one look at the other girls and decided we weren't going to "play," as she put it. "It's a beauty pageant," she'd said. "There is absolutely no way we're participating."

I've always gone to auditions alone, and in secret. She supports school- and theater-related projects, mostly because she thinks they are somehow "academic," but anything with film she's been against pretty much from the beginning.

I make my way to the reception desk, where a woman with a smile like a line hands me a sheet of paper. I take the form and fill it out on the edge of the table, careful to hand it back to her with a smile. She gives me a number in return and waves me off. There are no seats available, so I lean on the wall and put in my headphones.

For my birthday this spring, Jake made me audio recordings of all my favorite films. He even put them on my iPod. I can listen to *Empire Records* while I'm biking home from school or walking to work.

Today I choose a recording of *Singin' in the Rain*. It's corny, but I've always loved classic movies. There is something about seeing the screen without a ton of CGI or animation that just feels so cinematic. Important. Like the work those actors were doing meant something.

The sound of Gene Kelly's voice sweeps over me, and I sit back against the wall, knees tucked up to my chest.

I let myself think about what it would be like to get this part. To be in a real film. To prove to my family that this is more than an adolescent fantasy.

I let myself think about what it would be like to actually live my dream.

And just like that, I'm Debbie Reynolds. My eyes slip closed, and when she speaks, it's me. On the stage. In the spotlight. So much so that when they call my name and I hand over my number, hours later, I'm still singing my heart out. And when I read the lines, it's like I'm Debbie Reynolds reading the lines. And when they call this man in, this beautiful, tall, blond guy to read with me, it's like he really is Gene Kelly. And when they ask us to do the scene together, it's like we're in the film and it's raining all around us. A soft, steady pitter-patter.

"I'm Rainer." He holds out his hand to me, and I take it. He pulls me toward him, and before I've had time to even say my name, we've begun. We're August and Noah. And it feels right. No, it feels better than right. It feels perfect. It feels like every moment of my life has been leading to this one.

It's not until the audition finishes, what feels like days later, and I go outside that I realize it's actually raining. And the funny thing is I've lived in Portland my entire life and this is the first time I can remember ever forgetting an umbrella.

Three months later, we're on the set.

CHAPTER 4

"August and Noah are already household names, and soon Paige Townsen will be, too. The bestselling book series Locked is coming to life on the big screen, and we have the first pictures from set, where filming is already underway. Townsen will play August, the mortal girl caught between her human boyfriend, Ed, and supernatural crush, Noah. Rainer Devon, best known for his work in *Over You*, will play Noah. The role of Ed hasn't been cast yet.

David and Mark Hess penned the script, with Wyatt Lippman directing."

Rainer reads from the trades, and I crane over him to try to reach for it. "Watch yourself, PG," he says, and I snatch it out of his hands.

"Please," I say. "Can't we have five minutes in the morning without this stuff?"

Even though this is only our third week on set—and

we'll be here for a few months—it seems like we've clocked close to a thousand hours together. I pull my robe tighter around me and sip the coffee that has just been set down. There is a nice, cool breeze, and if you sit outside, like we are on the balcony of Rainer's condo, you can see all the way down to the ocean.

We're in Hawaii, by the way.

There were two more rounds of auditions in Portland, and then a trip to L.A. to meet and audition for the studio and about one hundred producers. There was the hiring of an agent and a lawyer and rounds and rounds of negotiations and more documents with my name on them than could fill a library. But I got the part. And the beautiful guy, Mr. Gene Kelly, and I landed in Maui to start filming *Locked*. The love story that has taken the world by storm. And I'm playing the lead. It still doesn't feel real, despite the evidence all around me.

The book is set on an island in the Pacific Northwest, but Hawaii was offering tax breaks that would allow us to start shooting almost immediately, so here we are. Beaches, palm trees. We've even turned an old plantation house into a soundstage and built the one set we have, the little hut Noah and August share on the island. They've rented nearly an entire hotel of condos for the cast and crew. It's where we're all staying and where a lot of the various offices and departments are—editorial, hair and makeup, props....

Rainer clucks his tongue. "Should we move our tabloid time to lunch, then?" He looks at me, an eyebrow raised.

"Funny," I say.

"*Charming,*" he says, shrugging. "But close."

Rainer and I are lovers. No, actually: Noah and August are lovers. Not us. We're just friends. He was the first one cast and the guy I read with in Portland. He's the producer's son and has been acting his entire life. Not theater, like me, but real movies. Television and film. The big stuff. He was in a movie last year with that actress Taylor, where they played neighbors whose parents get killed in a car crash, but it turns out to not be an accident. I'm not ruining this because I think every person on the planet saw it twice, but the big twist was that Taylor's character's parents actually killed Rainer's. They still ended up together, though. He saved her from her parents and then whisked her off to Europe with the inheritance his parents had left him. They changed their names and bought a villa.

The producers keep telling us to be prepared, that these roles are going to change our lives, but I'm not sure how his could get any bigger. He's already known as Hollywood's golden guy, and I've made a promise to Cassandra that if he's single, I will fly her out here to be his girlfriend. I don't think he is, though. How could he be?

He's famous and gorgeous and has the cutest dimple on the right side of his face. He's got shaggy blond locks and beautiful blue eyes, and his body looks like a superhero's. Guys like that are never single. It's, like, a fact of life. Or, you know, science.

There's also the slight issue that he's older. Twenty-two to Cassandra's (and my) seventeen. Even though he's playing a teenager, I hardly think he'd fall for one.

I look away from him. We've become good friends, it's true, but I don't share his nonchalance on set. I feel out of my element here, and not just because I've never done a movie before. This thing is on another level. The pressure to make August real, to make her loved, is something that stays with me from the moment I wake up until the moment I go to sleep. Rainer keeps telling me to relax, but I think that's easy for him to say. He's used to this.

Seriously, if you Google him, there are sixty-one million results, and that's not even counting news, blogs, or image searches. Up until a month ago if you Googled me all you saw was one track race I qualified for, and the news clipping for the production of *The Sound of Music* I was in. If you clicked on the link, though, the page had expired.

Locked—the first book, anyway—is mostly August and Noah on the island alone together. As they fig　 out why they're there, and how to survive, they begin love. There are a few smaller roles that they've cast, and we'll film those scenes near the end of shooting. They're still looking to cast someone to play Ed, August's boyfriend, who she thinks died in the plane crash. We won't meet him for a few weeks, at the earliest. For now it's just me and Rainer, alone in Hawaii. Well, us and the entire movie crew—which occasionally includes the author, Parker Witter. I've seen her around a bit, but from what I've heard, she's a recluse. She hasn't so much as spoken to us once since we've been here.

"How did you sleep?" Rainer asks me, rolling his neck out.

He's wearing a Hawaiian shirt that would look goofy on most people, totally corny on others, and maybe, at best, ironic on some, but on him it looks completely right. That's the thing about Rainer—everything he does is totally right. He's effortless on set. You can never see the work.

I lie, but it comes out a little sarcastic anyway. "Awesome."

Rainer cocks his head to the side. "It's that damn ocean, right? So noisy. I'll get Jessica to do something about it."

Jessica is the director's assistant. She's twenty-three and beautiful. The kind of girl you cross a room for just to be closer to her. Long blond hair and even longer legs.

She doesn't sweat, even in eighty-degree beach heat, or get bags under her eyes after an eight-hour night shoot. She also happens to be one of the nicest people I've ever met. She bought me a visor when I first got to Hawaii with the date of the shoot and LOCKED written on it. Stenciled in the corner was the movie logo, a cowrie shell—the necklace that August wears.

"Where is the espresso around here?" Sandy, Rainer's manager, appears at the screen door. As usual she is impeccably dressed and, despite the breeze, not a hair on her head is out of place.

When it really comes down to it, Sandy is the one who got me the part. She convinced my mom. It wasn't easy, but Sandy assured her she'd be around and that she'd look out for me. My mom considered coming herself, but I knew, in the end, she'd never leave her job, or Annabelle.

Sandy came with us for the first few days here and has been in L.A. since. I haven't seen her in over two weeks. I guess Sandy has kind of been acting as my manager. Everyone in L.A. has a manager.

Wyatt, our director, is on her heels, and I instantly freeze up. I'm still in my bathrobe, and Wyatt isn't exactly the most comfortable person to be around.

"You have to call the front desk," Wyatt answers. "The craft service stuff is poison." He's got on black jeans, a black T-shirt, and sneakers—a signature ensemble that

33

seems to say being in Hawaii is a serious inconvenience for him, not a privilege. And it's not just his style that resists the tropics. Even his hair, a self-proclaimed Jewfro, seems to be in retaliation against warm weather.

"We're starting at ten," Wyatt says. "I can't believe it takes six goddamn hours to fix the lighting in a room."

"You want a water?" Rainer asks. He's still his normal, relaxed self, but he stands up when Wyatt appears. He holds out a bottle.

"No," Wyatt says. He turns to me. "Shouldn't you be in hair and makeup?" I feel my face get hot, and my palms start sweating.

I open my mouth to answer, but Rainer jumps in. "It's my fault. I wouldn't let her leave." He glances at me sideways. "But yeah, kid, go fix your face." I get a wink.

"Thanks," I say. It's sarcasm, but I mean it. Another lecture from Wyatt is not what I need this morning. Although it could be worse. It could be on set, in front of everyone, the way it normally is.

Despite the fact that it's just Rainer and me acting, there are still eight million people on the set. Editors and production assistants and line producers. Lighting guys and stunt coordinators. There are so many people I'd need ten spiral notebooks just to keep track. I'm learning, slowly. It's a little like being tossed into college from kindergarten. Luckily I have Rainer to guide me through.

The crew loves him, and he's always pranking everyone. He's put plastic wrap on the sound-stage toilet seats at least three times.

"C'mon, PG. I'll walk with you," Rainer says.

When they did the press release revealing who would be playing August, the media latched on to the fact that I was an unknown. Latched hard. They've been calling me PG because of my "squeaky-clean image." I pointed out to Cassandra on the phone that I am not exactly squeaky. It's just that I haven't had the opportunity to get dirty yet, which sounded wrong. The point is Rainer now calls me PG, and I'd probably find it annoying if it weren't for that right-sided dimple of his. It makes it hard to get legitimately mad.

Sandy flicks her wrist, her Rolex landing dead center. "Yeah," she says. "Lillianna is already down there."

"I'm ready," Rainer says. He stands behind my chair, ready to pull it out for me.

I set my coffee cup down and wipe the back of my hand across my lips. I glance at Wyatt, but he's not paying attention to us. He's leaning over the railing, looking up at the clouds and down at the beach. Trying to get a read on the weather today. I know he's only in here because of Sandy, anyway.

She turns us both around by the shoulders and marches us through the suite, out the hallway, into the elevator, and down the two flights to hair and makeup.

"Sit, hon," Lillianna instructs. Rainer and I take our seats, and Sandy turns to leave.

"I'll see you guys on set," she calls over her shoulder.

"What if we need you?" Rainer teases. "Where will you be?"

Sandy stops, hands on her hips. "Give me a break."

"Where will you be?"

"You know where I'll be," she says, rolling her eyes.

"Just tell me," he says. He winks at me.

"Starbucks," she says through gritted teeth.

Rainer pumps his fist. "Every time. Why don't you just tell someone you hate the coffee here?"

Sandy glances at Lillianna, and then back at Rainer. "Just do your job, and I'll do mine."

She leaves, a whirlwind of cream-colored silk, and I sink down into my chair. It's only eight AM.

"We've got our work cut out for us today, love," Lillianna says, surveying my bed head.

Lillianna isn't just the hair-and-makeup woman; she's also our resident gossip. She's from Hawaii, born and raised, and she's been working on movies that film here since she was a teenager, almost fifty years ago. My first day she told me about the time she took a moonlit walk on the beach with Cary Grant. "I was a kid," she said. "I didn't even realize he probably wanted to kiss me." I didn't mention that almost everyone thinks he was actually gay.

She's pulling and attacking my hair, but the sound of her smooth voice and the comfort of the seat begin to lull me to sleep. I'm not getting much rest lately and sometimes, as embarrassing as it is to admit, the makeup session doubles as a nap.

What feels like a moment later, I'm nodding awake, wiping some obvious drool off the corner of my mouth. Rainer is gone, but Jessica is standing over me. She's fresh and bright in a light-pink tank top and denim shorts. "How's it going?" she asks. I can tell what she means is *why aren't you finished yet?*

"If your cute behind would stop interrupting, we'd be on schedule," Lillianna says.

Jessica blushes, and I bite my lip at her as if to say sorry.

"Got it," she says. She leaves the way she came, mumbling something into her headset.

I turn around to look at Lillianna. She's armed with a can of hair spray and a tub of makeup mud. She smiles and extends her supplies-laden arms. "Ready to get dirty, hon?"

I nod.

You know how at the dentist's office, the hygienist always waits until she has your mouth open, tubes sticking in and out and a metal pick hassling your gums, before she starts asking you how school is? Lillianna is kind of the same way.

"Tell me about the boys."

"What boys?" I mumble, my mouth half open as she paints my cheeks.

"The ones at home, the ones here." She clicks her tongue on the roof of her mouth a few times and moves her ample hips.

"There is only one here," I point out.

"Oh hon, but he's a good one."

I laugh. Lillianna is more boy crazy at seventy than most of my friends at seventeen. Well, besides maybe Cassandra. All Lillianna does is talk about how if she were fifty years younger, she'd never let Rainer out of her chair.

"I'm sure he has a girlfriend," I say. "You've seen him, right?"

Rainer acts single. I think. It's hard to tell. I wouldn't call him flirtatious, he's just being friendly, but he's never brought up his romantic status with me.

Lillianna waves me off. "That one, Britney? She's got nothin' on you."

"Who's Britney?"

Lillianna steps back and places a hand on her hip. "You ever pick up a proper magazine?"

"Not really."

"Britney Drake. Pop star, that's what they call her. Chin up."

I pop my head back into place. "Britney, huh?" I've heard of her. I want to say she was a Disney kid, but I'm not sure.

"If he knew what was good for him, he'd run in the other direction. Word is she's two-timing him with Jordan Wilder," Lillianna says. She holds an eyebrow pencil over me. "Any boys at home?"

I think about Jake briefly. "No. Just friends."

"Just a friend?"

I shrug. "There's this guy. We kissed. But we've known each other forever. It's not like that."

I have no idea why I've told her this. Stupid. I can never keep quiet. It's not like Lillianna is going to run to *Star* magazine, but I shouldn't be talking to anyone about anything. Sandy has been really specific about that part.

Lillianna eyes me. "How come you're never talking to him?"

"He's not that into phones," I say.

Lillianna crouches down in front of me so our eyes are level. "I never heard of a man who didn't want to speak to his sweetheart if he could. Sounds like he's not worth your time." She stands back up, puts her hands on her hips, and surveys me, then nods in approval. "All right, hon, we're all done here."

A familiar feeling of dread lands in my abdomen like a bird on the water. Every day on set feels like a giant audition, even though I already got the part. I know I need to relax—Rainer is right—but I have no idea how.

"Thank you," I say.

"You're welcome. You ever need someone to knock some sense into that boy, you let me know. I could get anyone on the phone." She raises her eyebrows at me. I kind of believe her.

The sun is blazing when I get outside. I walk down to set repeating the same words I chant every day in my head. *They chose you. You can do this. You belong here.*

CHAPTER 5

When I get down to the beach, Wyatt is squinting into the sun, talking to Camden, our cinematographer, about camera angles. Filming at the beach sounds sexy and sun-kissed and windblown but in reality is really just technical and itchy. It's a constant battle to get the right angle, to have the right amount of sand and dirt, to hit your mark without a gust of wind blowing or a wave coming in.

Rainer is a pro at it. I swear the elements sort of fold at his whim. I've seen it turn from pouring rain to blasting sun in a matter of seconds when he walks out onto the beach. Noah has powers in *Locked*. The weather does funny stuff when he's around. Rainer and his character have a lot in common.

Today we are filming what Wyatt has dubbed the

"washed up" scene. It's the one where August and Noah land on the island and he heals her. I'm covered in fake blood and dirt, and I have on what can only be described as rags, not clothes.

This scene is pretty early on in the book, but we're not going in chronological order. Wyatt says he likes to try to do that, for the emotional arc to feel as authentic as it can, but shooting schedules are complicated. We do what we need to.

Rainer is chatting with a production assistant who is building a mountain out of sand. He keeps trying to help her, and she keeps telling him to stop. I see her blushing, the corners of her eyes crinkling into a smile. He's not flirting, exactly. It's more like he's aware of the effect he's having on her.

"Come on, guys. Let's get this before sunset." Wyatt doesn't look at me but motions for us to come over, and Rainer flicks some sand at the PA. She shakes out her hair and laughs. Something flares up in my chest, but I shake it down with my nerves. We get miked, which always involves one of our sound guys getting a little too personal with my cleavage (or lack thereof). And then we head down to the water's edge.

I take a deep breath and focus on the ocean. It's this spectacular turquoise color. Cassandra would probably call it something ridiculous, like tortoiseshell green. From a distance the water is beautiful and bright, but when you get into it, right up close, it's perfectly clear. You can stare right down into the sand at your feet.

It's the same thing with acting: It looks a lot different up close. When you watch a movie, it's seamless. The story moves from one scene to another with effortless grace. But day to day, scene by scene, it's all broken up and choppy. Put your hand here, lift your chin right, square your shoulders center. Hit the mark on a certain word.

The real problem, though, is that I'm too in my head about it. Wyatt tells me this all the time. He screams it. *"Stop thinking!"* But I can't. I'm worried about getting August wrong and disappointing tens of millions of people.

I've played a hundred different characters before, characters of Shakespeare and Tennessee Williams and even one really chatty girl written by Steve Gleck, the eighth grader who won the one-act competition at my school a few years back. But this is different. August is a character beloved by the world, and it's my job to bring her to life. She'll have my face and voice and hair. She'll be *me*. And what if I'm wrong?

It seems so easy for Rainer. He doesn't even try. He jostles onto the set, makes some jokes, and as soon as Wyatt calls action, he becomes Noah. It's like an on-off switch.

Which is crazy because Noah is nothing like Rainer. Rainer is friendly and outgoing, and Noah is reserved and mysterious. They both have blond hair and tragically gorgeous blue eyes, though. And his abs. They're just... beautiful. There isn't really any other way to put it.

"We need to be better today!" Wyatt is yelling. I know he means me. *I* need to be better today. And I will. I have never been one to shrink from a challenge. Now hardly seems like the time to start.

For this shot I'm lying in the sand, in Noah's arms. I'm dying—there are shards of plane stuck in every which way in my body. Luckily they CGI most of that in later. We take our places in the sand. I lie down and then Rainer is there, right next to me. When his hands find my shoulders, I involuntarily suck in my breath. This is the most intimate scene we've done yet, by far.

"You're dying!" Wyatt is screaming. "This is fucking *painful*! Could we fucking *feel* that?"

"You got this," Rainer whispers to me.

Wyatt calls action, and I start choking. Noah is bending over me, frantic. I feel his fingertips glide up my sides. They search my rib cage. I focus on the feeling. Pain. Death. Darkness.

"Cut!" Wyatt yells.

I breathe out. Rainer sits back.

"I'm not buying it," Wyatt says.

Rainer squints up at him. "We could hit it a little faster," he says.

Wyatt shakes his head. "I want to *feel* it," he says. "I want to feel like you are losing her and you"—he points down at me; it makes my blood run cold—"you are barely conscious." He crouches down. "It needs to come from here," he says, and drops a hand roughly to my stomach. "Core."

He stalks off. I hear him mutter something, but I'm not sure what it is.

Rainer touches my shoulder. "Don't listen to him," he says softly. "You're doing great."

But I know he's wrong. I'm not. I want to be, but I'm not.

It's getting hot now, the sun climbing higher and higher. Jake knows how to tell time by the sun. He once tried to teach me, but I didn't quite get how you were supposed to go about it, since you're not supposed to look directly at the sun at all.

By the time we finish for the day, it's dark and I am exhausted. We must have done about a hundred takes of that healing scene. And then another hundred involving the crash. We were in and out of the water, and even though it was hot, my teeth have been chattering since the afternoon. Rainer kept putting his arms around me to warm me up between takes, and whispering encouraging things. He's been pretty protective since we got here, and I'm grateful for that. If he weren't on my side, I don't know what I would do.

We have to end at eight, and this makes Wyatt crazy. Usually our shoots get later and later throughout the week. Technically we can't shoot for more than twelve hours without a seven-hour break in between, and my hours are even stricter. Since Rainer isn't a minor, he can film late into the night and stay on set as long as he needs to. I, on the other hand, have all these stipulations and requirements—I can film for only five and a half hours and need to spend three hours a day in school. Sometimes, at the end of a shoot, I'll have twenty minutes of school left and I'll have to go up to the conference room in the hotel lobby with my tutor, Rubina. Wyatt will film my reaction shots, or dialogue, and then I leave and my double comes in to film the rest. It's weird to think that for a lot of the movie, I'm not even there.

Even so, once you factor in hair and makeup (which can take close to three hours), sleep is hard to come by.

I hop into a waiting van.

I turn to see if Rainer is coming, but I see he's cornered Wyatt, and the last thing I want is to interrupt that. We leave, and then I trudge back up to the hotel, discouraged. I had thought that getting the role was the hard part. That I'd proven myself and that was why they'd hired me. What I didn't realize was that getting hired was only the beginning.

I'm heading into my room when I hear footsteps behind me.

"Hey, PG, wait up." Rainer jogs to my door. He wiped his makeup off in the van and now has on a gray T-shirt and jeans.

"So," he says, "today was a little tough." He cocks his head to the side, like he's trying to get a read on me.

"It's okay," I say. "It's fine. It was my fault."

Rainer gives me a small smile. "Want to talk it out?" he asks. He moves around me to take the keys out of my hand and unlock my condo door. He's so confident, so comfortable. I know he's older, but it's something else, too—experience.

I shrug, caught off guard by our contact. "There isn't really much to talk about. I just sort of suck." I slip past him, and Rainer follows me inside.

"That's absurd."

"Oh really? Tell it to my core." I tap my abdomen twice like Wyatt did.

Rainer shakes his head. "He's being an asshole. I just told him—"

"Please," I say, cutting him off. "Please tell me you did not just tell him to go easy on me."

Rainer sighs. "You shouldn't have to be screamed at every day."

I drop my bag on the floor and slump against the counter. My condo has two bedrooms and a full kitchen. It's almost as big as my house back in Portland, and at one time six people lived in that thing. "I really wish you hadn't done that," I say.

"C'mon," Rainer says. "I got your back. We're in this together, kid."

I look at him as he leans casually against the cool marble, his arms crossed. He looks sophisticated, handsome, and self-assured. Like the world's never really given him a reason to not assume he could win.

"Thanks," I say. "But don't big-brother me to Wyatt."

"Big brother?" Rainer smirks at me, and I feel myself blush. "Hey, you want to grab dinner?" he asks, switching gears.

"I'm not all that hungry."

"Come on, you need to eat. What have you had today?" He uncrosses his arms, and some of his blond hair swings down onto his forehead. It's familiar, which is strange, until I remember it's the exact same pose he's striking in a poster Cassandra has on the back of her bedroom door.

My life is so weird.

"Okay, let me go change."

I hear him whistling in the next room, the tune of something I recognize but can't remember the name of. I think it's a Britney song. The one about summer love that played on repeat from April until August last year. Even I knew every word by heart. Maybe they are dating.

I yank open the dresser, and the photo sitting on top of it falls. It's a picture Jake gave me before I left—of him, Cassandra, and me from last summer. We're standing in front of Delmano's ice cream shop, chocolate and silly grins on our faces. I pick up the photo and place it in the drawer. I feel a sweeping sensation of guilt—for not calling more, for leaving. I think about the two of them in class, trolling around downtown on the weekends. All without me.

I choose a white tank top and a floral-print skirt I've had since sixth grade. I never wear it but figured it might be good for Hawaii.

I got my signing check last month, and it took me until last week to deposit it. I was scared, to be honest. The reality of those numbers is bigger than just money. It means something I don't totally understand yet. It's more money than anyone in my family has ever made before, combined and multiplied by ten. It makes me feel powerful, but not in a good way, necessarily. Kind of like Godzilla, who outgrew his family. Like I won't fit in my own house anymore.

Before I left I offered the money to my parents, but they refused. My dad actually left the room after I told them. My mother told me never to bring it up again, that I'm earning it and it's mine to keep.

But what do I do with it?

So far I've paid some lawyers and things like that. I gave my mom a check for the women's shelter she volunteers at. That she took. But I haven't gone shopping. I haven't bought myself a bag. Or shoes. Or a car. Maui doesn't have very many shopping destinations, besides this little center behind our condo, and even if it did I'd probably like the same things I've always liked—jeans and tank tops.

Maybe I'll fly Jake and Cassandra to set. She'd like that, I think.

"You look great," Rainer says when I reappear. He flashes me a smile.

I snort because despite the winning combination of my kiddie skirt and sand-infused hair, I'm pretty sure he's joking.

"Where should we go?" he says.

"Longhi's?"

The bottom level of the shopping center nearby has this Italian restaurant. We order from there just about every day for lunch, but their pasta is good, and the restaurant is open-air, so you can hear the ocean. Not that you can't hear the ocean from, you know, my living room, but it's still nice.

"Sounds good," Rainer says.

When we get to Longhi's, Rainer flashes his signature golden smile at the hostess, and she shows us to a table right at the edge of the restaurant, hidden discreetly behind a palm tree. She's the kind of girl you see in all those Roxy ads. Tan, tall, slim, and blond. I'm sure she surfs in the mornings, models during the day, and works here at night. If the acting thing fails, this sounds like a pretty good life. Minus the modeling.

"So I'm thinking of staying put this weekend." Rainer reclines in his chair and slips his arm casually over the back of mine. We're sitting corner to corner at a four-top, but Rainer has sat so close to me we're practically side by side. Next to us, two girls out with their parents audibly swoon.

It's never easy to forget he's famous.

"Yeah?" I say, pulling apart a roll.

Rainer has been jetting back and forth to L.A. pretty much every weekend. Now I think it's probably to see Britney, but I haven't asked.

He takes a sip of water, keeping his eyes down. "Yeah. I just figure I haven't really even been here. What am I running off for?"

"Britney?" I offer, and immediately regret saying it out loud.

Rainer frowns. "What do you mean?"

I imagine responding, "You want to make sure that your girlfriend isn't hooking up with Hollywood bad boy Jordan Wilder, right?"

Then I say, "Tabloids," when what I really mean is "Lillianna." I've heard about Jordan Wilder from Cassandra before, too. Bad news.

Rainer looks amused. "You read those?"

"Er, no, not exactly." I can feel my face start to get hot.

"It's okay." Rainer puts his hand on my bare shoulder. It feels soft and warm.

"I don't read tabloids." I exhale. "I probably should, because maybe then I'd know who people are, but I don't. My best friend used to fill me in." Normally I would have brought up Lillianna's comment with Cassandra, but I haven't had time. "Lillianna mentioned someone named Britney. It's not important. . . ." I'm rambling, I can tell, but it's hard to stop. The way he's looking at me—a combination of interest and confusion—is making me nervous.

Rainer clears his throat and retracts his hand. "We're not dating. We were but not anymore."

"Oh."

Rainer smiles. "How about you?"

"Britney isn't really my type," I say.

Rainer laughs. "Funny."

"I try."

He leans closer to me. "Anyone back home?"

I think about Jake, probably picketing some animal shelter or a Barnes & Noble right about now. "No."

"Really? You?"

"Surprisingly, yes, this doesn't make them come running." I hold up some stringy strands of hair, and sand immediately cascades down into my lap.

"You're a movie star, haven't you heard?" he says. His blue eyes sparkle. There is one movie star at the table, and it definitely isn't me.

"I'm an *actress*," I correct.

"In our position, sweetheart, it's the same thing."

I try not to let it affect me, I do, but the way he says *sweetheart* makes the nerves in my stomach begin to vibrate.

Rainer sits back and smiles. "So, what are you having?"

I notice the calm charm with which he talks to the waiter, the way he stands up and untucks my chair when I come back from the restroom, the way he smiles and makes light conversation when a mother and daughter come over to our table asking for his autograph. He's totally comfortable with it. More than that: He actually seems to like it.

"You get used to it," he says, cutting his salmon. "It's a little invasive sometimes, but it's also really flattering. It means they love what you do."

I don't have the heart to tell him that after today, I'm

not sure anyone is going to love what I do.

"It's going to get better," he says as if reading my mind. "You can't let Wyatt get to you."

"You're right," I say.

He puts his elbows on the table, bending his head close to mine. "So, will you tour me around this weekend or are you going to make me beg?"

I swallow. "Doesn't your family have a house here?"

Rainer raises his eyebrows. "You *so* read the tabloids."

I shake my head. "No way, you told me weeks ago."

He sighs. "Yeah, but we usually just sit by the pool and we've never been here for more than a weekend at a time. I want to see *your* Hawaii. You're the one who has been keeping it locked down here. I figure you have to have seen something." He leans a little bit closer, so close I can smell him. He smells like expensive cologne, like a department store. Combined with the sweet plumeria surrounding us, it's kind of heady.

My Hawaii is the inside of my condo, studying lines.

"I haven't been out much," I admit.

Rainer looks at me. "So we'll explore together."

It's definitely an offer I can't refuse. "Okay," I say.

"Great." He pushes back his chair. "Shall we?"

"Don't we have to pay?" I crane my head to look for the waiter, but Rainer stands.

"I have an account," he says. "Don't worry about it."

He touches the small of my back as I stand, and I can't help but look at the girl a few tables over. She catches my eye, and the strangest feeling comes over me. It's pride. I feel, for a brief moment, that he's mine. Maybe not in the real world, but in the fictional one, it's true.

I'm not one of those girls who gets swoony when she sees brides, and I'd rather watch a thriller than a romantic comedy, but there is something about him. The way he seems to know what I want before I say it, and how calm and confident he is. And when he walks me to my door he leans in, and I can't believe it—is Rainer Devon really going to kiss me? But he just brushes his lips against my cheek.

"Thanks for dinner," he says. "I'll see you tomorrow."

I say good-bye, and he turns to head down the hallway.

When I get inside, I immediately pick up my phone. I start to scroll to Cassandra's name, but something stops me. I can't call her—what would I say? I have a crush on Rainer Devon? Is that true? She'd probably only tell me the obvious—he's a movie star, not interested in dating a mere mortal like me. We're coworkers. He's being friendly. *Get a grip, Townsen.*

I fall asleep in my flowered skirt with the phone on my pillow. When I wake up, it's still there, Cassandra's name dark on the screen.

CHAPTER 6

I've started a ritual in Hawaii: Every weekend morning, when I don't have to be shooting and before the sun comes out, I go down to the beach and jump in the ocean. There isn't a soul around except the early-morning surfers, and even if they throw you a smile, it never develops into a conversation. We have an understanding that everyone is alone, but not in a way that's lonely. The opposite, actually. To me the ocean in the morning is like a good friend, the kind you can sit in silence with for hours.

I've never seen Rainer down here, or Wyatt, but then Wyatt works all the time and Rainer usually goes away on the weekends. I know he's sticking around today, but he seems much more like a brunch-at-the-hotel kind of guy than a wake-up-at-dawn-and-hop-in-the-freezing-ocean guy.

I toss my towel onto a rock and head toward the shore. I feel the water and then start walking forward, giving myself to the count of three before I dive in. It's the only way to go—if you edge in, it's pure torture.

The water hits—so sharp it feels like the wind has been knocked out of me—and I come up to the surface gasping for air. The ocean is new to me, but I've always loved the water.

Before my sister got pregnant and my brothers moved out, my parents used to take us camping every summer. My sister hated it. She'd stay in the tent and complain about how she hadn't brought enough magazines, or how the air was too cold or the ground too hard or how the food stank, but I loved it. I used to look forward to those trips every year.

We'd set up camp around a lake my dad had chosen, and the five of us would pitch tents while my mom unloaded the kitchen supplies. As soon as we were done, I'd hit the water. It didn't matter how cold it was—as soon as camp was set up I was in. My mom says I was born with a fish's tail, and I think it's probably true. When I was little, people used to ask me what I wanted to be when I grew up. I'd always say a fish. I didn't understand that a fish wasn't something you could work toward. That no matter how hard I tried, I'd never sprout gills and a tail.

Once I'm totally underwater, it's heaven. Cool and

crisp and deliciously refreshing, like biting into the summer's first slice of watermelon. The cold zings through my body, waking up my arms and legs and toes. I flip over onto my back and let the waves rock me out. It's just starting to get light, and I can see rays of pink and yellow and orange puncture the sky. It's like watching a painting being made. Long, leisurely brushstrokes that soften the darkness until the spaces between aren't pockets of sun, but the other way around.

I stretch my hands out in front of me and pump my legs forward, pitching my body underwater. It doesn't bite now and instead feels smooth, and soft—like a silk robe or velvet pajamas.

I spend about fifteen minutes floating and swimming, sometimes stopping to watch the sherbet sky. When I'm in the water, it feels like the whole world is on the same level—the beach and the sky are parallel, not perpendicular. It's so different from Portland. Portland is all rounded corners and hills. Hawaii feels level, like everything is happening at the same time here, all at once.

I finally let a wave carry me back. I sink my feet into the sand, hopping up and down a few times to get the water out of my ears and wringing my hair over my shoulder. It's completely light out, and if I stand facing the condos, I can see all the way up Haleakala, Maui's dormant volcano. When we first got here, Rainer's dad paid for Hawaiian culture lessons. The whole crew came, but most people left early. I was one of the few who ended up staying and hearing the entire thing. They told us that the Hawaiian Islands are actually a chain of volcanoes and that the "hot spot" moves from island to island, which is why only one volcano at a time is actually active—currently the one on Hawaii, the Big Island. The totally fascinating thing, though, is that the hot spot is moving now, creating another island. It will probably rise to the surface sometime in the next ten thousand to one hundred thousand years. It has already been named, too. It's called Loihi.

I wrap my towel around my waist and tromp back up to the condos. I'm looking forward to getting out of Wailea, our beach town, today. Jake bought me all these guidebooks, most of them focused on which species are indigenous and how to tell if ocean water is polluted, but he did get me one plain, straight-up tourist-trap book. The kind that tells you where the best burgers are and how to find the hikes with the waterfalls. I'm bringing it with us today.

The woman at the reception desk greets me with a smile. "You have a message, Ms. Townsen."

She hands me a note on hotel stationery with trim, precise cursive on it:

Get dressed and come meet me for breakfast.

—R

My pulse lights up, and my body suddenly feels warm. No more morning-water goose bumps.

"Anything else?" I ask the woman, making an effort to hide the slow smile that is spreading across my face. I have to figure out how to get it together. He's my coworker, not some school crush.

"No," she replies. "Just the one note."

I nod and take off toward my room, my flip-flops making smacking noises on the marble floor.

When I come down to breakfast, Rainer is waiting in another Hawaiian shirt and wraparound Ray-Ban sunglasses. This shirt is light blue, the color of the waves. He's smiling his signature dimply smile and tapping his forefinger on his watch.

"You're late," he says.

I hold up his note. "You didn't specify a time."

"I just assumed you'd see it and come running."

"Is that what the girls normally do?"

Rainer shrugs. "Pretty much, yeah." He shakes his head and smiles. "I'm kidding," he says. He looks at me to make sure I know it. "Sit. You know I would have waited all day, anyway."

"So, what are we doing today?" I say, trying to change the subject, determined to keep myself together. Cool. Collected.

A waitress has set an orange juice and bread basket

down, and I tear off a muffin top. I realize I'm starving. It's the morning swims. The ocean makes me ravenous.

Rainer watches me with amusement. "I thought that was on you, PG." He leans closer to me. "I get the car; you bring the plan."

I pull out my guidebook and open it to the page on Paia, this little town on the north shore I've been wanting to go to. There is supposed to be a restaurant there called the Fish Market that has the best burgers and sandwiches on the island, and the town is apparently cluttered with cute, artsy stores and shops. Not that anything could ever beat Trinkets n' Things, but, you know, one can dream. The guidebook says that from Paia you can go to Ho'okipa Beach and watch the windsurfers. I think that sounds kind of perfect.

Bent over my eggs and coffee, I tell all this to Rainer.

"I'm impressed," he says. "You learned all that from this?" He plucks the copy of *The Real Maui* out of my hands and fans through the pages.

I nod and parrot what Jake told me: "It's supposed to be the best one."

Rainer smiles slightly, like he thinks this is sort of funny. Cute, maybe. I internally cringe at how childlike I sound. So damn young. Then he pulls my coffee out of my hand, takes a sip, and sets it down. "Time is wasting, PG. Let's go."

Rainer has rented a neon-blue convertible, and when we pick it up at the valet, I can't help but snort. "You're kidding, right?"

"Oh, come on. Where's your sense of adventure?"

"You mean irony?"

He shakes his head. "You're impossible."

"I have a sense of adventure. It just involves things like hiking, not driving the tourist mobile."

"Well, I'm going to be the one driving." Rainer tilts his sunglasses up and looks at me. I can't help but note, even now with this aqua vehicle right by us, how blue his eyes are.

He holds the door open for me, and I get inside.

"Plus," he says, shutting the door, "I look good in blue."

It will be easier to spot us in this thing for sure, but so far that hasn't really been a problem. People are always complaining about the paparazzi, but I don't see what the big deal is. And truthfully, it might not be a terrible thing to be recognized, just a little bit. I mean, someone wanting to take my picture is kind of a new concept for me. Up until now I've had to jostle my way into Christmas card photos.

Wyatt keeps hammering into us, practically preaching, that this is going to change, that every day moves us closer to insanity, but I don't know. There was a big fuss when I got the part—magazine articles, one shot of me coming out of a Coffee Bean—but then everything settled down when we got here. No one recognizes me. How could they? I haven't done anything yet.

I take out the big map of Maui that was folded into the guidebook. We start driving west, the beach on our left and the hills climbing up into the mountains on our right. Every single second looks like a postcard. I keep wanting to freeze-frame the drive. The book says that the Hawaiian Islands are thought to be God's country, that if he ever chose to live anywhere on earth, it would be here. I get what they mean. It's paradise.

"What do you do in Portland?" Rainer asks. The top is down, and the wind is loud. My hair is blowing every which way, and I try to secure it back, my hands plastered to the side of my head like earmuffs.

"What?" I bellow.

"Portland!"

It's funny—Rainer feels so familiar, but we haven't actually spent a lot of time talking about our lives before this movie. I'm glad that we're getting the chance now.

The truth, though, is that I know a lot about *him*. The external stuff, anyway. All courtesy of Cassandra. Like his favorite color is orange and he has a dog named Scoot and when he was twelve his dad gave him a dinner date with Steven Spielberg for his birthday. He grew up in Beverly

Hills, his parents are still married, and he's an only child, despite occasional rumors to the contrary.

His parents have a bowling alley in their basement and a tennis court in their backyard. He's one of *People*'s most beautiful and his birthday is in June... although it could be January.

I realize, suddenly, the only thing Cassandra left out was Britney.

Rainer looks over at me and smiles. My eyes are watering bullets, and my hair looks like it's caught in an eighties music video. Sexy.

He says something I can't understand, but I don't pretend to, and we drive in silence until we reach Paia.

Paia is exactly like the guidebook described: a little hippie town that has more restaurants and character than the entire south side of the island combined. I can tell as soon as we pull in that this is the real island, the part no one sees on a beach vacation. Being on our part of the island is a little like being stuck on a cruise ship—it's beautiful and there is lots of good food, but you never get to see anything real.

Paia is composed of two strips. One that the highway runs into and another road that intersects it perpendicularly. There are no parking spots available, and every restaurant—mostly outdoor cafés—seems to be packed. I half expect Rainer to try to valet, but then he swings into a little parking lot at the base of town and proves me wrong.

"Seems like you picked the hot spot," he says. He parks, locks up the top, and then comes around to open my door. I've already done it, so we have this funny little moment where I'm getting out and he's trying to be helpful, but he gets stuck between the car next to us and my door. It's sweet, and kind of disarming.

Here's a fun fact: Even Rainer Devon looks silly caught between two parked cars.

We extricate ourselves from the parking lot and walk over to the Fish Market. Even though there is an insane line that wraps clear around the outside of the restaurant, I insist we stay and eat there. It's not like we have anywhere else to be.

"Don't doubt the book," I say, and Rainer consents.

"We could just go up, you know," he says, gesturing to the register about twenty people out.

"Cut, you mean?"

"For all they know, we need to be back on set."

"But we *don't* need to be back on set," I point out.

He crosses his arms and squints at me. "You still don't get it, do you?"

"Get what?" Who does he think he is, Brad Pitt? Would Brad Pitt cut in line? Probably. But only because he had to go save orphans or something. The only thing Rainer has to do is see a beach.

"Your naïveté is cute, PG, but you're a big star now.

It's time to start acting like one."

"That's not acting like a star," I say. "That's acting like an asshole."

He rolls his eyes and takes my hand. It makes me jump, but I don't fight him. He drags me up to the front of the line, excuses himself to the man who is at the register, and smiles at the cashier—a girl about our age. She looks at the cash register and then does this little gasp when she sees Rainer staring at her.

"You don't think we could put in an order, do you?" Rainer asks, beaming at her. He's still holding my hand and pulls me closer, showing me to her like I'm evidence he's providing.

The girl looks at me and then her eyes get wide. It's the same look Cassandra gives me when she has something really important to tell me and can't quite get the words out.

"Y-y-you're August," she sputters.

I glance at Rainer and then back at the girl. My first inclination is to correct her. I'm not August. I'm Paige.

But instead what happens is that I smile and nod, slowly, and then the whole restaurant falls silent. Where a minute before I felt like I was back in Rainer's convertible having to shout to be heard, now the only thing I want is for someone to sneeze to cover up the sound of my breathing.

And it's fast. My heart is going a mile a minute.

"I loved the books," the girl pushes on. "I'm so excited for the movie. Could I have your autograph?"

Rainer raises his eyebrows at me and smiles a *told you so* grin. I fumble in my purse, trying to find a pen. Are you supposed to keep pens on you when you're famous? Is that the deal? Or do people provide them?

I find one dangling from an eyeglass case at the bottom of my bag and take it out, cap first.

"Um, sure. What should I sign?"

The girl looks at me like she doesn't get the question, and Rainer hands me a napkin.

"Will this do?" he asks her.

She nods emphatically, and I take the napkin, pressing it down on the counter. At this point it feels like every single person in the restaurant has swiveled to look at me. I feel a little like one of those mannequins in the windows at department stores that are between outfit changes: naked and completely on display.

Except, you know, they're not alive.

I swallow and then scrawl my name. It looks messy, and you can barely make out the *T* in Townsen. I don't really have a signature. I never even signed my name, I don't think, until a few years ago when I had to get a passport. We were supposed to go to Vancouver to visit my dad's brother, who moved there like five years ago to start this woodchopping business, but we never did. We tried again a few years later, but it was right around the time Annabelle graced us with her presence and after that, travel...Well, it wasn't diapers, so it was out.

I hand the napkin to the girl, and she's beaming. Serious Christmas-morning smile.

"Thank you so much!" she says. "I'll take your orders. On the house."

"That's sweet," Rainer says. He hands over a hundred-dollar bill with a stack of twenties curled underneath. He cocks his head behind him. "Will you buy these people in line lunch, on me?"

The girl blushes fuchsia and nods. Rainer looks at me. I can feel my eyes go wide. "What?" he says. "I pay it forward." He orders and people start to talk again, the lunch-hour sounds resuming. Somewhere someone takes a picture and a little girl comes up to Rainer and asks for his autograph. He accepts and bends down, scooping her into a big hug. Her tiny little cheeks turn Pop-Tart pink. He signs one for the cashier, too.

We get our food, and I shove a twenty-dollar bill into the tip jar.

The restaurant is all community-style, long wooden tables with benches on the sides. Rainer takes our tray, and we head over to an empty portion of a table in the corner. I sit down. A stranger just recognized me. Someone I have never met before knew who I was.

"You feeling okay there?" Rainer leans forward, so I can see a few freckles on his nose.

"Yeah, fine." But the truth is the whole experience is surreal—like a dream. I keep expecting to snap back to reality.

"You'll get used to it," he says. He takes my hand up lightly, lets his fingers curl through mine just for a moment. "I don't want you to worry."

"Do you ever think it's strange?" I say. I have to swallow to keep my voice even.

"What?" he asks. He uncurls his fingers but lets his thumb glide over my wrist before he returns his hand to his side of the table.

"That people you've never met know your name?"

Rainer picks up his burger. "Yes," he starts. "Well, I'm not sure." He pauses, takes a bite, and chews thoughtfully. "It's always been this way for me. I mean, I was acting when I was a kid. I guess I don't know any different."

I nod and bite into my burger. It's delicious. *The Real Maui* was right: These things are incredible. Although it could just be that I haven't had a real hamburger in months. Jake is a vegan, of course, and is constantly trying to get me to consume the cardboard tofu crap he buys. He even convinced my parents to switch over, which royally sucks because now my mom serves soy dogs at our house.

We eat in silence for a few minutes, momentarily lulled by our food. We still get a couple of sideways stares, but for the most part everyone seems to have gone back to their meals.

After lunch we pull into the windsurfing beach. I read about an overlook where you can park and walk out to some rocks that hang over the ocean. If it's windy, chances are the windsurfers will be out. And at Ho'okipa, apparently, it's always windy.

The wind zips and howls around us when we step outside. But it's still warm, and the sun beats down strong and steady on my back.

Rainer squints into the sunlight and tosses me a baseball hat from the backseat. "Careful of that skin, PG. August is pretty pasty."

I roll my eyes and jam the Lakers hat down over my forehead.

"Looks cute on you," he says, giving me an approving nod.

My chest stumbles right along with my feet.

"Easy," he says, putting a hand on my back. "C'mon."

We climb through the railing, then walk down to the rocks. They make a shelf along the cliff, prime seating, like they knew people were going to want to watch the show. We take a seat, and as soon as I look out over the water, my breath catches.

Windsurfers are everywhere, but they don't look like humans. They look like little butterflies. Tiny, colorful butterflies that dip and sway and fly across the ocean.

"They're beautiful," I breathe.

Rainer nods beside me. "Yeah. It's pretty tough, too."

"Have you been?" I ask.

"Once," he says. "It was part of this pub shoot I did for *Wild Things*."

I remember *Wild Things*. It came out when I was in sixth or seventh grade, I think. It was about these young competitive surfers. Rainer played the lead guy, the one who gets injured the week before the big competition; they think he's going to have to sit it out, but at the last minute, he changes his mind, races into the water, and wins gold.

"Do you surf?" I ask him.

"I'd like to think I do," he says. "But no, not really." He places his hands in the sand, palms down. "You?"

I shake my head. "I haven't, but I want to. Everything about the water fascinates me." I'd have gone surfing the first day I was here if there weren't all this stuff in my contract about not getting injured and the "prohibition of impact-based sports" while filming. I asked the producers exactly what about surfing was "impact-based," but I never got a response.

The wind is picking up, and I tuck my arms around me. All of a sudden my skin has goose bumps. The sun has hidden behind a cloud, and the drop in temperature feels like twenty degrees.

"Here," Rainer says. He's brought out this lightweight gray cotton hoodie, and he slides it over my shoulders. His hand brushes my skin. Is it my imagination, or do his fingers linger there?

"Thanks," I say.

He clears his throat. "No problem."

Rainer rests his elbows on his knees and gazes out over the water. "Things feel so distant here, huh?" he says.

I thread my arms through his sweatshirt. "What do you mean?"

He keeps his gaze on the ocean. "What you were asking me earlier, if it's weird when I get recognized? It is, but I don't think because of what you meant. I think because it becomes your norm and that—" His voice breaks off. When it returns, it's softer. "That's a strange way to live." He looks over at me. His eyes have changed. They're darker somehow, stormier. They have more depth. "I want you to know that you don't have to go through any of this alone. Whatever is coming, whatever happens, you'll have me. I promise."

I can feel my heart hammering in my chest. I swear he can, too. "Thank you," I say.

He keeps looking at me, and I think he's going to say something more, something about what it's like where I'm headed—where we both are. The moment stretches, and the air seems to pause around us. Even the wind stills.

But he doesn't say anything, and after a bit I follow his gaze back to the water. There is one windsurfer in particular who catches my eye. He has a blue sail and is farther out than the rest of them. So far, in fact, that it's hard to see whether he's moving at all. The only way I know for sure is that he gets smaller and smaller. By the time we stand up and walk back to the car, his blue sail might be the ripple of a wave.

CHAPTER 7

I didn't swim this morning, and I'm lounging around in my condo, still in my pajamas and, yeah, thinking about Rainer. Listen, I don't think he's into me. Not like *that*. I get that he's a full-fledged movie star and I'm a total newbie. But something about our day yesterday makes me feel like my crush isn't completely unwarranted. God help me. I have a total crush on Rainer Devon.

A loud knock on my door jolts me back to reality. Two knuckle raps. When I swing it open, Wyatt is on the other side. My stomach instantly pulls back, like someone has socked me.

"Paige," he says. "We need to talk." He's wearing a Sex Pistols T-shirt and black pants, and his hair is standing up every which way.

"Fucking wind," he says, catching my gaze.

He follows me into the kitchen, and I take out some of the Evian water bottles the craft service people keep stocked in my fridge. They asked me what I liked to eat the first day on set, and since then coleslaw and peanut butter crackers have been showing up in my refrigerator and cabinets.

"So," I say. My hands are shaking so badly I can't even open my water bottle. "What's going on?" Wyatt has never visited me in my condo, ever. He sometimes goes to Rainer's but that's usually only when Sandy is there. This is bad. I know it is.

Wyatt shoves something at me. It's his iPad. And on it are grainy photos of Rainer and me from yesterday, splashed across a tabloid website.

I see pictures of Rainer and me driving with the top down, holding hands at the Fish Market. Snapshots of him putting his sweatshirt around me at the overlook and even ones of us talking, so close it looks like his forehead is pressed up against mine. And a stupid headline to top it all off: LOCKED COSTARS ALREADY GETTING COZY.

I suddenly become intensely aware of the crescent moons on my pajamas.

"Oh," I say.

He turns his face to me. He doesn't look pleased. "Yeah. *Oh*. Want to tell me what's going on?"

"Nothing," I tell him. "They were taken completely out of context, I swear. We were just exploring the island—" But I stop talking when I catch the look on Wyatt's face. It seems to say that any explanation I give him is only an excuse.

"I don't really give a shit what you do with your personal life," he says. "But I will not have my movie go up in flames because you two can't keep your hands off each other."

"Hey," I say. Anger flares up in my chest. "That's not what happened. This hasn't affected—it won't—we're not even—Rainer—" What I want to ask is why he isn't bringing this up with Rainer. Why this is suddenly all *my* fault.

Wyatt holds his hand up. "You might think this is just some teenybopper fantasy, but do you have any idea how much thought and attention and time has gone into this project? How many hundreds of millions of dollars? People's careers?"

"I know," I say, but I can't continue. My chest feels tight. I'm afraid I'm going to start crying.

Wyatt flicks his eyes across my face. "You think I'm hard on you," he says. "You think I'm unfair. You're wondering why I came to you and not him."

I don't blink. He continues.

"Rainer is who he is, but you're just getting started.

76

There are things you don't know yet about the way this business works."

"What are you saying?"

"I'm saying that he's the producer's son, but you have a shot at actually being an *actress*. Do it right. If not for yourself, then definitely for me, because I will not settle for anything less than the best. Do you understand?"

"Yes."

Wyatt takes off his glasses and tilts his head, the way he does right before he sets up a scene. I know he's picturing things in his mind, trying to figure out the best angle, how to get the truest version of the moment he's trying to capture. When he speaks again, his tone has softened, like a piece of plastic in front of a hot flame—it starts to melt at the edges.

"You know this is just going to get worse," he says.

I don't answer, just stuff my hands down into the pockets of my pajama bottoms.

Wyatt takes an Evian bottle and rolls it across his forehead, then twists the top and flicks the cap down on the counter. "I don't think you realize your responsibility yet."

"I do," I say. I'm fighting back tears because I don't need to hear this, not again, not now. "All I do all day long is think about the responsibility."

"Show me."

"What?" I just stare at him.

His eyes are fierce, just like they are on set. He's challenging me. *"Show me you get it."*

I want to ask him how, but I know that would make it worse. I should know how. I should *act* how.

"I will," I say. I stand with my hands on my hips.

"This is your life," he says. His tone is still strong, clipped, but his features have softened. "Once you put something out in this world, you cannot take it back. Do you understand me?"

"Yes."

Wyatt takes another swig and sets the Evian bottle on the counter. He doesn't say anything as he moves toward the door, and then he turns around. "We may have found our Ed," he says. "I'm bringing him over to test with you later this week."

I open my mouth to say something, but nothing comes out. Last I heard, Ed wasn't expected on set until the very end of filming. He doesn't have a ton of scenes in the first movie, or a very prominent role in the first book other than in flashbacks. Mostly he comes into play at the beginning and then at the very end.

Wyatt eyes me. "We'll see how you chemistry-test, but barring some kind of repulsion"—his eyes flick briefly to his iPad—"he's the one."

"Who is it?" I ask. Not that it matters. I always get celebrity names jumbled and anyway, I think they were considering another unknown for the part.

Wyatt looks at me, and I can swear his eyes twinkle. It's the strangest thing to see. "Jordan Wilder," he says, before disappearing out the door.

As soon as he's gone, I feel my eyes start to burn. My stomach feels sick, too. Did he just accuse me of trying to sabotage this movie? With an affair I'm *not even having*? The exhaustion of the last few weeks—my insecurities about the movie—all come bubbling up to the surface. This time I don't hesitate: I pick up the phone and call Cassandra.

"I can't believe you didn't tell me!"

Cassandra's voice charges through the phone, part high-pitched shriek and part baritone boom, before I can even get in a hello.

I melt onto a barstool at my kitchen counter. I should have known she'd already have seen them. I think she has a Google alert set on my name. "It's not true," I say.

"Have you seen these pictures?"

"Yes," I say. "And that isn't what happened."

I didn't think I'd have to defend myself to Cassandra like I did Wyatt. I suddenly have the intense desire to hang up and crawl back into bed.

"Pictures don't lie," Cassandra says. Her tone is indignant, and I imagine her on her landline (she talks less on her cell phone now—unlike me, she listens to a lot of what

Jake says), twisting the cord around her wrist the way she does when she's nervous or really focused on something.

"Neither do I," I say. My words are edged, and I know she hears them.

"I know," she says. Her tone softens. "But how do you fake that?"

I run a hand across my forehead. I think back to yesterday and try to explain what I couldn't to Wyatt. "Rainer grabbed my hand for a second to pull me out of the way and then later I was cold, so he gave me his sweatshirt. Those pictures are totally out of context. They just look real."

I hear her sigh, imagine the cord going slack. "Sorry," she says. "I wasn't accusing you of anything."

"No?"

Her voice gets quiet. "I feel like I barely know what's going on in your life—"

"I know," I say, cutting her off. I swallow. "It's just been really busy here."

"Apparently."

She laughs, and so do I. More out of relief than anything else.

"I miss you," she says.

"I miss you, too. How is everything?" The line goes silent for a moment. "Cass?"

"Yeah?" Her voice is quiet.

"What's going on at home?"

"Oh, the usual," she says. "Sit-ins. Protests. And I'm just talking about what's been happening in Mrs. Huntington's speech class."

We both laugh. It feels good. Familiar.

"How is Jake?" I ask. I bite my lip as I say it. Cassandra knows what I'm asking—does he miss me? Is he seeing someone?—but she doesn't really like to talk about it. Me and Jake, I mean. Cassandra makes a small grunt, and I imagine her nodding slowly, her blond hair rising and falling on her shoulders.

When we were younger, the three of us had a "three musketeers" pact. We'd put our arms into a triangle—hand to shoulder, hand to shoulder, hand to shoulder—and repeat the slogan "all for one and one for all." No one without everyone. There was a clubhouse in Jake's backyard and a rule book Cassandra made. We decorated the book with glitter and leaves and named it Bob, although I can't for the life of me remember why.

When Jake and I kissed, I told Cassandra, of course. I thought she'd be thrilled. She was always talking about how much she thought he liked me. But she wasn't happy. Not even a little bit. She said we didn't understand our own slogan, that we were breaking all the rules. It had just happened. The kiss, I mean. It was the night my sister ran away. She was always doing things like leaving for long weekends to go up to Seattle or stealing money from my parents and disappearing for forty-eight hours. Usually it was just to visit one of my brothers or something, but she never told anyone where she was going or how long she'd be gone for. It used to make my parents panic. Every single time she didn't come home for dinner they were convinced she was dead. I never understood it. She had pulled the same thing last weekend; odds were she was alive. But they never saw it like that. They were always terrified. Like this time would be different.

This was just a few weeks before she got pregnant, or at least before we found out. She had taken off on one of her sojourns, and my parents were furious with fear. They had called the police and were pacing our living room. Both my brothers were accounted for, and she wasn't with either of them. And I hadn't seen her in school that day.

Jake was over, and we were studying for something. It was probably geometry—I always needed help with geometry.

Jake and I were in the living room when my sister finally came home. She was drunk. Like stinking, stumbling drunk. You'd think my parents would have been pissed. They certainly would have been had it been me. But they weren't. They were relieved. Their little Joanna was back. The star soccer player, the first girl after two boys. The golden child. I know I sound bitter, and it's not that exactly. It was just this moment where I realized the supreme unfairness of life. I didn't get upset about it or anything. I don't think I felt it at all. It's more that I *thought* it, realized it. Like a date in a history book or a number on a math test. It was a fact. No matter what I did. No matter how many stage roles I got or how good I was in school or how well behaved, they'd never really worry about me like they worried about her.

Jake hung around for a little while after the commotion calmed down, a tearful Joanna going up to her room unpunished and laden with water and coffee. I watched the whole thing from the living room, and when it was over I remember Jake taking my hand in his and sliding the pencil out from under my knuckles. There were large red dents on my index finger.

"Are you okay?" he asked me.

I don't remember what I said, or what he said after that, but I do know that when he put his hand on my cheek and then his lips on mine, I let him. And it felt good. Because I knew Jake was on my side. Whatever side that was, he was on it. And I guess that was Cassandra's problem. There was a side after that.

She didn't talk to us for a month afterward, and we never called ourselves the three musketeers again. Not even jokingly.

That was almost two years ago.

"He's good," she says now. "Busy. We both are." Cassandra is silent for a moment, and I wonder if she hasn't seen much of him since I've been gone. A wave of guilt hits me—what if I was their glue? "Have you spoken to him?" she asks.

"Just a few e-mails," I say. "But you know Jake and the phone."

Cassandra laughs. "Ugh. Totally. So when are you coming home?"

I spin around on my stool. The sunshine and ocean greet me. "Isn't a better question when are you coming to visit? You do know I'm in Hawaii, right? And your favorite movie star is here?"

She laughs. Cassandra's laugh reminds me of twinkle lights at Christmas: bright and soft and a little bit magical.

"Clearly Rainer is more interested in you than me," she says.

"I was talking about me."

I'm almost sure I can hear her smile. "So you're calling yourself a movie star now, huh?"

"Only to you," I say, and when I do, I'm hit with just how much I miss her. Like the emotion is a stone thrown hard into a pond. It sinks, but the ripples keep on spreading. I wish she were here. Pulling at her long blond curls and wearing some crazy, colorful ensemble and making us dance around the living room to Madonna.

"Come visit," I say. "You and Jake. Next weekend. What do you say?"

"I don't know," she says. "There's school stuff. And I spent all my babysitting money on those new ocean underworld DVDs."

"I'd pay," I tell her.

"Oh."

"It's not a big deal," I say, all at once, the words knocking into one another. "It would mean a lot to me. You could see what the set is like, and we could spend some time together. The three of us."

Cassandra's tone brightens. "Yeah, good luck getting Jake on a plane."

"Please," I say, because all of a sudden I need her here. Both of them. It's like if they visit, if they see this, maybe I will feel more like myself. Maybe this will become real.

"All right," she says. "I'll talk to him about it. And in the meantime try to keep your affairs out of the international press."

I laugh. "It's crazy, right?"

"Crazy," she says. "Totally bat shit. But I kind of love it."

"That makes one of us," I say.

I hear her sigh, and the pop of her lips. "You'll come around," she says. "You always do."

We hang up, and I keep looking out my huge

floor-to-ceiling windows. They're the one thing in this condo that reminds me a little bit of home. My bedroom has one window that looks out into the backyard. I used to like to pull my desk chair up to it on the weekends and sit with a huge mug of hot chocolate and a good script. But now my sister lives in that room, and there's a playpen jammed up against the glass. Joanna wanted to be a massage therapist, and a while back she started to get her training. We all thought it would be a good idea because she could make her own hours and get pretty decent pay, but it never worked out. She ended up blowing off class, saying she missed Annabelle, and went instead to stock produce at our local Whole Foods. She works more hours now than she ever did in school.

That's the thing about my family: No one wound up where they wanted to go.

My mom didn't end up an actress; my dad didn't end up an architect. Both my brothers keep ending up nowhere, and half the time I don't think my sister even knows where she is.

It's not like our story is tragic or anything. Nothing that terrible has ever happened to us. Which I guess, actually, is the point. People are always saying the pendulum swings both ways—greatness and tragedy—but my family's seems to be stuck in the center.

I think about Cassandra and Jake. Jake will be great,

and not because he's destined for it but because he knows what he thinks and isn't afraid of hard work. He was volunteering at the animal shelter and starting a garden at five. He's wanted to help in whatever way he can since as long as I can remember and sometimes that drives me crazy (like when Saturday nights are spent pulling up non-indigenous weeds), but it also means he's committed to something. And Cassandra? She's passionate about everything, but especially the people she cares about. There hasn't been one of Jake's Saturday sit-ins she's missed, or one bio assignment she hasn't talked me through. They're both extraordinary because they care. About the world and the people around them. About me.

They have to come visit. If they do, this experience will be everything it's supposed to be. I just know it.

CHAPTER 8

"I can't believe this. Are you sure you heard him right?" Rainer is pacing the length of his condo, his hands knotted by his sides.

I tuck my knees up to my chest on the couch. "That's what he said. Jordan Wilder."

"Why would they hire Jordan? I thought they wanted an unknown." Rainer stops and looks at me.

I lift up my shoulders. "I have no idea. You should ask your dad." I think about Wyatt's words earlier: "He's the producer's son."

Rainer's eyes fire up. "You think he knew about this?"

"I mean, he's the producer, right?" I stick my thumbnail in my mouth and snap off the end. It's a nervous habit I have. Lillianna keeps yelling at me about it. I tried to explain to her that if August is on a deserted island with some tribe possibly intent on killing her, she's definitely biting her nails, too, but she didn't buy it.

"He wouldn't do that to me. He knows about Jordan."

"What happened?" I ask.

Rainer is unraveling right before my eyes. He asked me to come over to have dinner, and I was just catching him up on my morning, telling him about Wyatt coming over, when Jordan's name slipped out.

I've never seen Rainer like this. Usually he's so calm and cool and collected and together. The mere mention of this guy's name has completely unhinged him.

I know there are those rumors about Jordan and Britney but Rainer told me himself he isn't even with her anymore. And anyway, Rainer's not the kind of guy to go into a tailspin about rumors. Unless they're not just rumors.

He looks at me like he's forgotten I'm there. "Nothing," he says. "We used to be on a TV show together. It's not important."

"From the way you're pacing your living room, it *seems* kind of important."

"I'd just rather he not bog this movie down with his bullshit, that's all."

"*What* bullshit?"

Rainer's eyes flash and then fade out, like they've

blown a fuse, and he flops down onto the couch next to me. "I'm sorry," he says. "I just really hate the guy."

He lifts his head up, and he's wearing a small smile now. I realize, suddenly, that this is the first time I've ever seen Rainer angry. It's a weird realization. Like he's becoming human or something. Not so perfect. But it's not off-putting at all—instead, it's totally attractive. I like that he's let me into a part of him other people don't see. That he has his own demons. And apparently, Jordan Wilder is one of them.

"Hey," I say. I reach for his shoulder and place my hand there. "If this is so important to you, why don't we do something about it?"

He looks at me. His eyes narrow. "What do you mean?"

I suck in my bottom lip. I can't believe I'm about to say this, but I think about Rainer telling me yesterday we were in this together. Sitting on that couch, I think, I *know*, I'd already do anything for him.

"I'll flub my read with him," I say.

Rainer opens his mouth to say something and then closes it again. He looks at me, and a beat passes between us so long I think I might scream. But then he shakes his head, his mouth pulling into a smile. "I can't ask you to do that," he says.

"You're not asking."

He makes a noise somewhere between a laugh and an exhale. "But you're not going to," he says. "I can't let you. Not with how you feel about your current relationship with Wyatt."

I think about our talk this morning. Rainer puts a hand on my shoulder and glides it down my arm. I'm sure he can feel the goose bumps that prick up where his fingers trail. We've touched so much on set but so little, I realize, off. I've been anticipating August and Noah's kiss since we got here—I know it's coming. I guess at least they'll get there, even if we never do. "I'll just have to trust that Jordan's general assholery will speak for itself."

"Okay." I nod. Then, to change the subject: "Hey, I think my friends might come to visit next weekend."

"Jake and Cassandra?" Rainer eyes me, and I feel something rise in my chest. I don't even remember talking about them a lot. "That's great."

"Will you be here?" I pick at the edge of a pillow.

"Yes," Rainer says. His voice is soft. "And I'd love to meet them."

I look up at him. He's smiling. "I didn't ask," I say.

He cocks his head to the side. "But you want to."

I'm annoyed at myself. At how I can feel my blood heating up in my veins. "They're great," I say, because I don't know what else to say. "Cassandra and I have been friends forever, and Jake..."

Rainer picks up on the pause. "You haven't really clarified that one. Is he an ex?"

"No," I say hastily. "It's just strange being away from them. They've known everything about me up until now."

"It's hard," he says. "It's not easy to maintain relationships in this world."

"Yeah. And Cassandra is just—she saw those stupid tabloid shots." I already told Rainer about Wyatt's confrontation, but before I could gauge his reaction I brought up Jordan's name. I now really want to know: How does he feel about those pictures? About the world thinking we might really be together?

Rainer laughs. "All press is good press, right?"

"Isn't it 'not all press is good press'?"

He shrugs. "I forget. Was she upset or something?"

I glance downward. I can feel my cheeks flush. "She thought I didn't tell her everything."

I look up and see Rainer's eyes fixed on me. His smile has slackened a little, and he seems intent. "Did you?"

"You know those pictures were taken out of context," I say. "I mean, Wyatt totally overreacted. You were just being nice about the sweatshirt, and that hand-holding was..."

He unhooks his hand from the back of the couch and places it over mine, where it's resting in my lap. "I like you," he says.

I look at his hand and then up at him. All the hairs on

my body feel like they stand up at once. When the words come out, they feel small, like those firecrackers that barely spark before they die. "What do you mean?"

"You're sweet," he says, "and smart. And talented. I like your spunk and how unassuming you are. I like how new this is to you. You're so real."

There is a calmness to his tone, a candid softness, that makes me think he is letting me down easy. That he picked up on this stupid, totally inappropriate crush I have on him and is trying to move past it. To imply without calling me out that we should just be friends. Wyatt was right. Everyone but me knows that us getting together is a bad idea.

"Thank you," I say, because I have no idea what to say.

He laughs a little. "You're welcome, I guess."

He takes his hand away. Instantly, I'm sorry he did it. "Let's stay in," he says. "I think I have some sushi in my fridge. You hungry?"

I nod. "Starving." My voice sounds hoarse, and my mouth feels dry. But my stomach is rumbling at the thought of food. I try to push my embarrassment down low, shake it off. I'm an actress, after all.

Rainer goes to the kitchen, busying himself with containers. I swivel on the couch to look at him. "I don't suppose you have some pizza back there, too?" I ask.

Rainer laughs. "I have to be in a bathing suit

tomorrow." He's in front of the counter now, and he lifts up his navy T-shirt to reveal his perfect abs. He pats his stomach twice, like he's showing me his beer gut, except there's nothing there but muscle. I blink and look away.

"It's a challenge, being you," I say, trying to make my voice light, playful.

He smiles. "At least I have you."

I cross my legs under me on the couch and sink lower. My head hurts from thinking. Rainer. Jake. This thing with Jordan. But I'm still worried about tomorrow. Wyatt's visit looms in my mind like a smoke cloud—I have to get better. I must.

Rainer comes back with a bunch of rolls and edamame and some green, slimy noodles he informs me is seaweed salad. Gross. Thankfully, there is one greasy thing.

"Hey," I say, popping an egg roll into my mouth. "Do you think we could run some lines?"

"Now?"

I keep chewing. "Yeah."

He shrugs. "Sure, if you want to. You're not tired?"

"I am," I say. "But Wyatt—"

Rainer lifts a tuna roll with some chopsticks. "What did I say about letting him get to you, PG? You can't do it."

"I know," I say. "But I think he might be right. Something isn't clicking on set for me. And I don't know what it is."

Rainer shakes his head, still chewing. "You gotta cut yourself some slack," he says, swallowing. "This is your first movie. It's a lot to take in."

He stands up and goes over to the windows. He stops, opening the curtains all the way. I've been on the lanai only in the morning, never at night. It's dark out now. I missed the sunset tonight, and they're brilliant here. A million shades of pink and red and orange lighting up the sky. Way brighter than the sunrise. Like the sky has gained texture and depth since the morning. All the colors are more powerful at night.

"There. Better." He settles onto the couch next to me again, picking up his chopsticks. "So what do you want to go over?"

"Anything? Everything."

Rainer sets his sushi down. "You know what your problem is?"

"Split ends?"

He shakes his head. "You don't believe you can do it."

I fall silent for a minute.

"You're waiting for Wyatt to give you some magical pat on the head, but that's not going to happen unless *you* start thinking you can do it."

"So basically you're admitting I'm terrible," I say.

He rolls his eyes. "More like impossible. Listen, I think you're great. I think you're doing an incredible job. But I want you to *enjoy* this." He looks at me a moment too long. I can feel my heart in my throat. "I want you to be happy here."

We eat dinner and run lines. Rainer says his between bites of sashimi and smiles at me, reassuringly, when I fire back.

"See?" he says when we finish a scene. "No problem."

I want to tell him that there is a problem. A big one, actually. That I'm still terrified of letting everyone down.

The stakes are so high. Wyatt told me. Every tabloid and *Locked* fan site tells me. Rainer doesn't seem to notice. The way he approaches this movie, approaches Noah, is like it's a second skin. Like he's done this a million times before. And I guess, really, he has.

We run lines—over and over. Until two in the morning, until nearly the time I have to get myself to Lillianna, to begin becoming August.

Rainer walks me to his door and we're both bleary-eyed and half asleep. And then he does something he hasn't before. He pulls me toward him and hugs me. Not a quick hug, but a deep one, the kind that makes me loop my arms around his neck and roll up onto my toes. I breathe him in—warm and sweet and spicy. I bury my face in his shoulder. I feel his arms tighten around me. Then, just when I think he might never, he releases me, and I stumble into the morning and toward my condo door.

CHAPTER 9

It's Thursday morning, and I'm in Lillianna's chair, letting her attack my hair with a brush and grill me about the week. I don't mind, though. For one, I think my scalp is getting numb from all the hours I've spent in here, and for another, we're talking about Rainer.

This week has been nonstop filming, but on set things are different with us. So, okay, maybe he just wants to be friends. But I can't help but feel like I'm not crazy for having this crush. He's been so flirty this week. Using every excuse when we're on set to touch me. I can see it bugs Wyatt, and, yeah, everyone is watching us, but it's not like they weren't before. For the first time I just want to relax and enjoy this. I don't know exactly what's happening between us and maybe, for now, that's okay.

I'm thinking about yesterday when we were filming this waterfall scene. All we were wearing were the tiniest pieces of clothing, and it was freezing—the sun definitely did not want to come out. By the second hour my teeth were chattering, and between takes Rainer would put his arms around me and hold me against his chest to keep me warm.

"He's sweet," I say, looking at Lillianna.

She eyes me. "Something is cooking between you two."

I laugh. But I don't say no. I'm about to tell her about yesterday when there is a knock at the door. It's Jessica.

"Hey, Paige, we need you."

I glance up at Lillianna. "I just got here." I flip over my watch. "We're not shooting for another hour and a half."

Jessica smiles. "Jordan Wilder came to set early," she says. "You're doing your chemistry test with him later, so everything's moved up. We're already behind schedule."

I think about my conversation with Rainer last weekend. About how I offered to blow this thing. I know he declined, but the more time that goes by the more I know I'd do it for him. Things are so good on this set right now—we can't risk that. *I* can't risk that.

I nod to Jessica. "I'll be right there."

Jessica bites her lip, and I see her glance down. "Now," she says softly. She looks up at me. "I'm sorry, but Wyatt says we have to go now."

I stand up, and Lillianna gives me a shrug. "Good luck, hon," she says. "You keep holding your own with that boy." She pauses, looks me up and down. "Both of them."

Jordan Wilder is shorter than I thought, much shorter. Shorter than Rainer by far. He's standing by the edge of the water, the rising sun creating a halo around his frame. He doesn't immediately turn around, but I know it's him. I can tell from the scar down his neck, the one that starts just below his ear and scissors down to his jaw. The one that, according to *Hollywood Insider*, Jordan got from a fight last year. He was arrested for disorderly conduct. Between that and an ongoing lawsuit with his parents, he's constantly in the tabloids.

Okay, so, I'll admit it: When I first saw Rainer's reaction to Jordan being cast, I did a little research.

Here's what I found out: Rainer's not the only one Jordan has pissed off. Not by a long shot. He's been around Hollywood for a while and has been linked to countless actresses. And then there's his family drama. He emancipated himself from his parents because of money. He's been in prison. The list goes on.

Seeing him standing there now, even from far away, I can tell he's trouble. I can *feel* it.

I go over to where Wyatt is walking through something

with Rainer. I'm not sure if I'm relieved or terrified that he's on set, too. "Hey," I say. "I didn't know Jordan was coming today." My voice comes out shaky. I'm still not sure where I stand with Wyatt.

He doesn't take his eyes off the script in his hands. "You'll test with him later," Wyatt says. "We're filming now."

Camden comes over, and I grab Rainer's shoulder. He immediately loops an arm around my waist, and I have to swallow to continue my thought. "Is he going to watch?" I ask, slightly panicked.

Rainer moves his hand to my back. "It's okay," he says, but his face doesn't seem to agree.

I'm still holding on to his shoulder, and I lean my lips close to his ear. "Have you spoken to your dad?"

Rainer eyes me. "Are you concerned now?"

I shrug. "No. He just seems..."

"Destructive?"

"Interesting," I correct.

"Diplomatic." Rainer winks and runs his hand down the small of my back. It makes me inhale sharply. Wyatt turns away from Camden. He gives us a weary expression, the kind I've seen him wear a lot this week. The one that says *I don't have time for this.*

"While I'm under the impression that I'm young," Wyatt says.

Rainer still has his hand on me, and I keep my eyes on Jordan. He's facing the shore, his short-sleeved gray T-shirt billowing out in the morning breeze.

"Wilder, come here a second," Wyatt calls. I've never heard Wyatt use anyone's last name and the implied familiarity of it throws me. And then, slowly, Jordan turns around.

He catches my eye instantly. Did you ever have a moment that just solidified? Like the freeze-frame was so strong you could swear time stopped and hardened? Something makes my body feel tight, like my skin all of a sudden is too small.

Jordan's eyes pierce mine. They're jet black, the same color as his hair. It's impossible to tell where his pupils end.

He looks away, scanning the periphery slowly. I see him take in Rainer's hand on my waist, my grip on his shoulder. I untangle us quickly.

He keeps walking toward us. He's unshaven, but I can still see his scar working its way down his jaw to the back of his neck like a hiker on a mountain trail.

"PG?" Rainer is staring at me, and I have a feeling that isn't the first time he's called my name. I give him a distracted smile as Jordan reaches us.

"Jordan, Paige. Paige, Jordan." Wyatt glances back to where Jessica is waving him over. "Get to know each other for a minute," he says, before taking off for the tent.

I jump in. "Hi," I say. "Paige." I extend my hand to him, but Jordan doesn't reach out. He just tips his head to me and focuses his eyes on Rainer.

"Hey," he says. "It's been a while." His voice is low, but pointed. It curls around his words like smoke.

Rainer snorts. "I'm so delighted you decided to show up here." His tone is cold, biting.

Jordan crosses his arms. The edge of a tattoo peeks out when his shirt rides up. "I see not much has changed."

"Has it on your end?"

I take a step back. Whatever this is, I don't want to be in the middle of it. Jordan lets his arms fall, and it sounds like wind rushing by. Or it could just be the extreme sound of my own inhaling.

"Wouldn't you like to know," he says.

Rainer shakes his head. "No," he says. "I really wouldn't." He runs a hand over his forehead. "What did you think it would be like, showing up here?"

"Exactly like this."

Rainer moves closer to him, close enough that Jordan should take a step back, but he doesn't. "You bring this on yourself, and you know it. And it's just a matter of time before she realizes it, too."

Jordan's eyes narrow, and I can see his reserve breaking like thin ice—frown lines spreading across his face like cracks. "You'd like that, wouldn't you?"

"What I'd like is for you not to be here."

Jordan smirks, the corners of his mouth turning up at the sides like someone is pulling tiny marionette strings. "Then you just gave me even more motivation to stay."

He looks me over from top to bottom. His gaze is slow, halting, and I can tell by the way it brushes my shoulders and slides down my body that it's for effect.

Rainer gets this look on his face like it's taking every internal power he has not to close the two feet between them and punch Jordan right in the face. I wouldn't blame him.

I sidestep out of the way just as Wyatt yells, "We're losing the light. Can you guys hold your social hour for lunch? Wilder, stick around."

Jordan looks up. "I'd love to." He sends Rainer one more glance, a smile, almost scary in its sweetness, and then he casually heads back to the tent, slips into a producer's chair, and crosses one leg at the knee.

Rainer doesn't look at me as we start, and I feel something harden in the pit of my stomach.

I know that Ed is in the beginning and end of book one, and that August is torn between Ed and Noah. She loves Ed, she has a history with Ed, but she's drawn to Noah. She's had a crush on him forever, and without Ed on the island, her feelings blossom. But she is going to have a choice to make, and I don't actually know what she chooses. Contrary to popular belief, or what people are saying all over Tumblr and Twitter, neither Rainer nor I have read the final book. It's under lockdown at the publishing house. I have a sneaking suspicion that Wyatt knows. I think the author told him how things turn out.

The point is Jordan could be in our lives for the next two or more years. We could be cemented together as this trio forever. Which is why it's really, really important that he not get the part.

I've never seen Rainer so off his game.

He's vibrating next to me. He does this sometimes right before a scene, like he's shaking himself off. But this time it's more purposeful, like he's not just trying to get rid of himself but someone else, too.

Jordan.

He's sitting there. Calm and cool and collected and a total minefield. You don't even notice until it's too late— until you step on an unassuming piece of ground—and you're blown to bits. Rainer screws up a line and keeps fidgeting, resulting in someone having to fix his makeup like six times between takes.

By noon we haven't gotten close to what we need. And Jordan is still there. Arms folded against his chest, black eyes fixed on Rainer. Like a hunter looking through the barrel of a gun, lining up a shot.

When Wyatt calls for lunch, Rainer takes off toward

the vans to go back to the condos. He runs a hand over my hair before he leaves, but he doesn't ask if I want to come with. I let him go.

I take a breath and walk over to Jordan's chair. I want to say something, maybe even ask him to leave. But as soon as I open my mouth, he turns to Wyatt and starts talking. Like he doesn't even see me standing right there in front of him. He's branded me Team Rainer, so now he doesn't want anything to do with me. Well, fine. Two can play that game.

I take a van to the condos, and when I get there, I realize how starved I am. Everyone—cast and crew—usually has lunch together at a tent set up outside. When I get to craft services, the crew is already eating. I spot Jessica and head toward her. Wrapped sandwiches are set out on the tables, and I grab a turkey and Swiss on my way.

Jessica is wearing a baseball hat with her hair swept up into a tight ponytail; it swings like a pendulum when she turns to look at me. "Have you seen Rainer?" I ask.

She shakes her head. "You need something?"

"I'm good." I sit down next to her, unwrap the sandwich, and take a bite. It tastes like flavored sand. And I would know, I've been eating it pretty regularly during most beach scenes. I'd do anything for a burger from the Fish Market right about now.

"So, you meet Jordan?" Jessica spears a lettuce leaf

with a fork, keeping her eyes on her plate. Her tone is casual, but I can tell from the way her eyebrows move up that she's trying to get a read on me.

"Yeah," I say. "Rainer doesn't seem pleased that he's here. I guess they have some history."

Jessica gawks at me. "Some history? Are you kidding me?"

"Britney..." My voice trails off. I don't actually know which details are true and which aren't. Rainer hasn't told me, and I refuse to fill them in myself.

Jessica lowers her voice. "Britney Drake cheated on Rainer with Jordan." She clears her throat. "They're still together."

"Rainer said he broke up with Britney."

"Right," Jessica says. "Because she's with Jordan. Rainer is just trying to save face with you." She squints like she's just eaten a sour lemon and runs her hand over her forehead. "I'm sorry, I shouldn't have said that."

"It's fine," I say. I take another bite of my sandwich and chew carefully. So Wyatt isn't the only one who is watching us—so what?

"Those two are like natural enemies," Jessica says. "They have to be seated at opposite sides of the Teen Choice Awards." She spears a cherry tomato with her fork. "I get why he's here, he's a great actor, but I'm not sure how this is going to go."

"Well, hopefully he won't get the part," I say, attempting a smile.

Jessica nods. "Totally possible," she says. "Jordan playing the good guy? I just don't see it."

I want to ask her more about what she knows—like was he really in prison? But I have a feeling Google is going to have to inform me again, because I see Wyatt at the entrance to the tent, red-faced and script in hand. "PG," he bellows. "*Now*."

Jessica scoops up her tray, and I follow her over to Wyatt. "Good luck," she mouths. I can't help but think I'm going to need it.

CHAPTER 10

Jordan will barely look at me. We're reading together on the soundstage, and I try, again, to say hello when I get there, but he doesn't turn around. Wyatt walks in behind me, and Jessica follows. Our producers, David Weiss and Joe Dodge, are there as well. They're usually around, unlike our executive producer (and Rainer's dad), Greg Devon, who came once in the beginning. Apparently it's common practice for producers to be MIA on a movie this big. There are usually three or more producers to distribute the weight, and not all of them will be on set all the time. Some of them might never even come. David and Joe are the only ones who are in Hawaii regularly. The rest stay in L.A. to handle the business side of things. At least that's what Wyatt told me at the twenty-minute orientation he gave me our first day here.

"Can you guys just pick up at the top of the page?" Wyatt says. He hands us both a four-page script. It's a flashback scene—Ed and August are on vacation before the crash, and he gives her a love letter as her birthday present. It's a beautiful scene. One of my favorites, because it really shows what Ed and August have. And how much he loves her. It's a romantic scene, and I'm having a hard time seeing Jordan playing it. How is he possibly going to play sweet? The guy's a born brooder.

Jordan looks over the lines. He's still not talking to me, but I notice he's moved closer. There are only a few feet between us now, not a football field. His shirtsleeves are down, gone are any remnants of his tattoo, and I see that he shaved during lunch. The skin on his face is smooth now, lighter than I would have expected, too, like he took an eraser to the bottom half.

He looks over at me, catches my gaze, and smirks. I look away. Something about his gaze makes me feel exposed.

"You ready?" he asks. It's so quiet I think I've heard him wrong. Or it could just be that I'm surprised to hear his voice at all. It's deeper than it was when he was talking to Rainer this morning, softer.

"Yes." I haven't even glanced over the pages. I'm too nervous.

"Whenever you're set," Wyatt calls from his chair. Wyatt has changed this afternoon. He's got on a new shirt, but that's not what I mean. His tone is different with Jordan. He's not as rough or something. Or maybe it's just that we're not shooting. It's funny to not have any cameras around, and so few people. It's completely different from when Rainer and I film. It reminds me of all those rounds of auditions in L.A., and suddenly my body is full of anxiety—the kind that paralyzes.

And then Jordan starts, and the minute he does, I feel like the world has stopped, rewound itself. There is no more fear, no more anxiety. It's strangely calm and serene and peaceful, like we're two travelers walking through a silent, still forest. The only ones for miles.

"I'm always going to be here to tell you."

I set into August, and suddenly the space that has separated us, those rough edges that just didn't line up, fade seamlessly. I actually *am* her. The one torn between her old life and a new one. I'm stuck on a desert island with a man I'm falling in love with, and someone out there is the one who I used to love. I can't see clearly anymore. I don't know which choice is the right one.

As we continue through the scene, I remember something from a script I once read. It was an old version of a classic, and it had a director's note scrawled in the margin. His note to an actor. It said: *Frank—make me believe no one else could do it.*

Standing here rehearsing with Jordan, I know, without a doubt, no one else could do this part. Because something remarkable is happening. He's not becoming Ed, Ed is becoming him, and at the same time, August is becoming me. For the first time since I got here, I understand her perfectly. All these weeks of struggle melt away. *I* melt away. I'm losing myself in her. So much so that when Jordan stops reading, I blink to remember where we are. Like resetting my eyes might reset time, too. Bring us back here.

Everyone in the room is silent. Even Wyatt doesn't make any noise.

Then David starts to clap, and then Camden, then Joe, and then Jessica, and it's just four of them, so I can't say the sound is deafening or anything, but it's the best noise I think I've ever heard. Better even than the sound of Greg Devon's voice telling me I got the part. Because for the first time since I've been here I think I might actually be good at my job.

I look at Jordan, and for a moment our eyes lock. I see something in them. Something that wasn't there this morning. A flicker of light in the blackness.

"Thank you, Jordan," Wyatt says. He slides down from his chair, walks over to us, and puts a hand on my shoulder. The move makes me jump. He's never done anything this friendly. Not remotely. And then he says, "That was pretty stellar."

"Awesome!" Jessica pipes up. She winces and looks at David and Joe, but they're smiling, too.

"Come here," Wyatt says to me. "Jordan, give us a minute."

Jordan nods his head, breaking our gaze. I feel like I've just run a race and I'm beaming, the effects of exhaustion and pure adrenaline pouring outward, like my efforts are somehow outside of me, visible. Like a painting or poetry. I feel like if I tried, I could touch them.

But when I turn to look at Jordan again, he's already walking out the door.

"What do you think?" Wyatt asks me. He's tapping a pen against his clipboard, the way he does when he's trying to hurry our schedule along.

I think about Rainer, and how upset he was. I think about how he's taken care of me here—how much I already owe him. I think about how I really care about him, even if I'm not yet sure what that means. And I know what I should do for him. Even though he told me not to, I should try to get Jordan as far away from this movie as possible.

I take a deep breath and gear up to tell Wyatt I'm just not sure, I think we could do better, when I catch his eye. Wyatt's looking at me the way he does sometimes between takes. It's a hard look, and I know he uses it to inspire fear, but it's also a challenge. It's a look that says *what have you got?* And because of that, I can't lie. Not even for Rainer. The words tumble out before I can stop them. "He's perfect," I say.

Wyatt nods sharply. Triumphant. "The two of you together." He stops tapping his pen and peers closer at me. "I saw something today I hadn't seen before," he says. "I saw you stop trying so goddamn hard."

I'm not sure what to say, so I don't say anything at all.

Wyatt looks over at Joe and David and Jessica and Camden, who all have looks on their faces like the one Cassandra had when I told her I got the part. Like they just can't wait to scream *YES*.

So I say it first. And then they echo me, and soon even Wyatt is losing his cool, pacing the length of the sound-stage, his mouth moving, his arms swinging. He goes over to David and Joe, and they huddle up, like my brothers and their friends used to do when they'd play football in our backyard on Saturdays. There is some nodding, some muffled words, and then they call Jordan back in. And I stand there as Wyatt tells him he has the part. Camden, Joe, and David come over and congratulate him.

Jordan is still hard to read. He's smiling, lightly, but the only thing I have to compare to this scene is when I got the part, and I was, well, less composed. Hysteria comes to mind. And Jordan barely even seems to register the news. He simply says thank you politely, like Wyatt cleared his dinner plate.

Then he looks at me. Our eyes lock, for just a moment, but it's enough to make me feel the impact. Physically. Like he's thrown a baseball straight at my chest. It makes me waver and take a step back. There is something about him. Something that makes me feel like he could change me. That he *will*.

"Call Andrew," Wyatt is saying. "Talk it over. But we're saying, it's yours."

I learn later that Andrew is his agent and that Jordan came out to the audition overnight. That the producers had someone else in mind for the role up until the last minute, when Wyatt demanded they see Jordan read. In person. That he was his choice all along.

"Congratulations," I say.

He doesn't answer. Not with words, anyway. But I know he's heard me. I see his eyes flinch, one quick blink, like a firefly in the darkness.

And that's how it happened—how Jordan Wilder got cast.

People always say that there are a million ways to solve a problem, that no question has a black-and-white answer. It's not true. There are, at any moment, only two courses of action. The one that leads you toward something—stardom, love, disaster—or the one that leads you away from it. And at any moment, in any instant, you have to do your best to know which is which.

So Jordan gets the part.

And then we aren't just moving toward something. We're sprinting at lightning speed.

CHAPTER 11

Jordan disappears back to L.A. just in time for Cassandra and Jake to arrive. In the craziness of this week I almost forget that, come Saturday morning, I'm due at the airport to pick them up.

I talk Rainer into lending me the neon-blue car. "I thought you didn't want to be noticed?" he teases when I ask.

He's handling the Jordan casting news remarkably well. Not that I'm really that surprised. If Rainer had a life motto, it would probably be Keep Calm and Look Superhot Doing It.

"I need to pick Cassandra and Jake up."

"If you want me to come with you, all you have to do is ask."

We're in the doorway of Rainer's condo. He's not

wearing a shirt, just low-slung pajama bottoms, and I am trying really hard not to focus on the outline of his abs or the indents of his hip bones. His hair is still messy from sleep. It's barely six AM.

Unfortunately, we both have to work today. Rainer has to be on set, but I'm not scheduled to shoot until the afternoon, and Cassandra and Jake's flight lands in an hour.

"You can't," I say. "You have to work."

He leans against the doorframe and looks at me through his lashes. His face is still warm and open from sleep. "Keeping tabs on me, huh?"

"You're second on the call sheet," I fire back. "It's kind of hard to miss."

He yawns, and I try not to pay attention to the way the muscles in his jaw work. I think about this week. All our little moments. Maybe I have too many stories about costars falling in love running around in my head. Put there by Cassandra, of course.

I shake my hair out. "So can I borrow it or what?"

Rainer smirks. "Yes," he says. "If you let me take your friends to dinner tonight."

He looks at me, dead on, and I feel the blush rising in my cheeks. "If that's what it takes," I say, my heart flying fast up to my throat.

"See you on set," he says, before unfolding his hand to reveal the keys.

It has been a while since I was behind the wheel, and as soon as I'm in that ridiculous neon car I realize how much I've missed driving. My dad usually stays close to home on weekends, and he'd always lend me his car—oftentimes even if Joanna needed it. I'd pick up Cassandra and Jake, and we'd blast music. Sometimes we'd just drive, if I didn't have to be at work or Cassandra didn't have to babysit. Jake would occasionally protest about gas, but not always. He loved it, too, I think. I sometimes wondered why he wanted to spend all that time with the two of us. He had other friends. Guy friends. Cassandra used to say it was because he wanted to be with me, but I don't think that was totally true.

I can't wait to see them. I need to tell Cassandra all about Rainer, about what's happening, and the Jordan of it all. There is way too much to share, and I definitely need her advice, since I still don't really know what's going on with Rainer. Before they even get here, I start to feel sad they're coming for only two days.

I asked one of the women at the front desk to secure some leis for me, and I loop them around my arm after I park at the airport. They're plumeria, and instantly I'm transported back to that night at dinner with Rainer. I push the thought away, though. This weekend is about Cassandra and Jake.

I wait for them downstairs, near the baggage claim. The Maui airport is small, and everyone files down the same flight of stairs.

I see Cassandra first. Red patent-leather ballet flats, then denim cutoffs, a flower-print long-sleeved camisole, and finally her blond, cherubic head. "Paige!" she calls. She waves wildly and knocks into Jake, next to her; he turns and smiles.

Cassandra plows down the stairs and straight into my arms. I catch her and hold her tight. "You look too skinny," she says into my hair.

"Everyone eats sushi here," I say.

I pull back, and Jake has just reached us, and for a moment we're not sure what to do, but Cassandra rolls her eyes and pulls him in until it's the three of us—faces pressed together, arms around one another. Just like always.

"You're kidding me," Cassandra says, kicking off her shoes in the condo hallway. "This is all yours?"

Jake struggles behind us with the suitcases. Cassandra confessed in the car that it took some persuading to get Jake on the plane, but she reminded him that it was going to be flying whether he was on it or not, and he relented.

"This is incredible," Jake says. He sets the suitcases down and follows Cassandra into the living room. She yanks the sliding glass door back and waltzes out onto the lanai.

"Yeah," I say. "It's cool."

"One piña colada, please," Cassandra calls. I see her pitch the front of her body over the railing, taking in the ocean breeze.

I laugh, and Jake turns to me. "It's good to see you," he says.

I look at him. He's so familiar in his navy T-shirt and jeans. I'm looking at him now, but it's like I'm seeing him as a little kid—our entire history together. I go over to him and wrap my arms around his neck. His arms close around me. He's so much shorter than Rainer, and my head fits right on his shoulder. "I missed you, too," he says.

I pull back and see something cross his face. Hesitation, maybe.

"Everything okay?"

Jake nods. "Yeah, listen, I wanted to talk to you about something." He glances out to where Cassandra is still standing in the sunlight, her head thrown back.

"What's up?" I ask. I hop up onto a stool at the counter and gesture for him to do the same, but he stays standing, his hands in his pockets.

"Since you left . . ." He looks at me, and I see his right eye twitch. It always does when he's nervous.

"Hey, it's me," I say. "Jake, you can tell me anything." I have a feeling he might be about to tell me what I've thought—that since I've gone he hasn't seen Cassandra much. That things aren't the way they used to be, and I feel the guilt begin to bloom in my stomach.

He nods. "I know," he says. "I just—"

The condo buzzer goes off. I blow some air out through my lips. "Sorry," I tell him. "One sec."

I go to the door and find Jessica there. She looks frantic. She's talking even before I open it all the way. "You're late," she says.

I look at the clock: 11 AM. "I'm not supposed to be on set until two," I say.

She shoves a paper into my face. "Schedule changed. You must have missed it. You gotta move. Now."

I've never been late. Ever. And my stomach lurches as I think about Wyatt's reaction.

I look back. "My friends are here," I say. "Can you—"

"Yes," Jessica says, pushing past me. "Just get down to Lillianna."

She jams a script in my hand and hip-butts me out the door. "Tell them to come," I say, but she is already shutting me outside.

Lillianna rushes, cursing a lot, and I'm on set in forty-five minutes. We're filming on our soundstage, and I sneak in to see Wyatt, predictably, fuming.

"Are we interrupting your vacation?" he bellows, rounding on me. "You're an hour late. Do you have any idea how much an hour costs?"

I'm shaking. I open my mouth to apologize, explain, when Rainer steps in.

"Her friends are here," he says. "She was working off the old call sheet. She didn't know." He looks at me, and I feel a windfall of gratitude so big I think I might just throw my arms around him right then and there. But I don't. My feet are stuck to the spot.

"I see our little talk really had an impact on you," Wyatt says. He ignores Rainer. "Should we get to work? Or will we be interrupting a massage appointment?"

"No." My voice sounds small and fragile in my ears.

"Good."

As we get miked, Rainer glances at me. "Sorry," he mouths. I shake my head. Today we're filming the scene where August wakes up in bed and Noah tells her where they are.

I'm supposed to be naked under the covers. I'm wearing a nude strapless bra and boxer shorts. I climb into bed. It's really just a few pieces of plywood covered in old woven blankets. Still, the blankets are soft cotton, and they feel good as I slide underneath.

We rehearse. Noah comes and kneels down on the bed. We do our dialogue. He tells August that they're on this island. That no one knows where they are because it is magically protected from outside interruption. It's locked.

We do it a few different ways. In one, August is hesitant and a little afraid of and angry at Noah. In another, she's imploring. I put my hands on the sides of Rainer's face. He looks into my eyes. August is so in love with Noah. So painfully, deeply in love. She's committed to his best friend, who might now be dead, and yet she wants nothing more than to just fall into him, into Noah. She knows she can't. They both do.

We start shooting. I take a deep breath and focus my mind, the way I always do. I'll make up for lost time. I'll nail this.

"Why don't we reschedule the whole fucking shoot for when it's *convenient* for you to *act*?" Wyatt screams.

I bite my bottom lip hard. So hard I taste blood. I know Cassandra and Jake are here somewhere, and the humiliation is overwhelming. It sets my blood boiling. I want to scream at Wyatt to shut up, but I don't have to. Rainer does it for me.

"Why don't you go a little easier on her, man?" His tone is steady but pointed. "Cut her some slack once in a while."

Wyatt's eyes flash. I can feel the crew cower around us. "Is that what you want?" he asks, his tone icy. "For me to make your *girlfriend's* job a little easier? Maybe I could just leave and you guys could get back to whatever you were doing."

Rainer's hands clench and release. I can see the blood climb up into his face, making his normally calm, even features come to life.

"You don't have to be such a dick about it, is all I'm saying."

Wyatt stands there, staring at him. I can see something pass between them—some unspoken agreement—almost like they're calling up the same memory. But then Wyatt turns away, swears under his breath, and calls to start rolling again.

Rainer squeezes my hand under the covers. "You okay?" he whispers.

From the corner of my eye, I catch Cassandra and Jake, pressed shoulder to shoulder, sipping from coffee cups.

I don't answer. I push the emotions down. I want to be better. I want Cassandra and Jake to see I didn't leave for nothing. That there was a reason I was chosen. That I belong here.

Wyatt eases up, and we shoot the scene and one other. We work quickly, efficiently. Wyatt doesn't yell. I can't tell if it's because I am focusing superhard or because of his altercation with Rainer—maybe both. I don't even care. I just care that we're getting through things. I care that Cassandra and Jake are seeing me work.

Despite my schedule snag, we finish nearly on time. Wyatt walks off with Camden, and Rainer and I go over to where Jake and Cassandra are. Cassandra grabs Jake's elbow as we approach, and I know she's excited about meeting Rainer. The embarrassment I felt at Wyatt's words is nearly gone. At least I have this to offer her.

"Cass, this is Rainer. Rainer, Cassandra."

Rainer puts on a dizzying smile and extends his hand. "It's so nice to meet you," he says. "I feel like I know you guys already." He turns to Jake and for a second my heart leaps into my chest—how are they going to interact?—but Jake looks like he's just as happy to see Rainer as Cassandra is.

"Nice to meet you, man," Jake says.

"I heard you're a stellar activist," Rainer says. "We should discuss at dinner. My dad started Environment Now."

Jake's face lights up. "Wow," he says. "He's doing some amazing stuff."

Rainer throws me a light smile as if to say *see, no problem.* "His board is," he says to Jake. "C'mon, let's get food."

We go back to the condos and change. I have on a new slip-dress I bought at the shops, and I feel Rainer's gaze on me when he picks us up at my door. "You guys ready?" he asks, his eyes scanning my bare shoulders.

Despite the warm night, I shiver. "Yeah," I say. "Just about."

Jake appears in the doorway. "What time is sunset here?"

Rainer flips his watch over. "Whenever these girls get out the door."

Jake goes back inside and returns with a shoeless Cassandra, who says, "I'm not ready—" But Jake pushes her outside.

She giggles, which is weird. Cassandra usually doesn't like to be interrupted when she's putting an outfit together.

"Shoes," Jake says, setting down some of my flip-flops.

Cassandra slides them on, and the four of us leave.

Rainer drives us to a sushi restaurant. We haven't left Wailea a lot, and it's nice to be back in the car, top down, the sun setting around us as we head into town.

I give Jake the front seat, and Cassandra and I sit in back. She grabs on to my knee and squeezes so tightly she leaves marks. I know what that squeeze means. It means she cannot believe she is in a car with Rainer Devon. I squeeze back and hope it communicates what I can't right now: *I have so much to tell you.*

Rainer opens the door for us and offers me his hand as we get out. I take it. Then, all at once, he leans in. "You look beautiful tonight," he says. "In case it wasn't obvious." It's low, practically in my ear, but I know Cassandra hears. I know because when Rainer walks ahead with Jake, she grabs me by the elbow, hard, and turns me around.

"Bullshit," she says. "Bullshit that nothing is going on with you two."

"Cass," I say, but I know my face is giving me away. It feels on fire. "Nothing has happened," I tell her. "Yet."

Cassandra's eyes go wide.

"I know," I say. "Can you keep it together?"

She laughs. "I don't think that's the question. I think the question is, can you?"

Rainer is entertaining and charming at dinner. He lets Jake grill him about his dad's foundations and answers Cassandra's endless stream of questions about young Hollywood.

"Who is your favorite costar?" Cassandra asks. She's all elbows on the table, peering at Rainer like he's some kind of equation she's trying to solve.

Jake has his arm over the back of her chair, and he laughs. "This was definitely the price of admission for this trip," he says.

I wish Cassandra would cool it a little, but if Rainer is put off by her grilling, he's not showing any signs of strain. He arches around to face me. "You," he says.

I can see Cassandra look from Rainer to me and back. "I'm sure you say that to all your costars," I joke, hoping he doesn't, hoping he actually means it.

Jake removes his arm from Cassandra's chair. "I always knew you were talented," he says to me. I look across the table at him. Jake. Sweet, solid Jake. Something tugs at my heart. Not him exactly, but home. Who I used to be with them. All of a sudden I feel like the space across the table is an ocean—I suppose, really, it is one.

We say good-bye to Rainer in the lobby of the condos. I can see the exhaustion of the week wearing on him and I feel it, too. It's heavy. It bears down from all sides.

Jake takes the second bedroom, and Cassandra crawls into bed with me. She's totally keyed up. She wants to talk. I do, too, but now that dinner is over, I feel the grip of sleep. All these long hours. I'm not going to last long. I roll over onto my side to face her, my eyes at half mast.

"I have to tell you something," she whispers at me. Her breath is warm on my face.

"Yeah?"

"You didn't tell me about Rainer," she starts, but it doesn't sound like an accusation, not even a little bit.

"I told you," I say. "Nothing has happened. It probably never will."

"But you like him."

I look at her. I can't lie. Not now. Not to Cassandra. And despite my exhaustion, everything I've kept in, everything I've been talking myself out of, comes bubbling up to the surface and then spills right over. "Yes," I say. "I mean, I think so. It's not like I have tons of experience with this stuff, and it's just so confusing. Some moments I feel like we're totally about to, I don't know, become something, and other moments it seems like I'm completely in the friend zone. He's so hard to read, but then I think maybe it's me. Maybe I'm the one who doesn't see what's going on. It's complicated. This whole movie is just..." I shake my head, stifling a yawn. "I'm sorry. I'm blabbering."

"I know," Cassandra says. "And I've missed it."

I roll my eyes. "You wanted to tell me something."

Cassandra smiles. "It can wait."

I reach over and kiss her cheek. Her hair on the pillow tickles my nose. "I'm happy you guys are here," I say. "Really happy."

"Me too," she says.

When I wake up, it's light out. I haven't woken up after dawn in weeks, and the sunlight is momentarily alarming. I stretch, but my limbs don't reach anything. I roll over and realize that Cassandra is out of bed.

I swing my feet onto the floor and grab my robe from a chair. I pad into the living room. I hadn't thought about what to do with Cassandra and Jake today. Maybe we'll drive back into Paia. Or go to the beach. Or we could go get lunch in town. The possibilities swirl outward, making fuzzy patterns in my head against the warm sunlight.

I'm still rubbing my eyes, clearing sleep, so I don't immediately notice them. In fact I don't spot them at all until I'm practically toppling over the sofa.

Cassandra is sitting with Jake, her legs draped casually over his lap. Her hands are pressed into his shoulders, her fingers moving like she's searching for something.

And her lips? Well, they're right where his are.

I stand there in the open space gaping at them, absolutely no idea what to do, because my first reaction isn't what I'd expect it to be. It's not anger or confusion or even quick-footed sadness. My first reaction is that they look good together. The way he's touching her cheek and gently brushing her hair over her shoulder. The way, when he pulls back, right before he sees me, he looks right into her eyes. A look that makes my stomach and heart clench up like fists. Because he's looking at her in a way I've never seen before. I thought I knew everything about them. But I've never seen this. Which means I haven't really been looking.

"Paige?"

It's Cassandra who speaks first. She retracts her legs from Jake's lap like springs and flips around on the couch. "We didn't know you were awake," she says, like this explains something.

Jake looks at me. He stands up. "I made coffee," he says. "Do you want me to pour you a cup?"

He gestures to the kitchen, but I shake my head. "What's going on, you guys?" I ask.

Cassandra bites her lip. "We tried to tell you." She glances at Jake, her expression concerned.

I think about Jake saying he needed to tell me something, about Cassandra's urgent whispers last night. I feel so incredibly stupid. Here I was thinking they were losing touch without me, but really they were moving on.

I wish this isn't what I say—I feel like a petulant child—but what comes out, complete with dripping sarcasm, is "You obviously tried pretty hard."

Cassandra looks at me, her eyes wide. They fill up instantly. "I'm sorry," she says. Her voice falters.

I don't know what to say. I don't even know how I feel. Should I be angry? I wish I hadn't just walked in on this. I wish it were just the three of us watching a TV marathon. Not them making out on the couch.

No one speaks for a moment, and then Jake starts. "Paige," he says. "We wanted to tell you. It's just…" He walks over to me. He gets so close I can smell him. He smells so familiar—like laundry detergent, the unscented kind. It's underlying. Always there.

I want to hug him, to wrap my arms around him. I want Cassandra to come over to us and the three of us to embrace the way we did at the airport—the way we always have. But something is different now.

"Why didn't you?" I ask. "Why didn't you tell me while I was gone?"

Cassandra looks at Jake. "We didn't know how you'd react. Whether you'd be mad."

"Why would I be mad?" I cross my arms.

We all stand there. Jake and I no more than two feet apart, Cassandra on the other side of the sofa. All at once I wish I didn't know. I wish they had never come. That I could keep pretending that at least this hadn't changed.

"I'm sorry," Jake says.

I nod, playing with the skin of my elbow. "How long have you guys been…"

Jake shrugs. "A month."

I've been gone six weeks. They didn't waste any time.

"I wasn't sure we should have come…." Cassandra's voice trails off as she hugs her arms to her chest.

"No," I say. "It's fine. It's—" But I don't know how to finish the sentence. I clear my throat. When I speak again, I don't look at them. "I have to check in with set," I say. It's a lie; it's Sunday. Maybe they know that. From the looks on their faces, I'd say they do.

"Paige—" Jake starts, but I shake my head.

"It's okay. You guys should go down to breakfast. Order whatever you want. I'll catch up with you later."

Jake bites his lip as I turn to go. "You were off leading this fantastic life," he says. "You were far away. Cassandra wanted to tell you. We're—I don't know...." His voice trails off, but he keeps looking at me.

"I know," I say, because I do. There's something there. I don't know why it took this long for all of us to see it.

I suddenly remember how upset Cassandra was when Jake first kissed me. How she wasn't happy that we were together. How she said we didn't get it, that it wasn't the three of us now.

For the first time, I understand how she felt.

Cassandra walks around the couch, reaching out to touch my hand. "I'm sorry," she says. "You just weren't here."

I shake my head and turn away. "You can call the front desk if you want to order up something," I say instead.

"Do you want to go to the beach later?" Cassandra asks. Her voice is hopeful. It feels like it cuts right through me.

"I'll see how work goes."

I know I'm being unfair. I can feel it. My pride sings in my veins, pumping its venom right along with my blood. I want to get rid of it. To run to Cassandra and tell her of course I don't care, but I can't. There is something stopping me. I yank the door open, but before I can get outside, she moves in for a hug. I lean back, away from her, and her arm just catches my shoulder. I see the sadness in her eyes. It's so different from last night. This isn't the friendship I left six weeks ago, and we both know it.

"We'll see you later," she says.

I force a smile onto my face. "Yeah," I say. "See you."

"Paige," Jake says. I look at both of them standing there, their hands hanging by their sides.

"You're our best friend," Cassandra says.

The three musketeers. Except we haven't been that in a really long time. Because we haven't been together in a really long time. It's been the two of them before Hawaii. Maybe it's been the two of them always.

I smile, and then I turn and head out the condo doors. I'm not sure where I should go. To the beach? But even before my feet take me there, I know where I'm headed. And when I show up at his door, he doesn't seem surprised.

"Hey," he says. I see the outline of a pillow on his face—the remnants of recent sleep. He's not wearing a shirt, and his bronzed skin stands out in the sunlight.

"Can I come in?"

Rainer holds the door open for me, and then before I can stop myself, I'm throwing my arms around his neck. He pauses for a second, sways on the spot, but then his arms curl around me—warm and strong. "Come on," he says into my ear. "Come inside."

CHAPTER 12

Rainer and I have lunch and dinner with Cassandra and Jake. It's awkward, but honestly I'm not sure they notice. They seem to be so happy together. Out in the open. A couple in love on vacation in beautiful Hawaii. A vacation I paid for.

"I can't believe we have to go back to school tomorrow," Cassandra says wistfully at dinner.

School seems so far away—like a life that belonged to someone else. The thought of sitting in classrooms, taking history, studying for the SATs.

I just have to get my GED. Technically I'm not required to take a full curriculum, like I would if I were in school, so I just get tutored on the fundamental stuff: math, English, all the things I need to know for the test.

"And you're *staying* here," Cassandra says, her voice accelerating. "Everyone is freaking out that we came to set."

Jake and I exchange a glance. My face gets hot. I'm suddenly embarrassed. By Cassandra? It's not a feeling I like.

"Isn't this fun?" Cassandra says when we're walking to the car. She pulls my elbow, holding me back just a bit. "It's like we're on a couples trip."

But this isn't a couples trip. This is work, and Rainer isn't my boyfriend.

The fact that she doesn't see that, that she doesn't understand that this isn't some kind of fantasy, makes my heart ache. Because it means she doesn't really understand me. And when I drop them off at the airport later that night, the three of us at the curb, our good-byes are not what they would normally be.

"When will you be back?" Cassandra asks. We're standing by the car, and Jake is unloading the bags from the trunk.

"Not sure," I say. "After filming, I guess."

She shifts her carry-on backpack on her shoulder and nods. "Thanks for having us," she says.

"Of course." I pause, look down at my feet. "It was fun."

I look up, and she's staring at me. I can see her about

to crack, the words spilling out—the admission of everything that is wrong, in this moment, right now—how much she loves me and how nothing has changed—our friendship is forever, don't I know that? But she doesn't. Instead she takes Jake's hand as he comes around.

"Fly safe," I say. I give them both a quick hug, and then I'm back behind the wheel. I don't stop to see them go inside. I don't want to know if they look back.

A call sheet is waiting under my door when I get back to the condos. Five o'clock tomorrow morning in hair and makeup. But this time it's not for filming. We're shooting our first feature for *Scene* magazine. I make myself a cup of tea and fall asleep before the sun is down.

A few hours later I'm sitting on the floor of my bedroom in the condo, magazines covering the carpet. I've gotten a subscription to everything: *People, Us Weekly, Glamour, InTouch, Cosmopolitan*. Even the trashy tabloids. They're all here.

I haven't become Cassandra overnight or anything; it's just that I need some answers and figured this is as good a place as any to start looking for them. I need to know how to give an interview in about two hours, and I don't have the first clue what to say. It's time for some DIY media training.

Jordan will be back this morning, and I hope Rainer's

nonchalance continues. Something makes me think that once they're face-to-face, it may not.

I glance at the clock on my nightstand: 4:30 AM. I pick up the copy of *Scene* off the floor and hold it out in front of me. Some glossy, white-toothed girl I don't recognize is smiling back at me, pulling her shirt down so you can see the top of her bra. It's pink, the same color as the high-lighter I have bookmarked in the history textbook I'm reading for Rubina.

I flip to the white-toothed girl's article, where she's sucking on a lollipop, wearing a cherry-print dress in the middle of a field. HAYLEY'S HOME, the headline reads. "I'm happy with who I am. I feel like I'm finally completely in my own skin." I shut the magazine, using my toe to edge it to the far side of the room.

I used to think these plastic pinups were just that: unreal. But now I'm getting ready to do the exact same thing. I'm not sure whether I'm excited or totally embarrassed for myself. Both, probably.

I throw a sweatshirt over my tank top and denim shorts and slide into my flip-flops at the door. It's chilly outside, and I pop on my hood as I walk to set. Even though it's dark, I can still see the outline of the ocean, the first hints of sun picking up the rolling waves. I hope I can fit my morning swim in tomorrow. Since we're doing the magazine today, we'll probably have an early call time tomorrow, too. Everything on this movie is broken down to the minute. If you lose thirty seconds to sneeze, you have to make it up somewhere else, but this has to be balanced with union overtime.

When I get to base camp, Rainer is already there, wandering around the craft service table. His hair is a little matted down, and he's got a red dent on his cheek from sleeping. I can't help but think he looks pretty cute in his faded blue T-shirt and board shorts.

"Hey," I say.

He turns around, rubbing his eyes. "Hey there. Sleep well?"

I nod, although I did not sleep well. Sure, I passed out for a few hours, but I mostly dreamed about how disconnected and weird my time with Cassandra and Jake was. And then I sat on my floor, looking at perfect celebrities, trying to figure out (1) how people talk in interviews, (2) what I'm doing in this business, and (3) how to censor myself so I don't start telling *Scene* about the time I spilled hot chocolate down my jeans in second grade and everyone called me "Wets Her Pants Paige" for the rest of the year.

Jake once told me that it's hard to sleep when there's a full moon, and I make a mental note to check the sky tonight. I'd love to chalk my insecurities up to lunar patterns.

I reach to grab a coffee cup when I feel a hand on my waist. It startles me so much I spin around, and when I do, Rainer pulls me right up against him. He slides his other hand down my back and interlaces his fingers so he's holding me, chest to chest. It's like a quintuple espresso has been injected into my veins. My whole body wakes up. His arms are warm, and his T-shirt is soft. It's almost enough for me not to notice the reason he's got me all tangled up like this.

But then I see Jordan standing in the doorway. He's framed there by the first rays of sunlight, backlit in a way that Camden and Wyatt would probably kill for on film, and he's looking right at us.

The last thing I want is for Jordan to get the wrong idea. He hates me already, and my loyalty is to Rainer, I know that, but I don't want to start unnecessary problems between us before we even start working together. We're professionals. This is a job.

Rainer's arms, thankfully, slacken around me, and he plants a kiss on my cheek before letting me go.

I crane my head around to look back at the door, but Jordan's gone. So far we haven't spoken too much about Jordan being cast, but I know Rainer will suck it up. He's got to.

Wyatt is headed our way. He sends me a glance I'm plenty familiar with by now. *Keep that personal crap in your condos.*

I take a step back from Rainer, and Wyatt angles left for the coffee table just as Sandy comes sweeping toward us. You can really only describe it as sweeping because she's got on these ivory silk pants and a matching blouse that make her look like she's floating. It's not even six AM. I wince thinking about the rat's nest on my head. I still haven't taken my hood down.

"I didn't know you were coming," Rainer says. A wide smile breaks out on his face as they hug.

Sandy has spent the last few weeks in L.A.

"Just so we're clear, I'm back for the sun." Rainer shakes his head, and Sandy winks at me. "How's the shoot going, PG?"

"Pretty good," I say. "Learning a lot."

"Understatement of the year." She turns back to Rainer. "You look thin, kid. Are you eating over here?"

"He looks fine with his shirt off," Wyatt says, handing Sandy a coffee cup.

He smiles at her, an incredibly rare occurrence on his face, and she laughs. "You know I don't drink this stuff."

She wiggles her nose, and all at once she reminds me of Cassandra. I wonder what Cassandra's doing right now. It's eight thirty in Portland. Their flight got in at four AM, I think. She's probably at school. First period.

Last year Cassandra and I had art together first period. Early in the semester, we convinced Mrs. Delancey that we were working on installation art for our final project. We would take big canvases out to the lower field and just lie on them, looking up at the sky. It was always cloudy, and mostly we got rained on, but we didn't mind. We'd just lie there, sometimes talking, sometimes not, until the bell rang. By the end of the semester the canvases had all kinds of grass, dirt, and water stains. I was convinced we were going to fail, but Cassandra made us turn them in. We ended up each getting an A minus. Mrs. Delancey called our work "innovative and thought-provoking."

Wyatt angles his shoulders to the entrance. "Where's Jordan?"

Rainer snorts, so loudly I think it might actually have been involuntary, and I see Sandy narrow her eyes at him. A look that seems to say *watch it*.

Wyatt ignores him and motions to Sandy. "Walk with me. I want to run something by you."

Sandy nods, and Wyatt takes out a clipboard. He always has a notebook on him. Shot list, scene list, call sheets, etc. "You guys have until noon for this *Scene* stuff," he says, waving the clipboard around. "Then we're filming."

"Success hasn't made you soft, huh?" Sandy says. She smiles, and I see small lines around her eyes, like pencil marks on a page. I wonder how long they've known each other, and how they met. There seems to be a story there.

"Not yet." Wyatt looks at her, and for the first time I realize how little I know about him. I know he's not married and he doesn't have any children, but does he have a girlfriend? Does he live in L.A. when he's not filming? What was his life like before this? I know, and have always known, that he has a reputation for being the way he is—tough. But was he always like that? It's hard to imagine him any other way, but I saw something in him at that chemistry test with Jordan. I saw how much he loves this. How he'll do anything to make it what it needs to be.

A group of people I don't recognize have congregated in the corner of the tent. The *Scene* team. I heard something about them wanting to do a behind-the-scenes visit before our cover shoot. Jordan is standing with them. He says something, and one of the women nods intently. She lets her fingertips rest on his forearm briefly.

Wyatt and Sandy have disappeared, and Rainer is talking to Jessica, who has just arrived, orange juice in hand. "Does Urth Caffé deliver?" I hear him ask her.

She laughs, and Rainer blows her a kiss. God, he's cute.

Then Lillianna is there. She looks me up and down and declares loudly, "Oh, honey. If I saw you looking like this, I wouldn't put you on a soup can."

*

I'd never admit this publicly, but my favorite movie is not *Casablanca*. It's not *A Clockwork Orange*, either. It's actually *She's All That*. You know, the one with Freddie Prinze Jr. where he falls in love with the school nerd? It's not Hitchcock or anything, but I love it. My favorite scene is the one where the main guy is waiting for her at her house right before the big school dance, and she walks down the stairs and is totally transformed. All of a sudden, she's beautiful.

It's eight AM before I walk through the soundstage doors but when I do, I feel like I'm in a movie. Not acting in one, but actually *in* one. The way people's heads turn when I step inside. And the way Rainer and Jordan look at me, like neither one has ever seen me before.

Rainer turns around first, and I see his wide smile, mid laugh. His mouth actually stays open. He's gaping at me. Something inside me lifts. It feels good to be watched this way, wanted maybe. I can feel his eyes on me. The way his gaze sits—heavy, weighted. The way his eyes travel over my shoulders and up to my eyes like he's looking for something. Like I have something he wants. Then he whistles, and Jordan turns around.

You know how when you're taking a photo sometimes the shutter stalls and the picture goes into freeze-frame? My image of Jordan just hangs in the viewfinder. I see him swallow, his Adam's apple moving down his throat. I look at his hands by his sides. His fists opening and closing. Then his eyes look up into mine, and I recognize the same expression he shot me on the beach. His black eyes look like they're cut from glass. It feels like if he stared hard enough, long enough, he could slice right through me.

"Hot in here," I mumble.

No one hears me.

Usually stars bring their own hair and makeup teams to these kinds of photo shoots, but since I'm still new at this game and we're on set, Lillianna subbed in. And the look couldn't be further from August's signature soft, wavy locks and rose-colored makeup. Now my eyes are smoky ash, highlighted with black eyeliner and a light-gold shadow that travels from my eyelids down my cheeks like stardust. She's somehow got my hair to properly curl, too. It's got ringlets, and they bounce as I walk. Like they're dancing, set to music.

And I'm wearing a black dress. It's lace, with spaghetti straps and a ribbon adorning the waistline. It's so tight and short, I'm afraid to move my arms.

I have on four-inch platform heels.

My lipstick is red.

I feel…beautiful. Hot, even. The way I always imagined the cheerleaders at Portland High felt when they were opening the football games. Like they were worth people watching. Worth Rainer Devon and Jordan Wilder watching.

"Damn," Rainer says. I walk over to where he's standing, the *Scene* crew separating him from Jordan. In the time it's taken me to get ready, a massive stage has been set up inside. Big, black paper polka dots are everywhere—pasted onto the floor and walls. Red plastic balls float around vintage pinball machines, and giant Twizzlers are in big pink barrels. I feel like I'm in Willy Wonka's chocolate factory. I have to admit—it's kind of awesome.

"Are those edible?" I ask Sandy, pointing to the Twizzlers.

"Sorta," she says. "But I wouldn't recommend it."

Rainer puts his hand on my back again. I turn to look at him. "Seriously," he whispers. "You look ridiculously hot." He drops his lips down to my ear. "You're kind of making me crazy here."

"Yeah?" I say. The ends of my fingers feel tingly and numb all at once. I have no idea what is going on between us, but I know we're flirting. I know this isn't friendly. Or professional. Not anymore.

"Yes," he says. He nods his head down to mine. "You're gorgeous."

I don't know whether it's the makeup or the hair or the fact that I actually feel like a movie star today, on the set of what *People* just called "the hottest thing since summer," but I want to throw my arms around his neck. I want to kiss him right here.

Rainer is wearing a red-and-white-checkered shirt, open at the collar, and dark jeans. He looks dapper, and as I move back, I take a moment to appreciate how absurdly good-looking he is.

He smiles at me. "How are you feeling?"

"Good," I say with a nod. It's true, too.

"First official magazine feature," he says.

"Not yours."

I let my hand wander up to his collar. I pretend to pick a piece of lint off it, but there is nothing there. I just want to be close to him.

Rainer covers my hand with his. It's warm. It makes the rest of the soundstage get a little fuzzy.

"We're just filler," he says. "This entire thing is about you."

I open my mouth, but no words come out. He's looking at me with this expression that makes me feel nervous and excited and totally taken care of all at once. Like he's not going to let anything happen to me. On this photo shoot, on this set, or anywhere else.

The *Scene* crew parts, and then Jordan is there, right next to us. He's wearing black pants and a black shirt with a purple tie that's come undone. He has the slight evidence of a five o'clock shadow.

My heart trips, like it's fallen over a beat, and that familiar feeling of nerves comes rushing back. I force myself not to focus on Jordan. Every time I do, my stomach turns over. He makes me feel unstable. This is only the second time we've met and already his presence disrupts. And I don't want to be distracted right now. I want to keep standing this close to Rainer. I want him to keep telling me the way he sees me.

I blow some air out through my lips. I shake Jordan off. His issues are not going to ruin today. I'm here, right now, living this incredible fantasy. And the best part is that it's not a fantasy, it's real. I'm starring in a huge movie and about to be photographed for a magazine. And feeling anything but excited, joyous, downright *thrilled* feels like a betrayal of that dream. I won't let Jordan take this moment away.

Someone turns music on, and then the entire soundstage, all three thousand square feet, is filled with the Smiths, then Kanye, then Katy. The playlist pounds on as we start shooting. Me on Rainer's shoulders, Jordan watching us. Rainer with his arms around me, Jordan off to the side. They keep yelling things at us, and it starts to…work. Things click. This is the first thing we've done, the three of us, and I can feel the chemistry. It's not just me and Rainer or me and Jordan, but *all* of us. I feel it the same way I did with Rainer in Portland and Jordan here at his audition. Except this time we're all together.

It's enough to make me forget, momentarily, that

Rainer and Jordan can't stand each other. Rainer grabs a large Twizzler and rips off the end with his teeth. He swings it at Jordan, and the two mock-fight with the candy like they're wielding swords.

I pick up a red ball and toss it in the air, and when the camera snaps, just before the ball starts descending, I realize I'm having fun. Actual fun. I'm not self-conscious right now. I'm not worried that I'm not doing a good enough job or that I should be more this or that. I'm just enjoying being me, here, now. This world is crazy and strange, but also pretty spectacular. And I can tell Rainer and Jordan are feeling it, too. I can tell by the way they aren't sending each other looks or trying to rip each other apart. Suddenly the past and everything it holds—Cassandra and Jake and even Britney, whatever she means to these boys—feels a million miles away. Like it's not just an ocean that separates us but something else, too. Something solid.

The song changes, and Rainer lifts me up. He twirls me around, fast, and as the soundstage spins, I focus on his face. He's smiling and saying something, but between the speed and music I can't hear him. He sets me down and keeps talking, but I still can't hear him. I'm too hopped up on adrenaline and Madonna. Out of the corner of my eye, I see Jordan leaning against a wall, his hand on his jaw, looking at the camera. Someone hovers over him with a comb.

Rainer gets closer, and just as the music fades out, flipping songs, he says something to me again: "I want to kiss you." This time I hear him.

The bad news is, so does everyone else.

The *Scene* crew members look at one another like they're not sure what to do, and Sandy and Wyatt immediately leap to damage-control duty, watching the video replay and making sure you can't catch Rainer's words.

"The producers would love this," Sandy says to Wyatt.

"But I don't." Wyatt looks at me when he says it, and I'm reminded again of our conversation in my condo. How angry he appeared at the possibility of Rainer and me getting together. But now I think maybe he was wrong. And suddenly I'm incredibly annoyed at how big a deal this is. Because it's no one's business what I do off set. Rainer and I aren't Noah and August, and if we like each other, so what? It's not like we're going to stop doing our jobs. I look at Rainer again, standing there—waiting for some kind of response from me. He doesn't care. He's not concerned about Sandy buzzing around or Wyatt's pissed-off comments or the *Scene* people standing by, waiting to figure out how to move on. Because it's not about them. It's about us. I want to tell him I want that, too. I want him to kiss me more than I have ever wanted anything. I want him to put his arms around me and make this moment last, capture it right along with the camera.

Except something stops me. And it's not Sandy or Wyatt. My back feels hot, and I know, instinctively, that Jordan has heard. I can feel his stare. I can't explain why it makes me feel guilty.

I'm not hiding anything. Wyatt and Sandy are huddled up, and the *Scene* crew is setting up another shot, at least pretending they're not listening. I drop my voice, edging closer to Rainer.

"You can't do that," I whisper.

"What?" he says. His eyes trace over my face. I suck in my bottom lip.

"You can't say stuff like that at work." I look up at him.

"This isn't a *no*," I want to say. "It's a *not now*."

Rainer's face lights up into a grin. "It's hard to control myself around you," he says. He cups my elbow with his hand, runs his thumb along the crease there. Heat fires up my arm straight to my core. "But if it's what you want, I'll try."

My chest lifts; my temples throb. I take a deep breath, attempting to quell my rebellious pulse. "So much of our lives is already going out there." I gesture over my shoulder in the vague direction of the ocean, of whatever is at the end of it.

"It'll be okay," he says. He puts both his hands on my arms. They feel sturdy there—like they're holding me in place. His eyebrows knit together when he says: "I promise."

"No more funny business on set," I say.

Rainer laughs. "Ma'am, you insult my dignity." He takes his hands away and throws one against his chest in mock horror.

"I will if you insult mine."

He smiles, and his face gets soft. His features blending and setting into smooth, approachable lines. "Okay," he whispers.

The music starts back up, and Rainer goes over to Lillianna for a touch-up. I glance back, and when I do, I catch Jordan watching me. He turns immediately. I feel like I've lost whatever working relationship I could have had with him before it has even begun. My mother used to tell me that you can't have everything in this world. That's just not how it works. I guess she was right.

The magazine director, a woman around my parents' age, comes over to me.

"We need some shots of you," she says.

"Okay." I glance over at Rainer, who is filling a coffee cup now. "Should I—"

"No guys," she says, "just you." She gives me that smile that people at the DMV give you. The one that says *I've told you all I can. Now please go fill out the form and stop asking me questions.*

I nod, and let her arrange me so I'm sitting on this giant cupcake pillow. She has me bend my legs, my knees knocking together. She arches my back and puts my hair in front, then to the side. She steps back and squints at me, like I'm a painting she's not sure is hanging even on the wall. Then she sticks a wind machine in my face.

"Can you tilt your head a little more to the left?" she asks me. "Just the head, not the eyes."

I try to think what that even means, but by the time I start to work it out, the camera is already snapping, coming in on me, close. The wind is making my eyes tear, and I keep wiping at my cheeks, apologizing.

"Have some fun with it," she says.

Fun. Right. I try. I smile, I laugh. I try to access that feeling of power and awesomeness that I was experiencing a few minutes ago. I open my eyes wide and set my lips in a perfect semicircle. But it's not as easy as it was when we were all shooting together. Everyone's eyes are on me now, and I feel exposed, like this barely-there dress has been wiped off and I'm suddenly stark naked in front of the crew and my costars. I can feel them looking at me, their competing gazes. The combined impact is almost too much to bear.

Finally, mercifully, the camera stops, and Rainer and Jordan are called back. We do some posed shots now. Me still sitting, them standing on either side of me. We're close, all three of us, and the music is low, barely humming through the soundstage.

Rainer tucks his arm around me, and I lean back on his chest. Then we stand and do the same thing. Then the director motions for Jordan to get closer in the shot. "Grab her," she tells him. I keep my eyes trained on the camera.

Jordan turns.

"Hey," I say. I feel like it's the first word I've said to him.

"Hi," he says. His face is inches from mine.

Then he pulls me toward him. Fast. He smells like soap, like a shower, like Dove. It's so specific it makes me feel like I'm back in my shared bathroom in Portland. The one with Annabelle's rubber ducky toys, my sister's antifrizz shampoo, and the drain that never quite works properly no matter how many times my dad has fixed it. And that, more than anything, makes me melt into him. He tucks my head against his chest and closes his arms tight around me. I can't explain it, but the next instant I feel like putty. Like I'm Play-Doh in someone else's hands. Soft and pliable. Like I could be molded into anything. Anyone. Even August.

CHAPTER 13

Here is what the official kiss count at the end of today will be:

August and Noah: 1

Paige and Rainer: 0

We're finally filming their first kiss today—a scene that takes place in the hut-house during a huge rainstorm. Romantic, sure. Nerve-racking, definitely. Of course, the sun is out and blazing on our actual Hawaiian island, and for the moment we're inside on the soundstage rehearsing.

Here's the situation: Noah and August have been fighting their feelings since they got to the island. August is his best friend's girlfriend, after all. But as the days and weeks wear on, they start to realize they might never be rescued, and they give in to their feelings. *Cosmo* actually called our version of the kiss "the most anticipated lip-lock of the year." That's a lot to live up to, but I get it. It's supersexy in the book. And I want to do right by the scene. The truth is I've been equal parts dreading and looking forward to filming it, and I sort of can't believe it's actually here.

Noah and August seem to be on track. And Rainer and I are, too, I think. Last night we had dinner. We went to Longhi's, and a few girls around my age recognized Rainer and asked for his autograph. Dinner felt different from the way it has before. It felt like a real date. We shared a dessert. Our spoons clinked against each other, and he touched my knee under the table. I felt those girls watching us, watching me. The girl who was out with Rainer Devon—I liked it.

After dinner, he walked me back to my door and reached for my hand. He brought it up to his cheek. He was so painfully beautiful. I just wanted to wrap my arms around his neck and draw him in. I know he wanted to, too. All these weeks have built up between us like electricity.

But when he went to lean his lips down to mine, I couldn't do it. It suddenly felt terrifying. It seems like so much is invested in our story already. Like as soon as we kiss, everything will change. And I want to be ready for that, but I'm not sure I am. I need him. He's the one person in my life right now who understands me. Who is holding my hand through this. What if we get together and then it ends and I lose him? Is that a risk I'm willing to take?

"I'm sorry," I said. I reached my arms up and ran my thumb down the back of his neck. I felt my chest press closer to his, like my heart was trying to line right up with his rib cage. "It's—it's like if we kiss, it's more than a kiss. Do you know what I mean?"

"That's what all the ladies tell me," he said.

I shoved him. "Oh my God, are you ever serious?"

"Hey." He pressed his forehead to mine. "We have plenty of time." He put his hand on my face. Held it there. "We have three movies' worth of time."

I laughed, and so did he. Then he kissed me on the forehead and disappeared down the hallway.

And now here we are, ready to film this kiss. At least on paper. But we can't get started because unlike yesterday, today it's not raining.

Jessica has a big piece of bamboo filled with sand and painted with these crazy African hieroglyphics. It's her "rain stick," and she brings it out almost every day—trying to make it rain, or trying to make it stop raining. Because of the unpredictable weather, we've started prepping for five or six scenes in case we can't shoot the ones we had planned on for any given day. They've built sets in an old, abandoned shed by the beach and even one in Wyatt's condo. Anywhere we can physically film, we have.

Wyatt thinks this is nuts and is constantly yelling at

Jessica to "put the damn thing away," but I think that secretly, maybe, he believes it works. Because honestly, most of the time, it sorta does.

This morning Rainer is running around the set with the rain stick, singing that song about the rain in Africa. The second unit has gone out to get some extra pickup shots, and Wyatt and Camden are trying to figure out how and if they can set up the scene here and bring in fake rain, and Jessica is talking to the props department, trying to figure out what happened to the fake mud. I'm still not sure why movie mud has to be fake. It's not like blood, you're not harming anything if you actually take the real stuff. Although, I guess, Jake might think you were.

"Sing it with me, PG," Rainer says, holding the rain stick in front of me like a microphone.

"You're in a good mood," I say.

He looks at me and raises his eyebrows. "I get to kiss you today," he says. "Shouldn't I be?"

I blush what feels like fuchsia. I look away, over at Jessica, who is running by with a prop I can't see.

We're right on the edge of something, like the heavy, wet heat of the air right before a huge rainfall. Once our characters kiss, will it change things for us? Actors are always talking about how unromantic love scenes are, how there are a million people in the room, how strategic it is. But they're still *my lips*. They're still *Rainer's*. I know it's different, separate, but I feel the same way he does. It's like we can't take the leap, so our characters are doing it for us.

Wyatt makes an executive call: We're going to film inside. The props crew immediately goes to work on constructing a set that will match the one we've already filmed on outside. They'll use a green screen all around to be able to project the right background and match up shots in the editing room.

Wyatt has requested a closed set for this shoot, which means it will be Rainer, the immediate crew, and me. No Sandy, no extra crew members. No Jordan.

I remind myself of this as I run through lines in my head. It helps that he won't be here—that it will just be Rainer and me.

I watch Rainer from the side stage, dancing around with the rain stick. His smile and easy charm. He pokes Jessica, and even though it's obvious she's in the middle of a million things, she doesn't get mad. Rainer's older than Jordan and me by a few years, but there's something about him that's so childlike. He's just happy, like a little kid on Christmas morning. He makes other people smile, too. I used to think it was calculated—his celebrity charm. But now I know it's not. It's real.

Rainer is so different from Noah. Noah with his brooding, complicated past and mysterious aura. But they're both incredibly loyal. Supportive. And I think, as it turns out, they both might want to kiss me. My blood zings through my veins at the thought, and I once again have to steady my heartbeat.

"You look concerned, PG." Rainer sets the stick down and comes over to me. He places both his hands on my shoulders, and then runs them down to my elbows. I exhale. It feels good to have him close to me like this. It's calming.

"Not concerned," I say.

He tilts his head forward. "You sure?"

I shrug. "Maybe a little nervous."

"Okay." He turns me around, marches me over to a crate to the side of the soundstage, and motions for me to sit down. I tuck my costume, a white nightgown-dress, under me and fold my arms across my chest.

Rainer gently puts his hands on my knees, and kneels down in front of me so we're eye level. "Hey," he says, "it's going to be fine. It's just me and you." He smiles—that warm, approachable, melting ice cream smile—and my nerves start to slacken.

"People care about this," I say. "Everyone keeps saying how important this kiss is...." I bury my head in my hands.

Rainer squeezes my knee. "Don't think about them. It's just us right now. Hey." He lifts my fingers away from my face. "We'll do our best. That's all we can do."

"What if my best isn't good enough?"

He smiles at me. His eyes look into mine. "It will be. We have great chemistry." He touches my shoulder. "Right?"

I swallow. Nod.

"You guys ready?" Wyatt comes over, Jessica at his heels. He's wearing his Ramones T-shirt, which means today is a serious day. It's his lucky shirt, and I can tell how important a shoot is by whether he's wearing it or not.

"Ready," I say. I try not to let my voice falter.

Rainer puts his hands on my shoulders, just below the blades, and nudges me forward. We follow Wyatt to where a makeshift set has been created in a matter of minutes. Sometimes the things they do around here are kind of magical. Like there are elves hidden in the palm trees or something.

I snap my eyes closed and take a deep breath. Inhale and exhale. I'm trying to imagine what August is feeling right now. She wants to be with this person more than anything else in the world, and finally he kisses her. He lets them go there. It's wild abandonment—of their past, their future. It's all about this moment. Not thinking. Just *acting*.

The first take is clumsy. I lean in too swiftly, and my nose knocks Rainer's. I'm shaking. It's making it hard to have any actual contact.

The second take is worse. I have developed the hiccups, an old nervous habit, and when Rainer leans in, my entire body jolts backward.

"*Cut!*" Wyatt yells. He runs a hand over his forehead. "Look," he says to me. "What do we need here?"

"Sorry," I say, my body convulsing as another hiccup goes ratcheting across my shoulders.

"I don't know what's going on with the two of you, but just pretend you're someone else for a minute."

"I *am* someone else," I say. "I'm August." This is getting to be like Acting for Dummies over here.

Wyatt shakes his head. "Get out of her, too."

How can I tell Wyatt that kissing Rainer now, as August, feels like kissing him as Paige, too? All this flirting. All these glances and moments. They've been building to this, and I can't separate myself out.

"Who then?" I ask.

"A model?" Rainer offers. "Preferably French. Thanks." He smiles at me, shrugging his shoulders.

"You need to get out of your head," Wyatt tells me. He's frowning, and I'm afraid he's going to start yelling, but instead he says, "Sometimes you need to be someone completely different. Someone who would grab Noah and have her way with him. Who would do that?"

Britney? "I don't know," I say.

Wyatt waves me off with the back of his hand and keeps

talking. "Step out of the way. Take on a persona that would really make this happen tonight." He looks at me. There it is again. His signature intensity. "Just fucking *do* it."

"Okay," I say. Except what I'm thinking is that the problem is not my being someone else, the problem is Rainer being someone else. I'm nervous to kiss him because of everything it would mean for us, our relationship. But right now we're not ourselves. We're August and Noah. A lost girl and boy.

I make the first move. Practically before the camera starts rolling, I'm attacking Rainer, grabbing his face and shoving it down against mine. It's not very sexy, but hey, it's contact. Let's just get through it. Rainer seems amused by this, and starts cracking up. Wyatt, of course, yells cut.

Fourth take. Rainer places a hand on my elbow. He draws me closer, traces my jaw with his finger. I let my eyes slip closed. I lean closer. I feel Rainer right above me. Cut.

Wait, why? I glance over at Wyatt. "More intensity!" he yells.

Fifth take. I lean in, and so does Rainer, and our lips meet. It works. It way more than works. I wrap my arms around his neck, and he pulls me in closer. His hands are tight around me, and his lips are ziplocked to mine, so sealed I can barely even breathe. And I don't want to. I want him to keep kissing me like this—like it's just us on this island. His arms travel down my back, and I wind my fingers through his hair. My whole body feels on fire, and for a moment everything dissolves. We're not on a set. We're on an island. No one else matters. Nothing but this.

But then Rainer pulls back. I feel his lips leave mine, and I grope forward, not ready for the break in contact. My eyes are still closed when I hear him say, "You're not supposed to be here."

It's Jordan. I know before I even look. Faded gray T-shirt, arms crossed.

"It's raining," he says, like this somehow answers anything.

"Shit." Wyatt looks at him, then back at us. "It's a closed set, Jordan."

Jordan stuffs his hands into his pockets. "Okay," he says. "I'll leave."

Rainer's hand is still around my waist, and I feel him tug me in tighter. "Stay," he says to Jordan. I watch them look at each other, watch Jordan's eyes flit, briefly, to my hand on Rainer's shoulder. It's a challenge, and for a moment I feel a flare of anger that Rainer is claiming me right here, in front of Jordan.

"Then sit the hell down," Wyatt yells. He leans over to Camden, and they discuss whether we should move outside, now that there is actual rain to contend with.

Meanwhile Jordan has slipped himself into a director's chair. His scruffy sneakers dangle toward the floor, his arms draped over the sides. I can see the glint of raindrops on his forearms, the beads of water falling down his neck.

"Your heart is racing," Rainer says to me. He tucks my head under his chin. I feel his chest rise and fall against me—steady, strong.

But I still can't shake the feeling that Jordan's watching me. I want to ask Rainer why he told Jordan to stay, but I'm miked, so I can't. Even if I know the answer, I want to hear it.

We go again. Rainer bends his head down, and I pull him closer. His mouth is warm against mine, his hair soft. I try to stay focused. To not lose myself in him. I don't want to give Jordan the satisfaction of watching that. I can feel Rainer's heart hammering against mine.

"Cut!" Wyatt calls. He looks us over, then back at Jordan. "All right," he says. He checks his watch. "Let's break for lunch."

"Lunch" is any time when we're halfway through the scenes we have to do for the day. Usually it's around dinnertime, which means while I have a few hours left, the boys are gearing up for a night of shooting.

I glance over to see if Jordan is still there. He is. He's seated, watching us, but when I look over, he turns his head sharply and begins talking to Camden. I want to make an effort. I want things to be okay on this set. But I'm starting to get pretty sick of his attitude.

The sound guy comes and takes our mikes off. I'm happy to be out of earshot for now.

"Hey, PG," Rainer says. He's still so close to me, and his hand is resting on my side, right at the curve of my back. "Walk with me?"

I nod.

He takes my hand. I jostle to see if Jordan is watching us leave, but I can't meet his eyes, and Rainer is already halfway out the door. When we're outside, I find that it is, in fact, raining hard. We huddle to the side of the sound studio, where there is a slight awning but not enough to prevent us from getting wet. It's only been about twenty seconds, and already my nightgown is nearly soaked through. Rainer puts one hand on my waist, right where he last left it, and nudges me closer to him. "Come here," he says. He has this look on his face like he wants to say something. I hold my breath. But he doesn't talk. He doesn't say anything. He kisses me.

My chest tightens and then swells as his lips come down on mine. My hands travel up his arms to grip his shoulders. He presses me to him so there is no space between us. He's kissing me with so much intention. It's gentle and soft and strong and sweet all at once. It's everything I have wanted. I can feel us getting soaked, feel the rain on our faces, but I don't care. We're finally here.

CHAPTER 14

Rainer has to stay around set to finish filming, and I run back up to the condo, soaking wet and shaking. I feel exhilarated. It feels like it's the start of something, and I can't help but let excitement win out over fear. I want this. I want to be with him. He makes me feel comfortable and confident and protected. Safe in this new normal. I realize that the problem is not the way I feel about Rainer. I know how I feel about Rainer. The problem is the way I feel about Jordan.

He's gotten into my head. I know this recent development with Rainer will make it even harder for us to get along, but it's not like Jordan has been making any type of effort. He hasn't even tried to have a full conversation with me. It's all pointed stares and sharp hellos. It's so unbelievably stupid. I should just follow Rainer's lead. I should treat Jordan the way he treats me. But there's something about him. It's like I want to put as much distance as possible between us and at the same time figure out, up close, who he is. What makes him this way—his family? His history with Britney? I wonder if she knows Jordan's secrets. I wonder what he says to someone he cares about.

I can't sleep. I keep thinking about Rainer just down the hall.

I finally peel myself out of bed at 4:30 AM and slip into my bathing suit for a morning swim. I need to clear my head, and it's been a while since I've gotten into the water on a weekday morning. Call times have been so early lately.

It's dark as I slide into my flip-flops, sling a towel over my shoulder, and make my way down to the beach. I can see the outline of surfers in the water, their silver bodies illuminated by the predawn light. They look like those flying fish I read about once in a coffee-table book my dad has about lakes. I've never seen them live before, but their tiny bodies fly out of the water so they look like small silver arcs, moonbeams, almost like the reflection of shooting stars.

I set my towel down on a rock, tossing my shoes to the side. The sand feels cool under my feet, like it's been in the freezer, and for a moment, I doubt my ability to go in. But

I push the thought away, take a deep breath, and plunge headfirst into the ocean.

The water hits me, sharp and cold, and I start to swim. Long, fluid strokes. I don't take my head out until I've done ten. When I look up, sputtering and gasping for air, I'm already a few yards off the shore. I flip over onto my back and let the current carry me out a bit farther. The sky is changing—navy fading to gray fading to the palest shade of violet. Soon the sun will break out—like a solo dancer onstage—and start spinning, its rays reaching out left and right and center.

It's early still, and I swim out farther to where the surfers are congregated, straddling their boards, waiting for waves. I think about how Wyatt would kill me if he knew I was out here, and for some reason that makes me swim farther, faster. Past the surfers and the rocks off the coast. So far, in fact, that when I look back at the condos, they look like nothing more than sugar cubes: small and white and capable of dissolving in the mass of swirling water that is all around me.

I swim out a little bit farther. It's peaceful out here— expansive in a way things just aren't right now.

The thing about Hawaii is that there are no lifeguards. I remember them telling us this during our island orientation. When they told us about that moving lava chain. There are no lifeguards because the current is strong, very strong, and if you swim, it's at your own risk.

A lot of tourists die in the water here. Not from shark bites, although that's what I stupidly piped up during orientation, but from the current. They get dragged so far out to sea there is no way to get back, a big wave comes, and they drown. I thought that was ridiculous. Know your limits. I can handle the water, I thought. I'm a strong swimmer. Always have been.

Which is why what happens next is so crazy.

I know you're supposed to go under waves when they come. If it looks big, you dive to the base, because if you can't make it over the top, the force of the wave can knock you down and drag you under. But it's too late. I don't see it until it's already there, looming over me. There's no time to duck. I freeze, and in that split second, the decision is made for me.

The wave comes crashing over me, bearing down from all sides until I feel like I'm being pummeled to the ground. But it's too deep out here to hit the ocean floor, and I'm being pushed farther and farther underwater. I know all that's waiting for me down there is more water. More of the same, suffocating darkness.

And it is suffocating. My lungs feel like they're on fire, and I can't imagine that my mouth isn't hanging open, attempting to scream. I have a mental flash of water flooding my lungs, filling up my windpipe so much it bursts, like the water balloons Cassandra and I used to throw out my bedroom window onto the concrete driveway in the summer. Ten points if you hit someone square, three points if they were just sprayed.

My thoughts start to blur. I picture Cassandra and my brothers and my parents and Jake in my living room, the three of us joking around, and Trinkets n' Things. I picture a sunset full of orange and red—so bright it looks like the fireworks they set off in downtown Portland on the Fourth of July.

Then I see the beach and the sound studio and Wyatt looking angry. Except the image is faulty, grainy, and light, like a photograph that's been left out to fade in the sun. It wilts, and as it does, I see something else. Someone else. Someone I've imagined way before I knew what to picture. He's here. Real and human in a way I'm not anymore. I know I'm dying in much the same way I've known I had to shower or that I was going to get reprimanded for not taking the trash out. It's a practical kind of knowledge, and I don't even try to fight it. I just close my eyes and wish for it to happen quickly. For me to stop thinking. Because when I think about him, I don't want to go.

I hear him calling my name, quietly at first and then louder. I'm surprised because I imagined my senses would be fading. I thought that the closer I got to death, the quieter it would be. But it's not. It's full of noise. The screaming of my name, the sloshing of water, and then something else, too, something that convinces me I've already gone: his face, so close I can feel him breathe.

"Paige." He says my name sternly, and for a moment I'm reminded of my eighth-grade math teacher, Mr. Steeler. I'm not sure why I'd be thinking about him now, at my moment of death, but that's what happens.

It comes again: "Paige."

I open my mouth to answer, before I remember I'm underwater. I brace myself against the rush of pressure, the taste of salt, but it never comes. Instead I find myself coughing, sputtering like I did when I first got in the ocean this morning. And I open my eyes.

The first thing I notice is that I'm lying on something. I try to lift myself to see, but an arm gently nudges me back down. I can still hear the water around me, but it's softer now, less menacing. Instead of crashing, it's lapping, a soft *whoosh whoosh*, almost like a lullaby.

"Paige?"

I turn my head and see him bobbing in the ocean next to me, one arm tucked over my abdomen, the other fanning through the water. I'm lying on top of a surfboard, and Jordan Wilder is pulling me to shore.

He's frowning, the lines of his forehead pinched together like marionette strings.

"Jor—" I manage, and then start coughing again. His

hand that is over me reaches up to touch my shoulder, then smooths the hair away from my forehead. I close my eyes again. It's totally possible I'm dead. The odds of reality in this situation are not promising.

"Hang in there," he says. "We're almost back."

I see now that he's propelling the board forward with his legs, keeping me steady with his arms. I lift my head up and spot the shoreline a few yards off—the long stretch of beach is the best thing I have ever seen—wide and solid and steady.

"How are you feeling?" Jordan's voice comes next to me.

"Okay," I say. I cough some and then steady myself. "How did you . . ."

I look at him, and he shakes his head. "You were pretty far out," he says. "You can't do that in Hawaii unless you really know the ocean. You obviously don't."

"Did you *follow* me?" We're close enough to the shore that Jordan is standing. I swing my legs over the opposite side and stand, too. They're wobbly, though, and when they buckle underneath me, I keep my palms flat on the board.

"I had to," he says.

"No, you didn't."

He raises his eyebrows at me. "You sure about that?"

"No," I say.

"Right." He puts a hand on my back. I'm surprised at how warm it feels. My whole body is freezing.

"Thank you," I say.

"For what?" There is a lightness in his voice, playfulness. I haven't heard it before.

"Saving my life," I mumble.

"I'm sorry, what now?" he asks. He's teasing.

I look up and glare at him. Even after he's pulled me from the brink of death, Jordan Wilder is still obnoxious.

"You're welcome," he says.

I help him ease the board into the sand, then collapse. The sun is starting to warm the beach, and I can feel it on my back. I take a few breaths, lean back on my hands.

"Do you come out here a lot?" I ask.

He nods, sitting down next to me. "Every morning."

I turn to look at him. "Really? Why have I never seen you?"

He glances at me, water dangling off his lashes. "I guess you haven't been looking."

"Have you seen me?"

He opens his mouth to answer, but I'm coughing again—large, heaving, water-filled gasps. I feel Jordan's hands on my shoulders, and then one down my back, rubbing big, even circles. Even with the sun, it makes every inch of skin spring up with goose bumps.

"Thanks," I say.

"Maybe we should get you inside," he says.

"No." I don't want to go inside. I don't want to go anywhere. I am overcome with the need to remain—to stay on this beach with him for as long as I can.

"You should get some hot liquids in you. And maybe a proper towel." His voice is determined, and I gesture over to the rocks where my flip-flops are tossed, along with my pineapple beach towel.

"I have one," I tell him.

He stands, wipes his hands on his board shorts, and jogs over to the rocks. I watch his tanned body, the outline of his torso, as he slings the towel over his shoulder. He's so easy in the water and on this beach. He looks like the surfers who live here. Like he belongs.

He comes back with the towel and unfolds it, draping it over my shoulders like a cape.

"Oh, thanks," I say. "You didn't have to."

He sits back down in the sand. "You're a pretty priceless commodity these days," he says, brushing his hands together. I watch the sand fall between them. "The star of the movie. I'd probably have to pay to replace you if you got hypothermia." He looks over at me. "I don't think I could afford it."

"It's Hawaii. Hypothermia seems unlikely." I snatch my gaze away from him, because I'm worried he can tell, just by looking at me, what it feels like inside. How my heart beats faster knowing he's near me than it did when I thought I was drowning.

Jordan looks at me, and there is something new in his eyes. Something more than that fleck of gold—a star in the night sky. His eyes look softer, too. More brown than black.

"We haven't really gotten much of a chance to talk," I say.

He snorts.

"What?"

"Nothing."

"Tell me."

He leans back on his hands, stretching his legs out. "You're tied up, is what I meant."

"Tied up?"

He shakes his head. "Come on, don't do that. Don't act like you don't know what I'm talking about."

I think about Rainer's arms around me on Jordan's first day on set. Then again at the photo shoot. "Rainer," I say.

He raises his eyebrows. "You guys are a thing, right?"

I pull the towel closer around me. "I don't know." It's as truthful an answer as I've got right now. Plus... "I don't really see what that has to do with us being friends."

He holds his hands up like I have him at gunpoint. "Hey, it's your career, not mine."

"What's that supposed to mean?"

He sighs. "Rainer likes to be in the spotlight." He's talking slowly now, like he's explaining something to a second grader. "You get a lot more of it when you're dating an actress."

"That's not what this is," I say. "No one even knows who I am."

He looks at me intently. "But they will."

"Maybe," I say. "But who is Rainer supposed to date? He's an actor. Don't you do the same thing?"

His eyes narrow. "I don't date actresses."

"Just pop stars."

"I'm sorry?" he says, squaring his shoulders so he's facing me. "Is there something you'd like to say?"

"What about Britney?"

He lets out a long breath, picks up a handful of sand, and lets it sift through his fingers. "Britney is not, nor has she ever been, my girlfriend."

I can't help it, the words tumble out. "So you just hooked up with her behind Rainer's back?"

His eyes make my heart plunge down into my stomach. They're soft again. But not because he's concerned. He's hurt. "Is that really what you think?"

I shake my head. "No," I say. "I don't know. I was totally out of line. I'm sorry."

"Look, if you're going to be a part of this business, you

need to understand that there are things you don't share, or talk about, because they're sacred. People will come after everything. They will dig up graves for gossip. And if they can't find it, they will make it up."

Then he stands, like that's that. "Come on," he says. "We're going in."

He holds out his hand to me, and I take it. It's strong, and a little bit calloused—the kind of hand that's held things. That's gripped them tightly.

We walk in silence, a silence filled with the million things I want to ask but don't. It doesn't seem like he wants to talk, and after he saved my life, the least I can do is shut up.

"Thank you," I say when he drops me at my condo door.

He shrugs. "Luck," he says. "I'm glad I was there." His eyes meet mine, and we hold our gaze like that, not even blinking. I wonder if he feels it, too. I wonder if he wonders.

"Same," I say, softly.

Then he drops his head, tucks his arms across his chest, and turns to go. I watch him walk down the hallway until he vanishes around the corner. Even then it takes me another beat to pull out my key card, to not keep standing there watching the space where he once was.

CHAPTER 15

I'm reading some scripts my agent has sent over. The thought of doing another project is really exciting. It helps me remember that August is a moment—a big one—but a moment. There are plenty of other characters to play. There is a script about a mean girl who gets pregnant, one about a mermaid based on another bestselling book series, and then a period piece where I'd play the daughter of the male lead. It shoots in Seattle, so I'd be close to home, which I have mixed feelings about. I'm almost through it, and the script is pretty brilliant.

I set the pages down next to me and stifle a yawn. It's chilly outside, cooler at night than it was when we first got here, and I tuck my feet under me, readjusting myself on the lanai chair. If I close my eyes, I'm back in Portland in the winter. I imagine Cassandra and me trekking through the pouring rain to the Saturday Market, our umbrellas up, feet sloshing. Or drinking hot chocolate at Jake's, his mom rolling her eyes at me as Jake lectures us about the ramifications of cane sugar burning or the ill effects of some bacterial strain spread by seagulls.

Cassandra. Jake. They flash like photo negatives.

Something is happening out here, something I didn't expect. I'm forgetting who I was. It's becoming normal to be on a film set, to hang around with the crew, to have someone else cook all my meals and have my favorite snacks show up in my refrigerator without a Post-it or follow-up with Mom. I don't think twice about the fact that my hair and makeup are always done or that my inboxes—e-mail and voice mail—are constantly being clogged by handlers. I have a million messages from my agent about everything under the sun. I thought acting was just about acting, but I was wrong. There is so much more to all this—so many ins and outs I feel like I'll never learn.

I can't shake what Jordan said this morning, about keeping some things private. But I have no idea what in my life to keep hidden. What in my life is sacred? I thought my friendships were, but I haven't spoken to Cassandra or Jake since they left. And my family doesn't even understand what I'm doing, what my new life is. Perhaps my dream, this movie, is sacred. But isn't it also the very thing that has made me someone people are going to want to pull apart? And how do I know if Rainer is sacred when all I can hear is everyone's voices in my head, weighing in on us?

"Knock, knock."

I look up to see Rainer leaning into the lanai doorway, his aloha shirt blowing in the night breeze, a plumeria tucked behind his ear. The interruption makes me jump. It's freaky that he has appeared just as I'm thinking about him, and after this morning's near death I'm also feeling a little off. "Is that your idea of knocking?" I ask.

He nods slowly. "Yes."

"How did you get in my door, anyway?"

He smiles. "I wanted to see you."

My heartbeat speeds up. "Doesn't answer the question."

He walks toward me and takes a seat in the chair next to mine. "I have some friends in high places. Specifically the front desk."

I laugh. "So now you're flirting with the receptionist?"

"All in your name, PG," he says.

I won't tell Rainer about this morning. I'm not sure why except I know it has to do with Jordan. I just know Rainer wouldn't like us sharing something. Even if that something is mostly me not dying. Talking about Jordan seems loaded, too loaded for tonight.

"How was your day?" Rainer asks.

I loop my arms around my legs and tuck my head down on my knees. "Fine," I say.

"Why are you hiding then?"

"Not hiding," I say, turning my head to the side. "Just tired."

Rainer and Jordan had off today. We had to film some scenes where August is alone on the island. It was just me and Wyatt and the crew, and I can barely keep my eyes open right now.

"Come here," Rainer says. He puts an arm around me, and I feel myself being lifted out of my chair and into him, into his arms. It feels so good to be here. Some of the tension of today begins to drain out of me.

He settles me in his lap, pulls back, and puts a hand on my cheek. Then he leans in close, and I half expect him to kiss me, but instead he plucks the flower from behind his ear. He holds it out to me.

"For you."

"Thanks." I take it and run the stem between my thumb and forefinger. I put the petals up to my nose and inhale. It's sweet and spicy, like real vanilla.

"What's going on?" I ask him slowly, carefully, my eyes trained on the plumeria petals.

He shrugs. "I watched some TV today, grabbed a sandwich. It was nice to have some time off." I feel his hands on my back, traveling up my spine. I suppress a shiver.

I set the flower down. "That's not what I mean," I say.

He cocks his head. "What are you referring to, then?" His voice is light, singsongy. Flirtatious.

I knock him lightly on the shoulder. "Us."

The corners of his mouth turn up in a smile. "Us?"

I feel ridiculous. I'm sitting in his lap and his hands are on me, and I still don't even know what that means. "Yeah. Um, you kissed me."

"I'm aware of that," he says, still half-smiling at me. "Why do you think I'm here?"

The soft fluttering in my chest turns into full-on eagle-flapping wings.

He leans closer to me, but this time he doesn't hand me a flower and he doesn't pull back. "I'm here because you're smart." He leans closer. I can feel his eyelashes brush my cheek. "And funny." Closer. His nose grazes my jaw. "And beautiful." He hovers right above my lips. "And I really like kissing you."

My pulse is racing. It feels like it might run away from me. "Okay, but . . ."

"What else?" he whispers.

I inhale, try to keep my voice level. It feels like I have to struggle to get each word out. "What do you want?"

He sighs and places one of his hands on my knee, on top of my hand. It's soft and warm. "I thought that was pretty obvious," he says, threading his thumb through mine. "I want you."

"Rainer..."

He lifts my hand and puts it in his, right up against his heart. I feel it beat—strong and steady. "Just relax," he says.

I suck my bottom lip in. "Okay," I say.

"Good." He takes both his hands and grabs the sides of my face, and then he's pulling me toward him. He kisses my nose, and then my forehead, and then right over the creases of my eyes. When he pulls back, he is breathing hard. "You're so gorgeous," he says.

"You're kidding." I exhale.

"I'm not." He kisses the side of my neck, right below my ear. It's getting almost impossible to think clearly.

"Why me?" I ask. I clear my throat. I push him back. I think about what Jordan said, about how he dates actresses because he likes being in the spotlight. But how could that be true? I'm nobody yet. "Besides the obvious point that I'm the only girl you know on this island."

"Not true," he says. He threads his fingers through mine. I look down at them. "You forget about the receptionist."

"And Jessica," I say, keeping my gaze down.

Rainer nods. "And Jessica."

"So?" I untangle our hands and rest mine in my lap.

I have to hold them together to keep from sticking my fingernail between my teeth right now and biting.

"Why you?" Rainer asks. "That's what you want to know?"

"Yes." I pick my gaze up to meet his.

He shakes his head like I'm the one who's missed the point. "That, right there," he says. "You have no idea how people see you. You're incredible."

Then he kisses me. For real this time, right on the mouth. I want to say something, but it gets caught up in our kiss. Tangled in his hair and fingertips and the strong beat of his heart. *You're incredible*. With his mouth moving against mine, his hands on my waist, they seem like the only words that matter. The way he sees me. The way he feels about me.

His hands are everywhere—my back, my waist. He presses me against him. I reach forward and knead my hands into his shoulders, feeling the muscle there. I feel him sigh into my mouth, but he doesn't break our lips apart. He keeps kissing me, and slowly I start to feel it, too. That maybe he's right.

CHAPTER 16

"Are you with that boy?" My mom's voice is staticky through the phone. She always calls me on her cell because we don't have a long-distance plan at home, and the signal is never any good in our house.

"Since when do you read tabloids?" I ask. I'm standing in the condo kitchen, looking at an article with the headline: RAINER DEVON AND PAIGE TOWNSEN ARE *LOCKED* IN LOVE IN HAWAII. They've reused the photo of us from the Fish Market—me and Rainer, foreheads pressed together. Didn't that run weeks ago? How is that still relevant?

"Since my daughter ended up in them," she says. Even through the not-so-great connection, I can hear the shortness in her tone.

"Do you really believe all this?" I ask. I don't think

about what has actually changed since then. The fact that Rainer and I have now kissed. A few times.

"I don't know, honey," she says.

I put the magazine down. "Did you actually subscribe to *Star*?"

I still don't believe her. My mother wouldn't know how to locate a tabloid if it were the only book in the school library. Which, obviously, tabloids aren't. She shops at the local co-op, not the supermarket, and the only magazines there are *Yoga Journal* and a bunch of pamphlets on astrology. I have another theory.

"Cassandra called you," I say.

My mother sighs. It comes out in a crackle. "Please answer my question, Paige."

"She did, didn't she?"

There is a suspicious pause in our conversation. Then: "She really cares about you."

Cares about me. Right. That's why she's been so busy calling me since she and Jake came to set. "She just wants *information*," I correct her.

"Honey, I think if she wanted information she'd call you. It's very unlike you to doubt Cassandra. What's going on?"

I imagine my mom standing in our kitchen where she always uses the phone, her elbows on the counter, or fussing in the refrigerator, and I think about how long it has been since I've seen her. The longest since I was born. I should tell her something. That I love her. "It's not something I really want to make public," I say instead.

"It's Cassandra and your mother," she says. "Which one of us, exactly, is public?"

"She's dating Jake," I blurt out.

I don't hear a sigh or a gasp or even the silence of stopped words. "I know. I've seen them," my mom says matter-of-factly, like I've just told her I had a peanut butter and jelly sandwich for lunch.

"So you knew?"

I imagine her pausing in the refrigerator, putting the milk back and sticking her hand on her hip. "Honey, you have all been friends for a really long time. Things change."

"She's dating *Jake*," I say, slowly. Like if I place the words one at a time this will make sense to her.

"But don't they have a right to be happy, too?"

I inhale. "Of course," I say, "it's just—" My mom doesn't know about the times Jake and I kissed and how mad Cassandra got. "Cassandra always said it would ruin things if two of us got together."

"And what do you think?"

"I don't know," I say. I run my palms along the cool marble of the countertop. "It was just weird, having them out here and seeing them like that. I kind of freaked out." I sit down on a stool and swivel outward, toward the ocean. I don't usually talk to my mom about this kind of stuff, but it comes tumbling out. Seeing Cassandra and Jake on the couch. The dinners with Rainer. How awkward our good-bye was.

She doesn't answer right away when I finish. "Mom?"

I hear her inhale, the slow sigh of her exhale. "I understand, honey," she says. "But I think you need to give them a break. I don't think you're upset because they're together; I think you're upset because they moved on, too. Things change, sweetheart."

"I didn't think we would," I say. There is a lump in my throat I didn't know was there.

"You can't blame your friends for carrying on life without you."

"But did they have to carry it on *together*?"

I hear the slight jingle of her laugh. "Well," she says. "I think the better question is whether it's worth losing both friendships over." She changes the subject to my sister and Annabelle, then says, "I gotta go. I love you," and clicks off. I set the phone down on the counter. She's right, of course. And I miss them. I miss both of them. I want to call Jake and tell him about the Clean Ocean Initiative that Wyatt just started to offset any environmental impact the film might have. I want to call Cassandra and tell her that Rainer finally kissed me, listen to her squeal and ask me what it's like, whether his hair is soft, what he says to me when we're alone.

But I'm due at rehearsal, and I'm supposed to stop by the editing room this morning and look at yesterday's dailies. Yesterday we reshot the first scene of the movie, the scene where August washes up on the shore, bloody and broken. It felt better doing it this time, and I think Wyatt agreed. He actually asked me to take a look at the footage. He's never asked me for my input before, so I want to make sure to be on time. Hair and makeup is in twenty minutes.

Editing is located in conference rooms on the first floor of the condos. The blackout curtains are always drawn, so I feel sorry for the editors. They're stuck staring at these screens all day long while we're in Hawaii. At least we get to work outside pretty regularly.

Gillian, the special effects editor, greets me when I get there. She's incredibly tall with henna-red hair and multicolored wire-rim glasses. I've never told her this, because I don't really know her too well, but she reminds me a little of home.

"Hey, kid," she says. She puts a firm hand on my shoulder. "We got the whole thing set up for you. My office." She kicks the door closed with her foot and leads me into a room with gray walls and a large plastic desk with four computers and three keyboards on it. A frozen picture of the beach is on the screen.

"Sit." Gillian rolls a desk chair toward me, and I plunk down into it. She leans over and starts typing on the keyboard. "I'm glad you're here," she says. "Rainer joining you?"

"No," I say, craning around to glance at the doorway. "I don't think so, anyway."

Gillian flips a desk chair around next to me and sits, her chest pressed up against the back. "You ready?"

I smile to say yes. Give her a thumbs-up.

We go through the takes. It's strange to see myself on-screen like this. I have before—in commercials, and a few community theater plays that were filmed, but this is totally different. The special effects aren't even in yet, but there is no pretense of a stage or a set. It's just us, like watching a home video of yourself except it isn't you, exactly.

"It's raw," Gillian says. "But pretty cool, right?"

"Very," I say, nodding.

She winks at me, and clicks through to another take. Wyatt is always talking about matching shots, how my hand has to hit the same point in space when I say a certain word, so that later, when they slice the film together, they'll be able to match things up. I sort of got it, in theory, but now it actually makes sense. A movie is like a giant puzzle—pieces scattered on the living room floor.

It's only later, after it's together, that you realize it makes one single story.

Gillian's cell phone blares. "Dancing Queen" by Abba. "Favorite seventies song," she says. "I'm old. Don't tell anyone." Gillian snaps the phone open. She nods a few times, then covers the receiver with her hand. "I'm gonna go grab footage from set," she says. "Can you hang for five?"

"Sure." I should probably head out, but I want to stay. It's fun spending time with Gillian. She reminds me of the cool aunt character from the movies. The kind that lets you drink wine at dinner, and helps you "borrow" your parents' car to sneak out on the weekends. Both my parents are only children, so I never had that. One time my brother offered to buy me and Cassandra vodka for a sleepover we were having. We said okay, mostly because we were trying to look cool, I think, but he ended up not following through. What happened was that I asked about it, my parents over-heard us, and we were both grounded for a week.

I'm not saying Gillian would encourage underage drinking, exactly, but there are some adults who just don't seem to have the same reverence for rules. Generally they're the ones with no kids.

She leaves, firing some directions into her phone, and I'm left alone with me on the screen. It's a close-up shot of my body, still as silence, on the beach. I'm bloody, and my hair is splayed out like a spider web that's still being spun.

I feel like I'm bleeding to death, or she is, which is ridiculous because (1) August doesn't die, and (2) it isn't even blood. I was there when they mixed the hair gel with the chocolate syrup and food coloring, told me to lie down, drew an X on my abdomen, and started pouring the mixture right over it.

But still.

There's something about watching my body like this—my legs scissored out, my hand unfolded, the fingertips still reaching—that reminds me of the act of death. This is how it happens. You float up, above your body, and watch yourself like you're in some kind of movie.

"Strange, huh?"

I didn't hear him approach, but now I can feel Jordan's voice at my ear. It shocks me twice as much as what I'm seeing on the screen.

I brush my hair back and turn around to look at him. "A little," I say, trying to keep my voice level.

Jordan nods. He's watching the screen, his eyes flitting left to right. I'm incredibly aware that it's me lying there, that it's my half-naked body he's looking at. I want to throw a blanket over the girl at the beach, and one over me now, too. Because I can't separate us. It feels like he's not staring at the screen, but at me. When his eyes graze over her abdomen it makes me suck in my breath, and when he looks up to her still face my cheeks flush red, and when he reaches out and gently touches the screen I can feel his hand on my shoulder—like a spark plug.

"How come you're not at rehearsal?" I ask. My voice comes out hoarse, and I clear my throat.

"It's just you and Rainer today," he says. He turns from the screen to look at me, and I wonder if he's seen all those stupid magazines, too. I have the intense desire to tell him it's not true. To lie.

"Got it," I say. "What's up?"

Jordan turns Gillian's chair around and sits down. "I like to come in here and see how things look up there." He gestures to the monitor. "You?"

"Wyatt wanted me to take a look," I say. "I've never seen dailies before." Embarrassing. I should be in here. I should be taking advantage of every learning opportunity being on this set has to offer.

Jordan keeps looking at the screen. "I think it's interesting to see the process, you know? There is so much that goes into it."

He turns his head to look at me. "I've always liked watching how things come together. It's probably the thing I love most about acting. How collaborative it is."

"I guess," I say. "But acting itself isn't really collaborative."

He scans his eyes over my face. "Of course it is."

"I don't know," I say. "It doesn't feel that way." I have no idea why I'm being contrarian. All I've wanted is for him to talk to me, to not treat me like a leper. And now it's actually happening and I'm pushing back at him.

"This is the thing I can't understand about actors," Jordan says. "How you don't see that what you do is impossible without the help of dozens of people. No art takes place in a vacuum."

"But when you act, shouldn't it just be for you? I mean, does it matter who watches your play or movie or whatever? Don't you just do it because you love it?"

Jordan leans back in the chair and hooks his hands behind his head. "No," he says. "At its best, art is a dialogue. You do this thing so people can see it, and enjoy it, and engage with it. It's *for* other people."

I can see from the way he speaks—carefully yet easily, fluidly—that this isn't the first time he's considered this. It's an opinion developed through years of being thoughtful about his process. It makes something inside me tighten—a combination of admiration for his commitment, and disappointment at my own lack of the same.

"You've thought about this a lot."

He looks at me and squints, like he doesn't fully understand the question. "It's my life," he says. "Of course I have."

He has an ability to make me feel off-kilter, like the things I thought about the world—what I believed in and knew to be true—are all just a smoke screen for other things, bigger things. Talking to him makes me feel like I'm pulling back a curtain and I'm not sure what's behind it.

I'm trying to figure out how to respond when Gillian comes bursting back in. "Hey, J," she says.

He smiles at her. It's the first time I've seen one on him, and it changes his entire face. It's like how his eyes turned from black to brown—the smile softens him. "And I jacked your chair." He stands, and she waves him off.

"Sit. This one has to go, anyway."

"Me?" I ask.

"Wyatt's waiting, kid. We'll finish up later."

I mutter under my breath, and stand. I don't want to leave. "Well, thanks," I say. "I'll come back."

"They always do," she says, and winks at Jordan. She sits down in my chair, arms crossed. Jordan grabs the keyboard. The images on the screen move, my body coming back to life. He starts flipping through shots like Gillian did.

"Bye," I say. I expect him to keep his head down, to ignore me, but instead he looks up. "Bye, Paige," he says. "Nice talking to you." I try to find a hint of sarcasm in his tone, but I can't. It's possible he actually means it.

"You're late, babe." Rainer greets me as I walk into the hair and makeup trailer. He's dressed as Noah, and he looks amazing. He's shirtless, and his skin is perfectly tan. What you'd imagine those Greek gods would look like, come to life.

"Don't worry, hon," Lillianna says. "We'll make up the time." But I'm not worried. I don't feel like I need to scramble right now. After all, Wyatt was the one who wanted me to spend some time with Gillian.

"I should stop keeping you up so late," Rainer says, and my face immediately heats up with memories of last night. Us on my lanai. Me in his lap.

"I was in editing," I tell him.

"Editing?" He's looking in the mirror, adjusting some hair. "Why?"

"Wyatt wanted me to. Plus, it's interesting. Being a part of the process.... Acting isn't a vacuum," I say lamely.

Rainer looks amused. "I trust you," he says.

"I just like knowing more," I say.

"Cool."

I slump into the chair next to him. He reaches out and grazes my knee with his hand. "Hey," he says.

I lean my leg into his fingertips. He bends down for a kiss, but I turn away, smiling apologetically at Lillianna.

"I've seen worse, hon," she says. She pats the top of my head with her palm. "You make a darling couple."

"We do, don't we?" Rainer says. He lets go of my knee and hops down from his chair. "I'll go keep Wyatt off your back. See you down there?" He leans in again, but this time I let him get my lips. "Later, gorgeous," he whispers.

CHAPTER 17

Rainer is called back to L.A. the following week to do press for a movie he filmed last year. It sucks. I don't want him to go, and he doesn't want to go, either. But regardless, later tonight he'll be on a plane headed east. He'll be gone for eight days. They are going to L.A. and then New York and then London before flying all the way back here. "I wish you were coming with me," he says. "It's a rush. All those people. All that energy. I can't wait for you to experience it. It's like getting the biggest hug in the world."

"Soon enough," I say. We're standing in the lobby of the condos, waiting for his car to come around.

"What are you going to do this week?" Rainer asks. His tone is casual, but I know what he means. He wants to know about Jordan. Rainer would never admit it, but I can tell it bothers him that I've been going to see Gillian and that Jordan is usually there. Jordan always looks at the dailies.

"You don't have to worry," I say. I lift my hand to touch his shoulder.

"I know," he says.

"Hey." I tilt his face down. "We're all stuck in this hotel together. I'm just trying to be friendly, that's all."

"And you should," he says. Something passes across his face, but it's gone in a flash. "You should be friendly. I'm sorry." He shakes his head. "I'm just jealous of anyone who gets to spend time with you when I don't."

"Jealous?"

Rainer loops his hands around my waist. "Surprised?" he asks.

"Maybe."

He shakes his head. "Paige Townsen, you still don't get it."

"What?"

"I like you. A lot." Then he yells out, "Hey, everyone, I like Paige!"

I shake my head and feel his lips in my hair. "Stop," I say. "You're embarrassing me." But inside, my chest is soaring.

His car pulls up just as I see Jordan round the corner into the lobby. He pauses, leaning against a pillar. I can feel his eyes on us. Rainer notices, too. I feel his jaw clench. I untangle us but keep a hand on his arm. "Have a good trip," I say.

Jordan peels himself off the wall. "Where are you off to?" he asks. He keeps his tone level but lets his eyes drift over my hand on Rainer's shoulder.

"Press," Rainer says through his teeth. I feel his body tense up beneath my fingertips.

Jordan nods. I half expect him to say something like "I guess you're stuck with me, then," but he doesn't. Instead he says: "I'm going to visit Gillian. Come down after if you want."

I look at Rainer. He hands his bag to the driver. "Yeah," I say. "Okay."

Jordan leaves, and then Rainer's kissing me again, his hands in my hair. The driver next to us clears his throat.

"Mr. Devon," he says. "We need to leave now, sir."

Rainer nods. He presses his forehead to mine. "Be good," he says. "Stay safe." I lean into him. I wrap my arms around his neck. He's home here. But the driver is standing five feet away, and I pull back.

"I will," I say. "Hurry back."

"Always." He kisses my nose. I laugh as he ducks into the waiting town car. And then he's gone.

After I watch his car pull away, I head down to the editing rooms. When I get there, Jordan is seated at

Gillian's desk. He swivels around as I come in.

"Hey," he says. "Rainer get off okay?"

I try to read his face, but it's blank. "Come on," I say. "Don't do that."

"Do what?" he asks. His features are still impossible to read.

"Pretend that you care."

Jordan shrugs and holds out a chair for me. "Here," he says.

I sit and then glance back at the door. "Where is Gillian?"

"She's not coming," Jordan says, beginning to flip through footage.

"But you just—"

He turns to look at me. His eyes are dark. Stormy. "I know what I said. I thought your boyfriend might like it better if we had a chaperone."

"But we *don't* have a chaperone."

He keeps looking at me. It makes my chest feel tight, my breath come short. "Do we need one?"

I tear my gaze away from him and look back at the screen. "He's not my boyfriend," I say, like that's some kind of explanation. But it's low. Barely above a whisper. It's true we haven't had any kind of official talk yet, but it's almost irrelevant here, in this context. And Jordan knows it, too.

"You can call him whatever you want," he says. "It doesn't make any difference to me."

Something inside my stomach sinks, but I try not to notice. I try, instead, to focus on the pictures on-screen. We're looking at a scene Rainer and I filmed last week. Some stuff on the beach and the scenes we filmed with actors who came out for a few days to shoot the islander portions.

"Can you show me how this works?" I ask.

Jordan turns to me. His eyes flit briefly over my face. "Yeah," he says. "Sure."

He stands up to give me his seat. Then he leans over me and puts his hands on the controls. "This is how you get to the next shot," he says. His breath comes in my ear. I feel his body behind mine, warm, like he's emitting heat. "This is how you split the screen." He clears his throat. "I only know the basic stuff." His voice is so close I can feel his words landing on my neck.

"Thanks," I say.

He sits down next to me, and I feel the air leave my body in a rush. "You should just come in here and play around," he says.

"Is Gillian okay with that?"

His piercing black eyes look into mine. "If you're with me." I look away, but I can feel his gaze still on me. "Listen, I've been wanting to tell you—"

I swallow. "Yeah?"

"I'm sorry if we got off on the wrong foot."

I shake my head. "You saved my life," I say. "I think all is forgiven."

"Good point." He swivels his chair to face mine. He's serious all of a sudden. Brow knit. "But that Rainer stuff. It's not your problem."

"I know," I say. I turn to face him, too. Our knees are inches apart. "But it feels like it is."

Jordan shakes his head. Then he looks up at me. His face is steady, calm. "You're his girl," he says.

My throat constricts. I can feel the inches between us like the air is on fire. "It's not..." But I don't know what to say. He's right. I am.

"It's true," he says. He's still looking at me. "But it doesn't mean I have to feel about you the way I feel about him."

We look at each other, and I swear the silence passes between us like water. It has depth, weight. I can feel it flow from my chest to his.

Jordan tears his eyes away first. "We should get out of here," he says. "Our call time tomorrow is five AM."

I exhale. It feels like I've been holding my breath for hours. "I guess no time for morning ocean, then. Too bad."

He looks at me. He leans forward. "There is always time," he says. "If you want it."

"You'd wake up at three AM to surf?"

He turns back to the controls, his cool demeanor back on. "It wouldn't be the first time."

The next morning it's just Jordan and me on set. We haven't filmed anything just the two of us yet, and being around him still puts me on edge. But I'm also a better actress around him. Better (although I would never admit this out loud) than I am with Rainer. It's like his presence next to me challenges me to try more, work harder. To play at his level.

We're filming on the beach today. It's the scene where Ed arrives on the island and August sees him for the first time. And they kiss.

"This is someone you really care about," Wyatt tells me. "You love Noah. But you also love Ed. And you've missed him." Wyatt is wearing black jeans and a plain gray T-shirt. There is no band logo to be found on it, and I'm not sure how to take this. I'm not the only one who is different around Jordan. Wyatt is different, too. He's not less intense, exactly, but he screams less. Or it could be that I'm better, so there isn't so much need to correct. I'm not sure.

August is supposed to run into Ed's arms, and he scoops her up. They kiss, but just briefly. The kiss isn't as significant as the one with Noah in the hut we filmed a few weeks ago. It's softer, too. Not as charged.

"It's not as passionate as what she has with Noah," Wyatt tells us. "It's familiar."

Familiar. Right. Me and Jordan kissing. Totally an average day.

Jordan actually smiles at me when he gets to set. "Hey, Paige," he says. "Morning." His casual tone, his easy demeanor, take me by surprise. He's a different person. He jokes with Camden, slaps a call sheet playfully out of Jessica's hands. Is this all because Rainer isn't here?

"Let's go, guys," Wyatt says. "Run it a few times."

Wyatt sets us up. Jordan has to lift me, and we'll kiss in the air. It's a reunion kiss. "It's sweet," Wyatt keeps saying. "But for August, it's also sad. She's letting go of Noah here."

Usually Rainer whispers to me when we're filming. Between takes he'll make jokes, try to get me to laugh, that sort of thing. But not Jordan. From the moment Jordan walks in front of the camera, he is Ed. And today is no exception.

Jordan doesn't hesitate; he lifts me up easily. He wraps his arms around my waist and gathers me to his chest. I can feel his heart beat. I expect it to be like his eyes—solid and steady—but it's not, it's erratic. It's thumping like mine, like it wants to get closer to something. The sound, the feeling, makes everything else dissolve. Even when the camera comes, close up on my face, I barely even notice it's there. I feel last night between us. This burgeoning familiarity and something else, too. Something I can't even admit to myself in the privacy of my own head.

Jordan sets me down, and then, without warning or direction, he pulls me into him. His lips are like the silk ribbons tied around presents, and he kisses me so gently I can barely feel the weight of them. The impact makes me lean forward, wanting him closer. He follows my lead.

My hands start moving on their own. First up to grip his shoulders, then to his neck and finally threading through his hair. I don't even hear Wyatt call cut. I don't hear anything but the crash of the waves behind us, and his ragged breathing, the same as mine.

When he pulls back, he keeps me pressed up against his chest. I feel his lips brush over my forehead.

Wyatt is standing next to us, a look of bewildered fascination on his face. "That was good, but let's try a shorter take this time, okay?"

Jordan hasn't let me go, and when I look at him I see his eyes fixed on mine. Something in them has softened again, like a pond thawing in spring, and for a second I can almost feel myself falling inside.

Jordan lets his arms slacken slightly as Wyatt returns to Camden. I hear Camden say, "Are you sure it's not those two together?" I know I should correct him. I should untangle myself from Jordan and explain that, nope, no feelings! Just really good acting! I'm with Rainer! But I can't, because when Jordan releases me a moment later, I'm completely tongue-tied.

"Let's go again," Wyatt says.

I clear my throat. "Nice work," I say to Jordan, which is quite possibly the most ridiculous thing you can say to a guy who's just had his tongue in your mouth. Even if it was acting.

Not surprisingly, he doesn't respond.

We film again. And again. And again. Every time his lips touch mine, I feel like I'm moving closer to something significant, something I've been trying to get to the entire time I've been on this island, and possibly long before that. It's like kissing him explains it all. Why I'm here, why I got this part. That maybe everything that has happened in the last six months has been to get to this moment.

I remember something that Wyatt said to me when we were filming the Noah kiss scene. Something he referenced when trying to get me to understand what was going on in August's mind. "She finally understands what it means to fall into someone," he had said. "That part of loving someone where you're totally consumed by them."

We have off the next day, and it's pouring. We can't make it rain with sticks and potions and African dances, but the second we stop filming, the heavens open up.

I spend the morning in my condo, looking over the stacks and stacks of magazines that keep arriving in the mail from the various subscriptions I thought it would be a good idea to order. Then I try to organize my DVD collection, refold the clothes in my drawers. I'm determined not to have to go outside. The rain doesn't scare me so much as who might be out in it. I'm avoiding Jordan. Not because I don't want to see him—every single fiber of my being wants to sprint down the hall and find him—but I don't know what I would say. Or do.

Not that it matters. There's Rainer. Rainer, who is sweet and sexy and wonderful and who actually for some totally insane reason wants to be with me. And besides all that, Jordan probably has chemistry with a doorknob. It was acting, obviously, but I can't stop thinking about being that close to him. Is this why actors are constantly breaking up and cheating on each other? Is it this intimacy? *Is* this intimacy? I can't wrap my head around the possibility that Jordan didn't feel it, too, but maybe after you do this for a long time you learn to separate it out. Maybe I have it all wrong. Maybe it's really just playing pretend.

I wish Rainer were here. I'm sure this is all happening because he is gone. If he were here, I wouldn't be feeling this way. I wouldn't be feeling like I wanted to see Jordan. I wouldn't have to put myself on house arrest.

By two or so I'm going stir-crazy and the only thing left in my fridge is a bottle of mustard and a jar of pickles. I asked them to stop the magical food deliveries. I felt bad that so much of it went to waste, but now I wish I hadn't. Unfortunately the time has come to leave the premises. I brace myself against the elements with rubber flip-flops and a rain jacket. Then I pull the door open and head downstairs.

I wolf down a sandwich from the shops and then zip up my raincoat, the heavy-duty Oregon one I brought out here on a whim. It's pretty dry inside, and I decide instead of going back upstairs I'll take my chances and walk the beach. I need to clear my head, and if I haven't seen him in the lobby or at the shops, Jordan's probably in his room.

It's nice to have sunshine, don't get me wrong, but there's something about the rain that makes me feel at home. It's the smell. Even here, where the salt water threads its way into almost everything, it still smells the same. Like cool moss or strong pine or the heady, calming scent of lavender. The clouds roll in, my nervous system relaxes, and things feel quieter, less intense. Like the world softens.

The beach is pretty much deserted. I set my flip-flops down by the rocks' edge and sink my toes into the sand. The rain makes tiny pinpoints, nipping at my legs like insects. I start to walk west, down to where the beach curves around and then stretches forward. It's hazy, and the rain picks up, beating down in long, diagonal sheets. I walk with my chin tucked in, hands firmly in my pockets.

"Hey!" A voice comes from behind me, and I turn around to see Jordan jogging, a blue hoodie soaked through and pulled up over his head. The sight of him makes my stomach lurch forward. My veins feel like electrical wires.

"Jesus, I've been calling you for five minutes." He's panting.

"I didn't hear."

He steps closer to me. I can see him breathing. The slow rise and fall of his chest. The raindrops that hang on his forehead and his impossibly long lashes. "I saw you come down," he says.

"You're drenched," I point out.

He looks down at his sweatshirt, then glances around the deserted beach. "Come on." He grabs my wrist and pulls me up the beach. His fingers are cool, but his palm is warm on my freezing hand. His fingertips find mine, thread through them. I can't even see where we're headed through the rain.

I look up to see a line of cabanas being beaten down by the rain, strung across with rope. Jordan unclips the rope and holds the canvas flap open.

"It's hotel property," I say.

He gives me a look to tell me just how lame he thinks that response is and if I want to stand out there in the pouring rain, that's cool, but he's not going to. I duck inside. Jordan follows, looping the rope and knotting it back together once we're in. It's like a tiny tent inside, two beach recliners pushed together. They are covered with damp towels, and Jordan hands me one before using another to dry off. He unzips his sweatshirt and hangs it over the back of his chair, then runs the towel over his face and hair. I notice how his shirt clings to him. The outline of his chest and arms. Arms that, just yesterday, held me close to him. *On set*, I remind myself. *In a make-believe world*.

He looks at me. "Are you okay?"

I realize I'm sitting there, still in my raincoat, holding the towel and staring at him.

"Yeah." I take off my jacket and set it down. It's cold now, and the wetness seems to have soaked into my bones.

"Here." He takes a folded towel from the foot of the chairs, opens it, and reaches across to drape it over my shoulders. His arm skims mine, and I can feel his damp skin, the remnants of rain. It makes my goose bumps perk up even higher.

"Thanks," I say. I lay the second towel on top of me, tucking it down around my feet and pulling it up to my chin.

Jordan looks at me. "Snug as a bug." He lies down next to me, shoulder to shoulder, and does the same.

I laugh. "Did that seriously just come out of your mouth?"

"I have a little sister," he says matter-of-factly.

We're silent then, and I focus on the sound of the rain on canvas. Small, melodic beats.

"I like being in the editing room," I venture. "I like that you're showing me that stuff." Jordan doesn't say anything, but I can feel him inhale next to me. "I've been thinking a lot about what you said. About art not existing in a vacuum."

"Oh yeah?"

"Yeah." I roll over onto my side to face him, and he turns his head, his eyes meeting mine. I'm incredibly aware of how close our faces are now. No more than inches. I think about what it felt like to kiss him yesterday. How soft his lips were. How strong his arms were. "It's interesting," I say. "It makes me want to learn more about the whole process."

"You should," he says, his face still turned. "That's the best part about this kind of art. It's collaborative. Everyone relies on everyone else. You get to form a community."

"I like that," I whisper.

"I'm glad." He turns his head up to face our tiny hut roof. "I think a lot about why I'm here. Why out of everyone I'd be chosen to do this. You know what I mean?"

"Yes," I say. I don't have the heart to tell him that for me it's more a constant fear that someone will realize they chose wrong. That I've been miscast. That I'm not their August after all.

"I used to think I didn't belong in Hollywood," he says, like he's reading my thoughts. "But now I just feel a crazy amount of gratitude."

"You don't take it for granted, do you?" I say.

He rolls over to look at me, and when he does, I see something close to disbelief on his face. "Never. I know what it's like to have nothing. I'd never forget it. You have to keep reminding yourself of what's real," he says. "Who you really are, the people you love, your family."

"Family?" I remember that he's supposed to be this money-hungry bad boy who is suing his parents. That he's cut them out of his life entirely. Lying next to him now, his eyelashes blinking raindrops, it's hard to imagine.

"Do you want to ask me something?" he says, still looking at me.

I bite my lip. "Your family," I say. I jump in quickly, burying the words I just said. "My parents are clueless. And my brothers are crazy. My family is totally screwed up, too. And . . . I'm rambling."

"It's okay. I don't read tabloids, but I know what people say about me."

"I'm sorry," I say, pulling the towel up closer to my chin. "You don't need to tell me anything."

He scans my face. "I didn't sue for emancipation because of money. Money is a nice side effect, but it's not why I do this job."

"So what happened?"

His eyes settle on mine. "My dad isn't a great guy. He tried to take everything, and then when I wouldn't give it, he turned on my mom."

My chest feels tight, heavy. I want to put my hand on his cheek and hold it there. "What did you do then?"

"I had to get her away from him. I had to get all of us away, actually, and the only way to do that was to make sure I could support them." He inhales. "My sister and mom. I did what I had to do."

My eyes roam over his face, settling on his scar. Without even thinking I reach out and touch it, run my hands down the silver line of his jaw and down the back of his neck. He closes his eyes. "Did he do this to you?" I ask.

He nods, his eyes still closed.

A hot bolt of fire shoots up from my core. Anger. I want to find his father and kill him for what he did to Jordan. To his mom and sister, whom I've never even met.

"Why didn't you say anything?" I'm aware of how lame my voice sounds. Of how stupid and small my questions seem now.

He opens his eyes. "To the press? I would never do that to my mom."

"But she—"

"Has pride," he says, like there's nothing more to discuss.

"That must be hard," I say. "Don't you ever want to tell people the truth?"

He shifts his arms and puts one hand down on the space between us. "As much as I'd love to get back at my dad for hurting us, it wouldn't be worth it. And the people who I really care about know." He searches my face again, like he's looking for something. "That's good enough for me."

Something hits me, sharply, like the water on a cold morning. "How come you're telling me?" I ask. "I could tell anyone."

He looks at me and blinks, a raindrop sliding down his cheek like a tear. "You could," he says. "But I don't think you will."

Without even realizing, I've inched closer to him. My body is moving on its own, like when it's really cold in the winter and you go straight for the radiator. Like he's the only source of heat on this rainy, freezing beach. He is. "Why?"

He looks at me in a way that makes the world stop. Like some higher power has hit the pause button, and for a second I think he's going to say something. Something I really want to hear. But he doesn't. Instead he takes my face in his hands. He cups my chin with his palm, and gently brings my lips up to meet his. Everything fades. The sound of the rain, the cold chill, the goose bumps on my arms and legs. The only thing I'm aware of is how it feels to be close to him. His lips move against mine. They feel even better than yesterday. So much better because it's just us here now. We don't have to pretend to be August and Ed. There is no one watching.

His lips leave mine and find my neck. He trails kisses down to my collarbone and I gasp, my fingernails digging into his shoulders.

"Jordan," I breathe, but his lips are on mine again, devouring the words. He rolls me toward him and then I'm on top of him on the lounge chair. I feel his hands move on me. They grip my shoulders, then move down my back, pressing me against him. I can feel everything. His hip bones, the hard muscles of his abs. He keeps one hand on my side and with the other brushes my hair out of my face as it swings forward. I keep kissing him. I want to bottle this feeling. To have it forever.

Then he pushes me back gently, cups his hand to the side of my head, and tucks my hair behind my cheek. He drops his gaze down, lets his hand fall. "We shouldn't be doing this," he says. His breathing is labored, and I can feel the frenzied beat of his heart a few inches below mine.

"No," I say. It's the first thing I think. I say it automatically. The truth is when something feels this good, this right, it's hard to remember why it should be different. What reason could there possibly be that we shouldn't be here, right now, together?

But I know; we both do. Rainer. He doesn't deserve this. Even the thought of it, of him finding out, of what it would do to him, makes me feel like I'm going to be sick right here in the sand.

Jordan straightens up, and so do I. We untangle ourselves so we're just sitting side by side, not touching. My body aches for him. It feels like I've severed something. A limb, maybe an organ.

"Why couldn't you have come sooner?" I ask.

Jordan smiles. "I don't know," he says softly.

"Jordan . . ."

He shakes his head. "It doesn't matter," he says. "I can't go through this with him again."

"But I thought you said you never dated Britney."

"I didn't," he says. "But he doesn't believe me."

I clear my throat. "I want—"

But he reaches over and grabs my hand before I can finish. I want him. I want a different situation. I want to go back and rearrange everything. Make this feeling possible for more than this minute.

"Paige, don't," he says. He drops my hand. My heart sinks, like it's been submerged in freezing water. I don't know how it's possible to go from pure elation to devastation so quickly.

He sits up and pulls back the canvas flap. "Looks like it stopped," he says.

The light comes flooding in, bright and unwelcome, and I know that we're leaving.

He folds his towel and tucks it neatly at the edge of his chair, then he reaches across, his hand brushing my shoulder, and slides my own towel down.

"Thanks," I say. I try to hide the disappointment in my tone, but I know it comes through. I can feel it in the way he looks at me. His eyes seem to say it for both of us: *I wish things were different.*

He folds my towel and then stands, holding out his hand. I put mine in his, and when we touch, I feel it again. Like the final puzzle piece snapped down into place.

But it doesn't matter now. It's like an umbrella in the middle of a rainstorm after you're already wet. It's exactly what you need, what you want, but it's come too late.

CHAPTER 18

The final book of the trilogy comes out tonight at midnight, and Jordan and I are being sent to the Barnes & Noble in town to surprise fans. Rainer is on the last leg of his press tour and won't be back until tomorrow afternoon.

I've seen Jordan only once off set since the day at the beach. I ran into him in the hallway and awkwardly asked if he wanted to have dinner, but he said he was on his way out. He didn't clarify, just glanced at his watch and took off for the lobby.

He's been distant on set, and he barely looks at me when we're not filming. We haven't talked about what happened on the beach at all. Part of me feels like it didn't even happen, and I think that's what he wants—to pretend it never did.

Maybe it's for the best. I miss Rainer. I miss the way he makes me feel at home here. I miss watching movies in his condo, having dinner together. I miss the way he makes me laugh on set, the silly things he whispers to me, and how comfortable I feel around him. Sometimes I sleep in his condo to feel closer to him. Rainer makes me forget that the stakes are so high. He makes me feel calm. With him gone, everything feels too important, too serious. Jordan, this movie, the book release. It's like we're all at the edge of a cliff and Rainer is the fence, the thing that keeps us from spilling over the side.

We were supposed to go to L.A. for the book thing, but that got canceled because of our shooting schedule. I was relieved, actually, because honestly? The book and movie are linked and all, but the story is what won people over, not us. Rainer's and Jordan's fans are kind of established, but besides that girl at the Fish Market and a few curious tourists, no one has recognized me. I know that we're making tabloid headlines fairly regularly—PAIGE AND RAINER: SEPARATED BY DISTANCE; AUGUST PINES FOR HER NOAH—but we're pretty removed here. It's easy to forget the other side of all this.

Tonight I don't want to be anything more than a fan. I can't wait to get my hands on the final book to find out what happens to August. Does she choose Noah or Ed? When we started shooting the first movie, I thought they'd probably cast me in all three—if they made them, that is. But now that I've heard more of the behind-the-scenes gossip, the whispers of the producers hovering around set, I realize that it's far from a foregone conclusion. Will we get the chance to see this thing through to its end?

In the first book, we found out that Noah holds a special place on the island—he's descended from the people who live there. It gets complicated, obviously, and even now, having read the first two books of the series, I'm not sure where August's heart really lies. You think it's Noah in book one. How could anyone ever live up to the epic love they have? But then Ed comes back and she starts to remember what it was like to be with him. How he's family. I feel as confused as she does.

We're supposed to be getting copies of the book delivered to us this afternoon, and I'm going to try to get through as much as I can before we go out tonight. It's a Saturday, so that shouldn't be too hard to swing. I go for a swim in the morning, dragging myself out of bed at six. I could go later, given that it's not a filming day. I tell myself this isn't about trying to see Jordan, but I know that it is. No matter how hard I try, no matter how much I think about Rainer and miss him, I can't get Jordan out of my head.

He's there when I wake up, like a dream that doesn't fade. I keep thinking about him in the tent, the way my fingers traced across his face, the silver sliver of his scar. I know I just need to focus on Rainer, on the fact that he's coming back tomorrow, and on our plans to go to the other side of the island next weekend. I was so happy to hear his voice from London when he called. "I miss you," he said. "I love that next time we do this, we'll be doing it together."

It's probably a good thing that Jordan's not at the beach this morning. I'm disappointed—I can feel the emotion palpably, like it's sitting inside me—but it's better this way. Seeing him leads to more of the what-ifs. And it doesn't help to think that way. It's the reality that matters.

I hang out in the water for a while, floating on my back, watching the sunrise from the corner of my eye. When I finally peel myself out, it's almost eight and my skin is shriveled and prickly.

I wring out my hair and wrap my towel around my waist, then walk back up to the condos. When I get inside, I find a package sitting on my counter. It must be the book, ahead of schedule, but I'm surprised at how tall the envelope is. I tear it open, excited to see the cover, but when I look inside I realize I'm wrong. It's not the book at all, but a copy of *Scene*, the shoot the three of us did last month. I peel back the tissue paper and flip to the page with the Post-it on it, but the photo isn't the one I expected to see—one of the three of us. Instead, it's just me. I'm sitting on one of the giant polka-dot chairs, my hair half over my shoulder, half back, and I'm wearing the black dress. The look on my face is one I don't recognize. It's hard, cold. I'm not smiling. My expression is blank. I look older with my hair curled and styled. I look pretty in a way that's hard to distinguish. If I were passing a newsstand and flipping through the magazine, I would know I'd seen the girl in the spread before. That she was vaguely familiar. I'd just never, ever, think it was me.

"Paige Townsen on *Locked*, Becoming a Movie Star, and Those Rainer Rumors."

I scan through the article quickly. It seems harmless enough. I remember them asking me about how I got the part, what working with Wyatt Lippman was like, whether I liked living in Hawaii. Then they'd asked me about Rainer.

Scene: "What's it like working with Hollywood heartthrob Rainer Devon?"

PT: "It's great. He's been so key in helping me adjust and understand this business. We're really good friends."

Scene interviewed both Rainer and Jordan, too. Jordan is brief and professional. He talks about the film, his respect for the books. He refuses to comment on his "family drama" or the rumors about Britney. His reserve is impressive. He doesn't hint at anything, not even slightly. His answers are crisp and clean and completely one-dimensional.

Rainer's are about the same until the last question.

Scene: "Who is your celebrity crush?"

RD: "Paige Townsen."

It should make me smile. The guy who likes you says in a national magazine that you're his crush—that's swoonworthy, I think. But it doesn't make me feel weak in the knees. It makes me feel annoyed. The entire crew already knows, but is it too much to ask not to involve the world as well?

Every girl would kill to be with him. You actually are. What's the problem?

Jordan. Jordan is the problem. This interview, this photo shoot, feels like it took place years ago. I remember the feeling of having their eyes on me, both of them. Rainer and I were hovering on the edge of something, but we weren't there yet. So much has happened since this shoot that it might as well be someone else in the pictures. I'm not the girl who answered these questions anymore because Rainer isn't just a friend now. Maybe Jordan isn't, either.

I leave the magazine on the couch and go into the bedroom. It's only nine AM, and the book probably won't be here for a few hours. I pull out the first book and flip to the first page. The last time I read it I wasn't August. I was just a girl from Portland going to an impossibly improbable audition. Now everything has changed. Now I've kissed two movie stars, and Rainer Devon has told an international magazine that he has a crush on me.

I start to read. It's strange to see scenes in my mind's eye now. What we've filmed, what we've left out, and what we still have to cover. It's a little like being thrown into your own diary—and I find, as I read, that something has happened over the last few months: This book has become personal. It holds the key to my future. Whatever is dropped off on my doorstep in a few hours will most probably determine how I spend the next two years of my life. Like the hands of fate—something greater, higher, deciding the course my life will take. And it's already been written.

I keep reading until a knock comes at my door. When I open it, Jessica is standing there, a package tucked to her chest.

"You ready?" she asks. She hands it over.

I take it, and when I do, I notice my hands are shaking. All of a sudden, I don't want her to leave. "Are we still going tonight?" I ask, trying to keep the interaction going.

She nods. "Be ready at eleven," she says. "We're planning to get there at midnight and stay for an hour. You'll sign books. You okay with that?"

"Sure." I shift the package under my arm and pull my

hair over my shoulder, twisting it around my thumb.

"I saw *Scene*," Jessica says, changing the subject. "Great interview. It's going to fly off the stands." She smiles at me, a warm, bright, open smile, and I'm met with the desire to pull her inside, sit her down on my couch, and beg her to tell me what she thought of Rainer's answers, whether people are going to make a big deal out of this—to make her my friend.

She squints at me for just a moment, and I think maybe I've said something in my head out loud. But then she turns to go. "Enjoy!" she calls over her shoulder. "I'm actually going to try to get to the beach!"

I close the door and toss the package on the counter. I pour a glass of water and stare at it. Then I set the water glass down and pick the package up. I flip it over. I wiggle my finger along the edge, just enough to break the seal. It reminds me of my mom at Christmas. How she always opens her presents end-first, peeling the tape back carefully, never ripping the wrapping paper. "We can reuse it," she says whenever we complain she's taking too long.

But now I just want to prolong the process. I don't know what I'm going to find in here, but I'm not sure I want to know. Whatever happens to August is going to happen to me.

When the cardboard comes undone, I survey the cover.

It's a forest, tall oak and pine trees, and in the middle is a group of people. One I clearly recognize as August. I notice immediately that she has more of my features than the girl on the cover of the first one. Her hair is redder, her forehead higher. She is flanked by Ed and Noah, who bear a striking resemblance to Jordan and Rainer. In the background there are three people I don't recognize: a woman, a man, and a girl about my age.

I flip open to the first line: "If it is in forgetting that we forgive, then we are brought back only by ignorance, and never by love."

I flip back to the inside cover, pick up a pen, and write down two lines. I know that I should say them out loud, but I'm still not sure how.

I'm sorry. I love you.

Then I snap the book closed and put it back in the packaging. I'm grateful I was so careful in opening it—it fits back in exactly.

I mark down the familiar address, the one where I've spent most afternoons since I was five. The one I know by heart.

Then I tape the ends of the package, sling it under my arm, and race out the door in search of a post office. She was a fan first; she should read it first. If it weren't for Cassandra, I wouldn't even be here.

*

Jordan is sitting next to me in the back of the car. His manager, Scotty, is driving. Scotty is about sixty-five and looks like he just stepped out of an investment bank. He's professional, curt, and totally unchatty...which I guess fits Jordan perfectly. He doesn't seem like he wants to talk to anyone, least of all me.

Unlike Sandy, Scotty hasn't been popping in and out, which makes sense. Jordan isn't the kind of guy who would like to be babysat. But Scotty showed up today for the book release.

There are two town cars behind us with Wyatt and Jessica and a couple of public-relations women I haven't met and two bodyguards. I don't think a few teenage girls are really something to prepare an army against, but I don't ask. I don't say anything. Jordan and I are sitting so close I can feel the static between us, but we still haven't spoken. He's gotten more and more distant since that day on the beach. He keeps pulling back.

I clear my throat. It's been sixteen minutes, someone should say something. "Did you get the book?" I ask.

He inhales. "Yes."

"Have you started reading?" I turn toward him. He's still facing front.

"Yeah." He doesn't look at me, but I can see his eyes dart slightly, the gold in his pupils shooting to the left.

"Okay." I sit back and stare out the window, away

from him. I feel him shift next to me. "Do you think there will be a lot of people there tonight?" I push on.

He clears his throat. "Probably."

We sit in silence for another few minutes, the questions building up in my head like water bubbles, ready to burst: "Why does it have to be this way? Why won't you talk to me?"

What ends up coming out is "I miss you." It sounds so stupid. How could I miss him? I barely even got to know him. But still, I do.

He exhales. "Paige..."

"Please," I say. I'm completely facing him now, my seat belt jumbled. "Just talk to me."

He turns to me then, his expression dark and solid, like a piece of clay baked in the oven—he's no longer pliable. "What do you want?"

"I don't want to pretend that what happened at the beach didn't."

"And how would that help things?" His tone is cold, sharp. It feels like his words could stab like icicles.

"Should I remind you that *you* kissed *me*?" I bite my lip hard. I taste blood. It doesn't matter who kissed who, and I can tell by the look on his face that he knows it.

He surprises me when he says, "I know. And I'm sorry for that."

"I'm not." I can feel something blaze up in my

chest—that stubborn streak.

Jordan shakes his head. "You gotta stop, Paige. It was a mistake. That's it."

And just as quickly, that thing in my heart deflates. "Jordan, please. Don't shut me out."

He looks at me for a beat so long I swear an entire song goes by on the radio. Then he says, "You're lonely. Your boyfriend is gone. I'm sure once Rainer is back, things will return to normal."

"How can you say that?"

"Trust me, it's easier this way."

"For *who*?" I ask. "It's not easier for me. It's awful." I can hear myself pleading, my voice cracking. I'm distinctly aware of Scotty in the front seat, but I can't help it. Something about Jordan makes me incapable of acting like a sane, rational person. Not the most awesome influence when you're supposed to go to a very public event in about five minutes.

"I told you. I'm not getting in the way of anything."

"But we can try," I say. "Can't we at least try to be friends?"

His black eyes flash. "We were never just friends, were we?"

I open and close my mouth. "No."

Jordan's eyes soften, for just a moment. "Things are hard enough. You know how much Rainer hates me…

what he thinks about Britney." He's whispering now. "I can't be close to you. That's just the way it is."

"What happened between you two?" I ask.

"It doesn't matter."

"It does," I say. I can feel the edge in my voice. The pleading. I don't care. "It matters to me. Why do you guys hate each other so much? Is it really all about her? I won't take sides. I just want to know."

I realize that I've moved closer to him, so close that I'm inches from his face.

"What happened?" I say again. My hands become disconnected from my body, or my brain, and the next thing I know my fingertips are tracing the line of his scar, just like when we were at the beach. They brush over his ear and down his neck.

"Stop," he says, but his voice is breathless, soft. I can tell they're just words, that they don't mean anything, not even to him.

"Please," I say again.

He looks at me, the same look he had in the beach tent. The one that makes me want to take his hand and press it up against my heart right here in the backseat of this car. "No," he whispers. He brings his hand to my cheek. My eyes reflexively close.

"Why?" I whisper back.

I open my eyes and see his spark. They're gold in the

center, bright—like a camera flash. "Just trust me," he says.

We're pulling into Barnes & Noble now. I can see the lines of people twirled around the shopping center like a long, sleeping snake—ready to rear its head awake at any moment and swallow us whole.

Jordan unsnaps his seat belt and moves away from me as we pull forward. I open my mouth to argue, but Scotty turns around and gives us a pointed look. "You guys ready?"

Jordan doesn't respond; he just opens the door. One of the guys who works security at the hotel meets him outside. "This way, Mr. Wilder."

That's when I hear it—the screaming. It's sharp at first—a few voices—and then louder and louder, like a stereo system that's been cranked up to full volume. But it's not melodic. It's manic. Loud and shrill and high and raging. I suddenly have the desire to jump under my seat and beg Scotty to turn the car around. But he's outside, too, and before I can dive into the trunk, my door opens.

I was once on a trip to New York with my mom—the second and only away audition we ever went on together. It was for a role on a soap opera—and after a lot of negotiating, I convinced her to go. I saved up all my summer money and worked straight through winter break to pay for it, too. We went in February. I had never experienced cold like that, ever. I remember walking out of our hotel room and being blasted by it, so overwhelming that it knocked the wind right out of me. That's how it feels now. When I step out of the car, I can't breathe.

The first thought I have is to look around and see what all the fuss is about. It's ridiculous. I *know* what all the fuss is about—it's about us—but I still turn my head and glance behind me, like maybe it's John Lennon, back from the dead.

But no, there is no Beatle. One Direction isn't here, either. These are *Locked* fans. *Our* fans.

They seem to be everywhere, and when they spot Jordan, then me, it's like they multiply. I imagine those scenes from movies where ants or spiders or cockroaches come crawling out of the walls and cover the characters in a prickly, suffocating mass. A different security guard leads me over to the line where fans are waiting to get into the bookstore. They chant our names like they're war cries.

"We love you!" they yell.

How can that possibly be true? They don't *know* me.

One girl hands me a photograph. It's of me, some promotional pic I don't recognize. I guess they've been taking stills from the set and releasing them. I kind of just stand there, holding it. I feel like a complete idiot. I should sign it. I should do something. A pen materializes out of thin air, and on autopilot, I sign the photo and hand it back to her. She presses it up against her chest when I do, and I have the fleeting hope that it's not permanent ink. I hope my words are not scrawled across her shirt, smudged and unreadable.

I wish Rainer were here. He would know what to do. He would whisper something funny in my ear, make a joke to the crowd. He'd wink at me or catch my hand, and I'd feel centered somehow, tethered to something.

Jordan may have saved me on the beach, but right now, in this tsunami, he is totally content to let me drown. I can't see him from where I am, but I know he's in front of me somewhere, winding his own way through the crowd.

I've been a total fool. I don't know what I was thinking. It's the classic bad-boy appeal. The same thing that got my sister into all that trouble. And I'm not her. I'm not willing to give up what I love for someone else. This job is what's important to me. This opportunity, screaming fans and all. And Rainer is someone I can navigate all this with. Someone who will hold my hand and stand by me. Not someone who puts me in danger of losing everything I now have.

CHAPTER 19

"Close your eyes."

I'm sitting with Rainer on the living room floor of his condo. I managed to avoid Jordan almost entirely yesterday. Once we got inside the bookstore we took pictures with people and signed books for an hour, and then we were whisked back to the condos—this time in separate cars. Now Rainer is back, and things feel as they should. I told him about the book release, and he told me that next time he'd be here to do it with me.

"Just give it to me."

He shakes his head, his golden-blond hair falling into his eyes. "Nope. Closed."

"Fine." I close my eyes, and when I do he takes my hand. He holds it for a moment and then uncurls my fingers one by one. I feel it then—a cool piece of metal. Like a raindrop in my palm.

"Okay, open."

I look down. Inside my hand is a cowrie charm. It's almost identical to the one we're using in the movie. The one August wears around her neck. The one that Noah gave her.

"It's beautiful," I murmur.

"So are you." Rainer holds his own hand out to reveal a thin gold chain. "Do you want me to put it on for you?"

I nod, and Rainer lifts the charm from my hand and strings it onto the chain. It slides down and then dangles, dead center.

"Here." He brushes my hair back and loops the chain around my neck. He fiddles with the clasp until it catches, and I feel the gold shell cold against my chest.

"Looks good," he says, letting his fingertips graze my neck.

"Thank you."

He smiles, tucking some of my hair back behind my ear. "I had it made. I'm glad it came in time."

"In time for what?"

Rainer frowns. There is something written on his face, but when I try to read it, it's gone. "Just in time for this." He kisses me gently, his fingertips brushing my shoulders.

"Okay," I say when he pulls back.

"I can't believe we're almost done here," he says. He pulls me into his arms and runs a hand through my hair. I snuggle down into him.

"I know. Only a few days left—it's weird."

"I'm sure they won't wait too long between movies. I bet they give us four months off, at the most."

I loop my arm around his neck. "But the second movie isn't even guaranteed yet."

Rainer looks at me and laughs. "You really need to call your agent more," he says.

I shove him back. "I call her," I say. It's just that every time we talk, she wants me to get a manager, and I'm just not sure how I feel about that. I know Sandy can't keep doing everything forever, but I don't know if I'm ready to commit to someone else yet. I don't know who I trust.

And it's not like my parents are particularly good at business. My mom still thinks this movie is a hobby, some flyer she can fold and stuff into her jewelry box. She fully intends for me to come back to Portland and finish my senior year when we wrap the shoot.

At the thought of Portland, I feel that familiar pinch in my stomach. I wonder if Cassandra has gotten the book yet.

"So," Rainer says. "Are you going home next week?" He pulls me closer and places his hands on my neck again, to touch the necklace. They linger there and then move down an inch, sliding against my collarbone.

"Yeah." I swallow.

He leans in now, his lips meeting mine. "I missed you," he says. He draws me in, and I fold quickly. He runs the back of his hand over my cheek. I'm in his lap now, my hands reaching up to his hair. I try not to think about Jordan, about the guilt I feel at that kiss. That betrayal.

"I missed you, too." Seeing him makes me realize even more just how much.

Rainer raises his eyebrows. "Really?"

"What do you mean?"

He scans his eyes across my face. "Nothing. I just sort of felt like..."

"Like what?"

"Like maybe this isn't what you want." His eyes hold my gaze. His hand stops moving on my back.

I feel like I used to when I'd sneak home late on a Friday night. My pulse would pound in my ears if I heard a noise before I was safely back in my room.

"You're Rainer Devon," I say, trying to lighten the mood. "Every girl is into you."

He shakes his head. He's not biting. "We're not talking about every girl. We're talking about *you*." His face is calm, and I remember, suddenly, that he's older. Right now, in this moment, he's not acting like a boy. He's acting like a man.

I feel my breath catch in my throat. Like it's forcing me to shut up—to stop and tell the truth. "I know," I say. "This is all just a lot."

Rainer nods. "It is. I know that. That's what I'm saying."

My stomach turns over. He keeps going. "At some point, you're going to have to choose."

"Choose?" I can tell my voice is high and squeaky. How does he know? It's not like there is a choice, since Jordan has taken himself out of the equation. But Rainer doesn't know anything about that. Panic sets in, and I can feel my muscles begin to knot up with tension.

"Yeah," he says. "You're going to have to decide whether you want to be with me, or not."

The air leaves my body in a rush. Relief. "But I thought we already were. Together, I mean." Immediately, my face flushes.

Rainer notices and cups a hand over the back of my neck. It's soft, gentle. "That's been mostly my call, not yours. I don't want you to feel like I'm pressuring you into anything."

"Okay," I say, cautiously.

Rainer pushes on. "It's not just about us," he says. "Being together means a lot more than that."

I don't say anything, just wait for him to continue.

"It'll mean more press. And less privacy. But to me it's

worth it." He moves his hand from my neck to my cheek. "It's worth it to get to be with you."

I think about what Jordan said, about Rainer only dating actresses for the press. About how wrong he was.

Rainer's thumb traces a small circle on my face. "What I'm saying is, I won't make this decision for you. But I realized while I was gone how much I want to be with you. To make sure nothing happens to you. I want to get to be that person for you." He gently moves me off his lap, and takes my hands in his. "Could you say something?" he asks me, his green eyes wide. "I'm kind of dying over here."

"I don't know what to say." A million thoughts are scrambling to take center stage. One threatens to push through, but I clamp it down, shut it out.

"Why don't you take some time?" I can see the hurt in his eyes. I know it's taking everything in him to suggest that, and my heart swells so big I think it might burst. I just want to leap back into his arms and stay there.

But he's right. Being together means something. We're not just a couple. If we do this, it's for real.

"Okay," I say.

He smiles. "Okay."

"How long do I have to think for?" I ask.

He laughs, and so do I. It feels good. It cuts the tension.

"You're going home, right?" he says. "See your family. Think about it there. I'm going to be in Europe shooting for a while, anyway. You can tell me at the premiere."

I nod, remembering he's doing a movie in Prague while we wait for the release of *Locked*. I suddenly think of the scripts stacked up in my condo. Of how my agent keeps saying I should line up a project.

"All of that seems far away," I say. "It's months."

His eyes look into mine. He nods. "It is. Feel free to cut to the chase and tell me you're ready now. But I think you need time."

I drop my eyes to my hands. "I know."

He makes a move to get up, and then decides against it because in the next instant he's right next to me—his hands on either side of my face. He kisses me, parting my lips with his. I reach up and thread my fingers through his hair. I breathe him in—plumeria and vanilla and warmth and something else, too. Comfort. Home. "Something to consider," he says. Then he holds out his hand and helps me up.

The end of filming comes too quickly, like a cold blast when the leaves haven't even changed yet. When Wyatt calls "that's a wrap" for the last time, it feels like everything is coming to an end, not just this movie. I can't shake the feeling that maybe this was all some fluke, a glitch in the system, and come next week I'll be back on a plane to Portland for good.

But that's also not entirely true. I'll be back in Portland, but not forever. I'm going to do that small daughter role in the indie script I read a few weeks back. It shoots in Seattle, so I'll be close to home, and it should only take two months. It will keep me busy while Rainer is in Europe.

"I'm proud of you," Rainer tells me at the wrap party that night. The cast and crew are having a bonfire on "our" beach, and they've set up a projection screen outside underneath the stars.

"For the gag reel," Jessica tells me. Tonight she has on a white dress and dangly gold earrings, and her hair is piled on top of her head, a few wisps hanging down, skimming her cheeks like angel wings. She's beautiful. Totally stunning. Even Rainer looks at her, impressed. I don't blame him.

"It's the best part," Rainer says. "We used to do one every season on *Backsplash*."

I remember watching *Backsplash*. It was on the Disney Channel. Britney was in it, too, and a few other child actors who graduated to star on television shows Cassandra obsessively watches.

"It's true," Jessica says. "It's kind of become a traditional part of the wrap party."

They've set up benches on the beach—long logs—and Rainer and I take a seat on one toward the left, in front of the projection screen. Sandy floats over in some combination silk-and-crepe outfit and squeezes Rainer on the shoulder before sitting down behind us. One of Gillian's assistants is fiddling with the video equipment, and the rest of the crew make their way to the benches as well. I try to focus center, willing my shoulders to stay squared. *Don't turn around.*

Jordan probably isn't here, anyway. Gag reels don't exactly seem like his thing. And I'm not sure he's so interested in being in the same time zone as me or Rainer. But despite whatever rational-thought blocks I try to impose on my mind, the feeling slips in like fog through the slits of a fence. I can feel him. The same way I can when he comes on set when I'm in the middle of filming a scene.

Don't turn around, I tell myself again.

Rainer's sitting next to me, and I can feel the guilt seeping into my limbs like a drop of food coloring in water. It turns everything red.

"I really hope they got that shot of you puking salt water," Rainer says.

I nudge him in the ribs, and he laughs. He's got his hands tucked under him, and he's looking at me and smiling. He's been so gentle with me since our talk in his condo a couple of weeks ago. He doesn't kiss me. Or talk about our relationship. He's just been a friend. But sitting here, looking at his impossibly gorgeous face, I feel like I don't need until the premiere. I want to tell him right now that this is what I want. I don't care about what comes with it. I'm ready. I'm about to open my mouth when Gillian comes into view in front of the screen.

"All right, guys, we're going to get started. Dan over here"—she points to her assistant, who gives us a half wave—"has put together some fun stuff that I for one can't wait to see." Gillian squints, and folds her palm over her forehead. "I can't see here, so I don't know where you are. Where's Wyatt?"

I see him standing on the sidelines, shaking his head. He rolls his eyes when Gillian calls him out. "Wyatt," she says. "You're not the easiest taskmaster." I hear Rainer mutter something under his breath. It sounds like *understatement*. "But you are," Gillian continues, "an incredible director. It has been a pleasure to serve you on this movie."

I look over at Wyatt. He nods once and then looks at me, and in that moment I feel an overwhelming sense of affection for him. The first months seem to have boiled so long they've evaporated. He's taught me hard and strong and at some points, without much delicacy—but he's also made me *better*. I don't feel like I used to on set. Going to this new movie in Seattle, I don't feel afraid.

Gillian is saying something, and Rainer whistles and throws his hands over his head. "Excellent," Gillian says.

"You two." I feel my face get hot and pinch my hands together. "You've given us some amazing material—both intentionally and unintentionally." Everyone starts to laugh, including Rainer. "It's been a real treat to watch you guys work."

Rainer blows a kiss, and Gillian smiles. "Where's Wilder?" she asks. My heart leaps into my throat so fast I swear Rainer can see it.

Gillian's smile softens, and she motions with her hand for Jordan to come forward. I swivel around. He's walking this way, arms folded across his chest, T-shirt pulled tight against his shoulders. He nods at Gillian and glances around nervously. Almost like he's not sure he belongs. He slides onto the bench across from Rainer and me and keeps his head ducked down.

"Jordan, you already know how I feel about you," Gillian says. "You're a force to be reckoned with, kid. I love ya." She turns her gaze back to the larger crowd. "Thank you to our crew. Camden, Jessica, Andre. Everyone. You have all been amazing. So let's roll this thing."

Everyone starts clapping and cheering, and then Gillian flicks a remote behind her and sits down next to Jordan. I watch her sling an arm over his shoulder and then him reach around and pull her down into a hug.

The gag reel starts—10, 9, 8—and then it's our audition tapes. First it's me in my jeans and sleeveless button-down at the Aladdin in Portland. I look nervous, bumbling. God, this seems like a long time ago. I want to shut it off, or at least for Jordan not to see. Rainer puts his arm around me and squeezes.

He lets me go as the scene changes—now it's us practicing that kissing scene. There are some whoops from the crowd; Lillianna yells, "Hot damn!" They've set the whole thing to eighties pop music, and the effect is sort of funny. We look ridiculous.

Next it's Wyatt yelling. There's a montage that transitions to him ranting at Rainer about how Mumford & Sons is the most overrated band since Coldplay. Rainer is laughing so hard I see tears sliding down his cheeks.

Then it's some outtakes from the *Scene* photo shoot. Luckily they either didn't capture or didn't include the footage of Rainer saying he wanted to kiss me in front of the entire cast and crew. Beyoncé is playing, and Jordan, Rainer, and I are laughing on the polka-dot set, the only time in the entire duration of filming I can remember the three of us getting along.

There's Jessica dropping things. I glance at her and see her standing next to Wyatt, watching through her fingers, but Wyatt puts a hand on her shoulder.

Then it cuts to a clip of Rainer giving the second unit crew a tour of his condo. "I'm really into pineapples," he informs them, holding a throw pillow up to his chest.

Everyone laughs around us, and Rainer stands up and gives a little bow.

There's a montage of us filming. One shot of me getting salt water sprayed up my nose and running around the beach like I'm on fire. Everyone laughs again, even Jordan.

There's stuff with our production assistants and our boom-mike operator, Tyler, who I'm pretty sure has hooked up with every single one of the girls at reception. He's pretty hot.

Then there is footage from the scene of August and Ed's kiss. I shrink as soon as I see it flash on the screen. Jordan's arms around me, my lips on his. I can feel Rainer next to me, the extended exhale of his breath. *Please cut away*, I silently pray. *Please*.

But the camera only moves closer. There are no hollers or whoops like with the footage of Rainer and me. There is just dead silence, so still I can hear the buzz of the projector.

Jordan-as-Ed's hands move from my face, through my hair and down around my back. I pull my own arms tighter around me. I feel a little like I did in Gillian's office that day. Like the on-screen me and the real me here, right now, are connected somehow, fused. When he pulls back and looks at me, I half expect to see the Jordan sitting here doing the same.

The camera lingers on the two of us post-kiss. Somewhere you can hear Wyatt call cut, and we just keep standing there stupidly. Suddenly I'm angry. How did Gillian's assistant think this was funny? It's not. It's mean.

Finally after what feels like years, the screen flips to Sandy talking on her cell phone. There's a montage of her in silk, on her phone. I hear some nervous laughter, and then by the time the opera music starts up and there are close-ups of her face and the phone like the two are lovers, there is a rolling, raucous applause.

Except for Rainer. He isn't laughing. I bite my lip and turn to face him. "It's good, huh?" I quip. He doesn't look at me. He keeps his eyes fixed on the screen. I ramble on, like if I push ahead I'll somehow push away whatever he saw, too. "I wonder if Gillian cut the whole thing herself. She's pretty talented. I thought that thing on the beach was hilarious. I totally forgot about getting water up my—"

Rainer interrupts. "What's going on?" he asks. His tone is cold. Not angry, just cool, like steel.

"Nothing," I say. I try to talk around the tremor in my voice, but I know he hears it. The gag reel has ended with a picture of the three of us, one they took a few weeks ago—my arms over both Rainer's and Jordan's shoulders. The screen fades, and everyone starts to clap.

"I was so stupid. I didn't even notice it." Rainer shakes his head. "Did you hook up with him while I was away?"

No no no no. "What are you talking about?" I reach for him, but he moves away.

"I'm talking about you and Jordan," he says. "I'm not blind, Paige. I saw that kiss on-screen."

"In what? A video? That's acting, Rainer." I'm trying to keep my voice low, but people are beginning to look at us.

He opens his mouth, then pauses. What comes out is, "No one is that good."

He stands. So do I. "You mean *I'm* not that good."

He exhales sharply. He steps closer to me and keeps his voice low. "Commit, then," he says.

"What?"

"Tell me you want to be with me. That you're all in. Right now."

"I . . ."

Rainer shakes his head. "You can't. And can you honestly tell me there is nothing going on between you two?"

People are starting to get up. I imagine Jordan somewhere behind me walking with Gillian over to the fire pit, sipping a mai tai and sliding down next to Wyatt. Did the video upset him, too? Did he even notice? I don't know why I keep assuming he cares.

Because I do. I care.

"No," I tell Rainer. "I can't."

If he is surprised, he doesn't show it. He holds up his

hands. "I won't do this," he says. Then he turns and starts walking back toward the condos.

I watch him go. The moon is shining—a silver, glittering mass on the water, like the shadow of a stranger—and for a moment I feel more alone than I have in my entire life. I'm used to being surrounded by people and feeling alone. It's the way I grew up—a million people around but no one really with you, and tonight reminds me of what I've known all along: *I don't really have anyone.* Not Jake and not Cassandra. Not Jordan. Not even Rainer.

This was my dream. The only thing I can ever remember wanting to do. When I was four, I told my mom I was going to be an actress. She even filmed me at the dinner table, her red lipstick swiped across my lips, as I declared it to the camera: "Someday I, Paige Townsen, am going to be a star."

It's everything I ever wanted. I'm acting. I have a film contract. People the world over will soon know my name. I'm living my dream. But all I can think about is how my heart seems to be falling through my body—down down down.

And then I hear footsteps behind me, and a familiar voice at my heels. "Hey, can we talk?"

I know it's Jordan. I recognize his breathing, the curve of his words, but I don't turn around. I don't want to talk, to be reminded, again, of everything that has gone wrong.

"Paige." I hear his voice like in the car—quiet and pleading.

"I'm sorry," I say, and then head back toward the condos.

That's the thing about success. It changes a lot, but not everything. You still have bad hair days. Friendships that have fallen apart won't miraculously be fixed. And people who didn't love you before still won't. Because the one thing success never changes, no matter what level you reach, is what has already happened.

CHAPTER 20

I wake up at three thirty and go into the kitchen for a glass of water. I see a note slipped under my door.

I care about you, but you need to decide what you want. I can't do it for you. Good luck on the movie. I'll see you in L.A.—R

I put the note on the counter. The living room curtains are open, and I can see the moon reflected on the water. Rainer's gone, and somewhere on this island Jordan is still here.

I know I won't be able to go back to sleep, so I decide on the next best thing—a swim. I put on my bathing suit, grab a towel, and pad my way down the now-familiar trail. I'm not scheduled to leave until tomorrow night, which means I'll have an entire day here to lie on the beach and have lunch at Longhi's and maybe even go shopping. To enjoy Hawaii, and forget, for twelve hours, what waits for me after this.

I'm surprised that a different feeling greets me at the shore—the feeling of possibility, like the entire world has been unzipped down the center and something hidden, something new, can now be seen. It's electrifying, and coupled with the cool, sharp sting of the water as I plunge forward, it's enough to make me forget the note on my counter.

I keep swimming—long, fluid strokes. It's hard to believe tomorrow I'll be on a plane back to Portland. It feels like I just got here, and at the same time, like I've been here forever. Like I never had a life before I met Rainer and Wyatt and Jordan. Like I've always been an actress.

The first play I ever did was a neighborhood production of *The Sound of Music*. I played Gretl, and we used our neighbor's back porch as the stage. I was probably no more than five or six, but I remember being really upset that we didn't have a curtain. That the guests were just going to show up and see the set. There wouldn't be a hushed silence as the curtain rose. There'd be no reveal. I always wanted that moment. That crest of a second where your stomach is in your heart and time stretches, slows down so much you think you can see it.

I duck my head under the water and then pop up, turning toward the shoreline. After my brush with drowning, the deep sea doesn't tempt me quite as much as it used to. Plus, it's pitch-black out. Not exactly an ideal time for long-distance swimming.

I wipe the water out of my eyes as I bob up and down, and then suck in my breath—there is a figure on the shore. It startles me, but not for long. After a beat, I know it's Jordan. He's sitting in the sand, legs crossed, bent over, almost like he's praying.

I blow some water with my lips and propel myself forward, swimming fast. It doesn't take me more than a minute to reach the wave break, and I ride a small one back to the shore.

I stand, shaking the water out of my ears. "Good morning."

He looks up, startled. "What are you doing down here?"

"I could ask you the same thing."

He shrugs, looks back down. "I couldn't sleep." He's wearing board shorts and a tight T-shirt. I can see the muscles move underneath the material.

"Me neither." I think about Jordan following me yesterday, about turning away from him. "Can I sit?" I ask.

His eyes flit downward, and I suddenly realize how naked I am in my skimpy nylon bikini. He's seen me like this before, but after last night I feel more exposed. I want the darkness to be heavier. Opaque.

He gives me his towel. "Here."

"Thanks." I unfold it and slide it over my shoulders, then around my waist, and sit down next to him.

"It's not morning," he says, looking out at the dark horizon.

"What?"

"You said good morning. It's not morning."

"Oh."

I loop my hair around my finger and pull. A trickle of water slides down my shoulder and into the sand.

"I'm sorry about last night," I start. "That really caught me off guard, that clip. I wasn't expecting—"

He turns to me. "Do you want to go somewhere?"

My mouth is still open, ready to continue. "Now?"

"Yes."

"It's, like, four AM."

"I know," he says. "It's perfect timing."

"For what? Murder?"

He squints at me. "I'm not looking to off your boyfriend, if that's what you think."

"I..." I exhale. There is no point in getting into that. What Rainer is or isn't. I'm tired of it, anyway. Instead I say, "Where do you want to go?"

He stands and holds out his hand to me. I take it.

When our fingers touch, I feel heat snaking up my arm. His palm is rough but familiar now.

"I want to show you something," he says.

Ten minutes later, we're sitting in Jordan's pickup truck, the wind howling through the windows. I'm still wearing my bathing suit, and it's wet against the inside of the sweatshirt Jordan gave me. I pull it closer around me and inhale. It smells like him. Like wood and fire. Like the elements things are made of. Pure and essential.

"Where are we going?" I ask him again.

He shakes his head. "Don't you want it to be a surprise?"

"Not if you're kidnapping me."

He looks at me and raises his eyebrows. My heart starts pounding away in my chest like a prisoner dying to escape. I cross my arms.

"Kidnapping?"

"Haven't you already been to prison?"

He makes a sound halfway between a sneeze and a sigh. "You really believe everything you read, don't you?"

"No." I gather his towel that's still wrapped around my waist and hike it up higher. "But that's true, isn't it?"

He turns his head to me. Almost too long for someone behind the wheel. "No, it's not."

"You were never in jail?"

"I've been there." He shrugs and looks forward.

"See?"

"To help with an inmate literacy program I started." He takes one hand off the wheel and brings it up to his neck. He rolls his head from side to side and one tiny bead of water rolls down the length of his scar and nuzzles itself in the crook of his collarbone. "Things aren't always the way they seem."

I tear my gaze away from him. "I know. I mean, when you told me that stuff about your family—"

"You thought I must have spent time in prison?"

"No, that's not what I mean." I roll up my window. It's instantly quieter in the truck, and I'm aware of my words now more than ever. "I just mean you seem like someone who'd do anything to protect the people he loves."

I feel him glance at me, and I keep my eyes pinned on my lap. I'm grateful we're in a moving car. That we're not sitting opposite each other. He can't see the way the blood is pounding in my veins, making it almost impossible to hear.

He doesn't say anything, and neither do I. The sun hasn't caught up with us yet, and we keep driving in the darkness. It's tough to make too much out, but Jordan seems to know the way. He doesn't check a map or squint to read street signs. He just goes, like he's got some internal magnet that's pulling this truck, and us, toward our destination.

We take a turn, swing right, and then we're climbing—up and up, like the sun in the mornings at the beach, and all at once I know where we're headed.

"Are you taking me to Haleakala?"

Jordan smiles. "Yes."

"Really?" My face cracks into a smile the size of a California fault line. "I've been wanting to do this since I got here."

"Then how come you haven't?" He rolls down the window a little. The air is cooler up here, thicker. Almost like the ocean this morning.

I shrug and flip up the hood of his sweatshirt. "Busy, I guess."

"Rainer not a morning person?" He smiles. He's kidding. I exhale. Maybe we can joke about this. Maybe it doesn't have to be the way it has been. But then I remember us at the beach, his arms rolling me on top of him, his hands on my face.

"Can I ask you a favor?" I say.

"Of course."

"Can we not talk about Rainer today?"

He nods. "If that's what you want, sure."

We drive in silence for a while, the wind whistling in through the open window, the sound of turning tires on the pavement. We keep heading up—winding along the side of the volcano. I've heard the view on the drive is spectacular, but I can't see much now. Just the eerie mountainside, the rolling hills tumbling down into a still-black sea.

Finally, we reach the top. There are a surprising number of cars there, but watching the sunrise from Haleakala is a popular tourist activity, so it makes sense. Jordan parks, and we get out. It's freezing, and the wind is fierce. It zips and hollers and screams, like someone wailing over a lost love. Maybe love has been lost here—swallowed up by time and space and stars.

"Come here." Jordan takes my hand and starts walking past the tourists huddled by the cars, thermoses of hot chocolate and coffee clutched in their fingers. I pull the towel tighter around my waist and the sweatshirt in closer.

When we round the corner, I squeeze his hand so sharply he flinches. The view is like nothing I have ever seen, not even in movies. It's a giant landscape of crater—red and orange and deep browns, stretching so far it's impossible to think this is all on one island.

"It's beautiful, isn't it?" He cocks his head in the direction of two rocks, and we take a seat. It's still dark out, but the first rays of sun are starting to poke through the blackness. It's completely unlike the sunrise at the beach. This is epic, massive. Closer. I feel like we might be at the center of the world up here.

"It's spectacular."

We're protected from the wind in this little nook, and its absence makes the mist hang. We're actually in the clouds.

"Thank you for bringing me here." I slip my hands into the sleeves of the sweatshirt and tuck them in between my legs.

"You're welcome." He clears his throat, and then there is quiet again. But this time it's not calm, it's charged. Lit with all the things we're not saying.

He picks up a rock. I look at his hands—rough, calloused. Even though it's freezing up here, they were warm just a moment ago. "I'm sorry about the video," he says.

"It wasn't your fault."

He nods, turns the rock over. "Even so, I am. I'm sure Rainer wasn't thrilled."

"I thought we weren't talking about him," I say, jabbing him playfully in the side.

He looks from the rock to me and then back down. I can tell he's not kidding, and I sit very still. Even the blood in my veins seems to halt. "I don't want to complicate things for you."

"You're not," I say quietly. "I mean, do you think you are?"

He studies the rock carefully, like maybe the answer is written on the underside. "Yes," he says. "I do."

"Tell me why you and Rainer hate each other," I say. "I need to know."

Jordan sighs. I watch his chest rise and fall. "I don't hate him. I never have. Things just got complicated."

"Complicated *how*?"

He looks at me, his eyes dark like charcoal. "Do you really want to know?"

I swallow. Nod. "Yes," I say. "I really want to know."

He drops the rock and wipes his hands on his shorts. For a moment, I'm scared of what I'll hear. How permanent this rift is. How irreparable.

"You remember how I told you my dad isn't a great guy?" His eyes are fierce but kind. I can tell he wants to protect me from this, whatever it is. "Well, Rainer's isn't, either."

"Greg?"

Jordan nods. "Right. He used to produce a show we were all on—me, Rainer, and Britney."

I nod, catching up. "*Backsplash*?"

Jordan frowns at me. "You know it?"

"No. I mean, yes. I watched it a few times. What about it?" I flip my hood down and tuck the stray hair behind my ears. The shiver of cold makes me edge closer to him.

"It was the first thing any of us did. It's how we all met. We were friends." He rubs his palms together like he's trying to generate heat. I see the muscles in his arms work.

"The three of you?"

He exhales, and I see a small smile play on his lips, like he's remembering something. "Yeah, the three of us."

I think about Jake and Cassandra. About our tree house and rule book and secret pacts. All the things that made us friends. That bound us together.

"We all went our separate ways after the show ended. We were still really close, though. We had monthly dinners, that sort of thing."

"What does this have to do with Rainer's dad?" I ask.

Jordan picks his gaze up, and I can see his eyes are sad, restrained. Like he doesn't want to tell me what happened next.

"Rainer and Britney started dating. This was a few years after we were finished with the show." I see the pulse in his neck. I wait for him to continue. "I was fine with it. I always figured something would start up between them, and I didn't have feelings for her. Not like that, anyway." He glances at me sideways, and I drop my gaze to the ground. I can feel a little knot form in my stomach, like my insides are fingers curling into a fist.

"She started spending a lot of time at his house. And one night—" He breaks off. "Rainer wasn't home, and she came early to wait for him. Greg was there."

I start to feel sick. All of a sudden, I think I know what's coming.

"Oh my God."

He takes a deep breath. "She managed to get away before he could, you know. She came over to my house. She was in really bad shape, and nothing really tears Britney up." He smiles, and I see the warm flush of familiarity on his face. Affection. "She's tough, but she wasn't then." His face clouds back over, and his eyes find mine. They're black. Opaque. Like marbles cut from solid stone. "She kept saying he told her that if she said anything, he'd make sure her career was over."

My hands are shaking. I knot them together and press them up against my pounding heart. "Wouldn't his have been over, too?" I ask.

Jordan exhales. "I wish it worked that way. She was basically an unknown. Some girl from some kids' TV show. Her music career hadn't taken off yet. People would have just thought she was looking for attention. And she's not—" Jordan looks at his hands. "She's kind of a loose cannon. She always has been."

"But she told Rainer," I say, piecing it together.

"It's complicated," he says. His voice has gotten quiet. Above the wind, it's almost hard to hear. "But yes, Rain thought she had made it up."

I've never heard him use a nickname for Rainer before, and it catches me off guard. The intimacy of it. This whole history I'm not a part of.

"Why would she have made that up?" I ask. "Why

wouldn't Rainer believe her?" It doesn't sound like the guy I know. The one who has been so supportive of me in everything here.

"He thought she made it up because she was desperate." He exhales, runs a hand over his face. "Because he found her with me."

We both get quiet. His head is in his hands. I reach out and touch his shoulder gently. I feel him flinch and then relax under my fingertips.

"After what happened with Greg." I see the muscles of his jaw work as he says Rainer's father's name. "Rainer came to my house. She was in my arms. She kissed me," he says. I feel the skin of his back heat up, like the memory itself is generating fire. "She was upset. It just happened. But Rainer saw and he thought—Britney started relaying this crazy story about his dad. . . ." He trails off, and I take my hand back. It's warm now. Heated up by his contact.

"He hasn't forgiven me," Jordan finishes. "How can I blame him?" He smiles a small, sad smile, and I realize something else: He misses him. Like I miss Cassandra. They were friends, and now they're not anymore. Who was it who said you can't have hate without love?

"So you see why this"—he points slowly from him to me, from his heart to mine—"isn't really a good idea. He already thinks I tried to take someone he cared about from him."

The sun has started to crawl up the mountain like a hiker climbing to safety—with intention, purpose. Every millisecond makes him more sure of his own survival.

"But what about what I want?" Once the words are out, I wince; but it's too late, I can't take them back.

"What do you want?" Jordan's breath is short, and for a moment I think maybe he is as nervous as I am.

"I want to know you," I say. It should feel like a betrayal of Rainer, but it doesn't, because it's the truth. I slide closer to Jordan. Without even thinking, I've picked up one of his dirt-dusted hands with my own.

He smiles down. "I want that, too."

We sit in silence that way for a good ten minutes, our fingers wrapped together like vines as we watch the sunrise—shades of colors I never even knew existed thrust across the sky like shooting stars. It feels like the whole world is waking up here. Like the first light that ever existed was created on this volcano.

When we get up to leave, Jordan stands and holds his hand out to me, his face lit up with the morning.

"One more minute," I say. I look out over the sun-drenched canyon. It feels like if I called something out, I wouldn't get an echo, but an answer. I want to ask what to do, what's the right choice, but I'm afraid of my own voice. Of what I'll hear myself say. I just wish I knew when I would get this chance again.

"We'll be back," he says, as if reading my mind. He stretches his arms out wide, like he's trying to touch both ends of Haleakala at once.

"Maybe," I say. "We don't even know if they're going to make the next movie. We could just go back to our normal lives. We could forget."

Jordan shakes his head, like I don't get it. Then he takes his hands and puts one of his palms, gently extended, on my cheek.

It feels right there, like recognizing a familiar road sign after hours of being lost. Relief. Joy. The feeling of going home. "Haven't you ever heard of faith?"

The wind slows down, stops, so his words just sit there, like upright children on the first day of school. Full of potential and infinite possibility. Hope, even.

"Yes," I say back. He leans in slowly, and for a moment I think maybe he's going to kiss me, he's that close, but he doesn't. Instead he brushes his lips up against my hair.

I want to tell him that what I do know is that I have faith in him, that I've never been so sure of anything in my life. That when we're together I feel like I do when I'm acting: like everything else falls away and I'm totally, completely, exactly where I should be. But the wind starts up again, threatening to carry my words far from here, all the way east, if necessary, and instead what comes out is "We should get back."

Because it's true. We should. I remember Wyatt's confrontation with me from months ago, and for the first time I get what he was trying to say. He was trying to tell me to take responsibility. That it is my choice how things turn out. How I'm not at the mercy of a moment, a feeling, the soft stream of fate. Maybe there are some things that are out of my control, but not this. I have to make things right. I have to talk to Rainer. I can't run just because what's in front of me is hard. As Jake would say, "You need to recognize the impact you make in the world."

Jordan and I listen to the hum of the radio on the way down the mountain. The day has crept in, and it's keeping us company. Gone are the stretched silences. It's calm, peaceful—comfortable, even. Like the day breathed a sigh of relief as soon as the sun rose.

I doze off, and when I wake up, Jordan's hand is on my arm, rocking me awake. We're back at the condos.

"Come on," he says. "I'll walk you upstairs."

We walk through the lobby, his arm tucked around my waist. When we get to my door, he takes the key card gently out of my palm and unlocks it. Then he comes inside with me. I face-plant onto the bed, kicking my shoes off and snaking up to the pillows.

"Thanks," I murmur.

I feel something soft on top of me. The blanket I keep

on the edge of the bed, the one I brought from home that's been mine since the day I was born. He pulls it up and over, and when he reaches my shoulders, his hand brushes my skin. Instinctively, I reach up and curl my fingers around his. "Stay," I say. "Just sleep."

My eyes are closed, and I can feel myself falling into the seductive grip of unconsciousness. Before I succumb completely, I feel him sink down next to me. He pulls me against his chest and locks his arms tight around me. He kisses my cheek, and I can feel his breath on my face, his heartbeat at my back. It beats against me, through me, the same as my own.

CHAPTER 21

Being the last one to leave sucks. No matter what the situation, you always feel like you're being left. When I wake up, I'm alone and it's evening. My flight leaves at midnight, and I still have packing to do. I pick up a sandwich and wander leisurely through the lobby. I know Jordan won't be there, but I try, anyway. Even though the hotel is exactly the same—the furniture and pillows and lamps and even that spectacular, panoramic ocean view—the entire place feels empty. Like by leaving, he took everything tangible with him.

I miss them both. I can still feel Jordan's arms around me this morning, his nose pressed against the crook of my neck. And I miss Rainer, too. I miss his laugh and beautiful blue eyes and easy charm. I went seventeen years without

269

having a boyfriend, without ever even having more than a crush, and now there are two of them. These two guys who are so different, like separate species, and yet the way they make me feel....I never thought you could really care about two people at the same time. That seemed ridiculous. Cassandra falls in love constantly, and I always called her fickle. But now it's like Jordan and Rainer are fighting it out inside my heart. And I don't know who to root for because just thinking about one makes me feel like a traitor to the other.

I replay the last few months in my head like a highlights reel. Dinners with Rainer at Longhi's. Jordan's kiss in the cabana. Editing. The Fish Market. Our time on set. And just like that, I know where I need to be.

I sprint across the hotel floor. I get to his room totally out of breath. I knock twice. *Please be there. Please be there.*

I hear the shuffle of feet and the door swinging open, and his head of curly hair appears in the doorway like an apple in a barrel. Wyatt.

When I see him, I get nervous. Crazy nervous. It's Wyatt, after all. We haven't had the best relationship. But I have to tell him. Even if he slams the door in my face, which he very well might do.

"I didn't say thank you," I start. "And I thought you had already left, and I never got to tell you what this has meant to me and how—"

And then Wyatt does something remarkable. Something that seems totally out of character and perfectly right, perfectly *him* all at once. He hugs me.

He reaches out and pulls me toward him. I'm so surprised that I can't say anything, I just stiffen up like a piece of plywood. But as soon as his arms are around me, I start to soften. There is something familiar about his hug—warm. It reminds me of when my brothers used to wrestle me to the ground in our living room and then help me up afterward. It was moments like those that let me know they cared. That they might have even loved me.

"All right, kid," Wyatt says. He pushes me back and holds me at arm's length, his hands on my shoulders. He surveys me, in much the same way a painter might admire a newly completed work. "I'm proud of you," he says. "But don't expect me to say it again."

I nod once. Understood.

"You're here all by yourself? Isn't security at least keeping an eye on you?" He peers down the hallway, and sure enough, one of the guards is standing by. Has he been following me? For how long?

"Rainer left yesterday," I say.

Wyatt drops his arms from my shoulders and crosses them. He raises his eyebrows like he's questioning me, and all of a sudden I cough up the words, like a confession: "Jordan left today."

Wyatt clears his throat. "You two got close."

I wrap my hands around my elbows. My voice sounds small in my own ears. "He's different from what people think."

Wyatt doesn't take his eyes off me. "I agree."

"I wish Rainer could see that," I say.

Wyatt leans on the doorframe. "They've got history," he says, and for a moment I think about all the things I don't know about him. What his own history is.

"I know."

"But I think they'll come around. As long as nothing else further muddies the waters." He looks at me then, dead on.

"I know," I say again, but this time it's light, soft. I can barely hear the words.

We stand in the doorway for another beat. And then he smiles. "Now get out of here, will you? I still have to pack."

When my plane takes off, it's so dark out that I can't see the ocean or the green landscape, but I know it's there. It's comforting somehow, like a movie you've seen so many times you can leave it on as background noise and still know exactly what's happening if you catch even one line.

I close my eyes and see the soft roll of the hills, Ho'okipa Beach with its windsurfers, who won't be out for another few hours at least. I see Longhi's, and our condos, and the beach with its clean white sand and pebbled stones, and the cabanas, their tops pulled tight to protect against any night rain. I think about last night and this morning, turning the memory over in my mind like a shiny penny.

I imagine myself back in that bed with Jordan, back in his arms. His stray hair falling on my cheek, his breath warm against my neck. I want to reach out and touch him, curl my fingers around his hands, shoulders, neck, face. Draw his nose to mine and never let him go. But something stops me.

Someone taps my shoulder. "Excuse me?"

I blink. A girl is leaning over me. She's probably around thirteen or fourteen with the most freckles I have ever seen on a girl's face. She's a little bit sunburned on her cheeks but then again, so are most people on this plane, I think.

"You're Paige Townsen, aren't you?"

I nod. I feel a bit like I've been caught in a lie. Hand in the cookie jar. Which makes no sense. It's true. I am Paige Townsen.

"Wow." Her eyes get wide, and she blinks, remembering something. She lunges forward and rummages through her bag, producing a book. She hands it over to me proudly, like a cat with a mouse in its teeth.

"Do you think you could sign it?" she asks. "It would

really mean a lot to me. This book"—she holds it to her chest like a valentine—"is my life. I've read it four times." She pauses, inhales briefly. "I don't have any brothers or sisters, you know." She gestures to a woman across the aisle wearing a silk sleep mask, her mouth slightly open. "My mom and I travel a lot together. She sleeps and I read."

I remember what it was like to be this girl. To want to spill your heart to strangers. To feel like if you kept talking you could somehow make it all better, get to the answer. It occurs to me, looking at her freckled face, that I no longer feel this way at all, and for a moment, the realization saddens me. I can't pick up the phone and call Cassandra; it's clear she doesn't want to talk to me. I can't talk to Rainer because I don't know what to say, or how I really feel.

I smile and take the pen she hands over. "Who should I make it out to?"

"Jen," she says, tapping her chest. "Jen Sparrow."

I write her name across the title page and then add, *To Locked's biggest fan—Paige Townsen.*

It's strange, looking at my name like that. Like signing the bottom of a painting in elementary school or the top of a paper for English class. The only difference is this isn't my own. It's someone else's. The responsibility hits me again, but it's not as scary this time, not as overwhelming. It doesn't feel like it did when I first got the job, or the way it has on set—at times crippling. It feels good, almost. *Right*.

My mom used to lecture my sister about responsibility. How it wasn't just about her now, how she had to start thinking about Annabelle. Annabelle, whose happiness was now more important than her own. I think, looking at Jen Sparrow, that I have a responsibility to her. To her happiness. To somehow, in some small way, live up to the meaning she's given this book, and my role in it.

We talk for the rest of the flight. She lives in San Francisco, but her dad just moved to Portland and her mom is going to drop her off. I give her my phone number (a big Sandy no-no) and tell her that she should stop by Trinkets n' Things. Her eyes get big. "You'll be there?" she asks me. "Just at a store?"

"Sure," I say, "why not?"

She looks at me, her eyebrows furrowed. "You're a movie star. I don't think you can work in a shop." She winces, like she's said too much. "I'm sorry," she says, "let's talk about something else. Rainer Devon?" She bites her bottom lip, but I can tell that she's not going to be able to keep in whatever she's about to say. "Are the rumors true? Are you with him? He's so cute." She keeps talking, about his movies and how she thinks I am "way better than Britney." She only pauses, hiccuping in some air, when the captain announces we're going to be landing soon.

I laugh, the absurdity of this situation grounding itself

in my stomach like our plane on the tarmac. A girl I have never met before wants to know who I'm dating.

"It's complicated," I say.

She nods, but she doesn't say anything. Her mom snores awake across from her, and we both giggle. I suddenly miss Cassandra something fierce. It's been what seems like forever since I giggled with another girl.

"I think you have to follow your heart," she says. "I'm not sure love is actually that complicated."

I want to say "I wish it were that simple," but maybe it is. Maybe it always has been. I think about Rainer's hands on my face, his note, his promise of protection, and I think about Jordan—about how it feels to be with him—like he's waking something up in me, some part of me I never even knew existed. I want to be able to give Rainer an answer. I want to be able to tell him yes. But if I do, if I commit to him in front of the world, there is no possibility of Jordan. Not ever.

She smiles, and so do I. "I can't wait to tell everyone I met Paige Townsen."

"Make sure to point out my total lack of plane hair," I say, picking up a frizzy strand.

"I will," she says, laughing. "I promise."

When we get to baggage claim, I see her dad. He's standing by a luggage cart, looking nervous. He pulls her into a hug when she gets to him and kisses her on the head, his eyes briefly snapping closed.

I wonder if he thinks about his responsibility. To keep her safe and happy. To love her. I hope so.

I'm turning when I spot my own father. He's standing to the left of the double doors. He smiles, lifts his hand to wave. Then I do something I have never done in my life. I run to him and throw my arms around his neck. He pauses, sways, obviously surprised by the attack. But then he puts his arms around me, and smooths my hair down with his hand.

"Welcome home, baby," he says. "I missed you."

CHAPTER 22

"Business has been booming!" Laurie says. She's holding up an empty crystal basket as evidence. "We're the store that used to employ a star. People love it."

"How do people know?" I ask. "It's not like you have a poster in the window. Oh God, do you?"

Laurie waves a dismissing hand at me and goes to the door. She hands me a wooden sign: FORMER WORKPLACE OF PAIGE "PG" TOWNSEN.

"Wow," I say.

"Honey, it's like gold." She frowns. "You're not upset, are you?"

"No?"

"Good. Because I tell everyone the Patchouli Petal Body Scrub is your favorite. We can't make it fast enough!"

It's nine AM, and the store doesn't open till ten, but I already see a few tourists eyeing the entrance.

"Sometimes we have a line," Laurie tells me. "Imagine if they saw you in here!"

"That's okay," I say quickly before she gets any ideas. "I just stopped by to say hi. I have some errands to run today."

I hand her back the sign, and she takes it. "Oh, I almost forgot, I have something for you."

She ducks into the back room, and I run my fingers across the counter. The same ancient computer buzzes in the corner. I think about how many days I've spent behind that thing, dreaming of being on the other side.

There is a basket of "*Locked* lockets" and a little box filled with "August amber." I imagine Laurie coming up with these names. She must have gone to the library to Google the book. She doesn't read, and no way that ancient computer behind the cash register could do an Internet search.

Laurie emerges in a cloud of basil and orange. "Here," she says.

I take the package wrapped in purple tissue paper. Inside is a little incense box.

"Turn it over," she says.

I flip the box and see two dates, four years apart.

"The dates you worked here," she says, finishing my thought.

A lump catches in my throat. "So there's no chance of a part-time job this summer?" I ask her.

She smiles, the wrinkles around her eyes softening. "You don't belong behind that computer anymore, honey."

"No one does," I say. "That thing is basically dead."

She laughs. "Just don't be a stranger, okay? I can handle you being a star but not a stranger."

"You got it."

"And you tell that friend of yours Jake that he's welcome to keep his flyers up, too," she says.

I don't have the heart to tell her about Jake, or Cassandra, who I still haven't seen even though I've been here for close to a month since I got back from Seattle. I've been holing up at home, which is essentially what I did on that film set, too. Hole up. Hibernate. It was so different from *Locked*. It was a bigger cast, but I was the youngest by a lot, and everyone really bonded. It was cozy and warm and light—a welcome reprieve from the pressures of *Locked*. And the pressures are here now. I'm starting to get recognized on the street. All the promotional stuff is up for *Locked*, which opens in two weeks in L.A. I'm set to fly back at the end of next week.

Rainer, Jordan, and I have seen each other three times since Hawaii. Rainer has been filming a movie in London, and Jordan has been lying low in L.A.—I only know that from some online stalking. Okay, a lot of online stalking. I haven't spoken to him. Jordan, that is. Even though I've seen him, it feels like our relationship ended on that mountaintop. Holding hands, our fingers intertwined. Even Rainer has been suspended somehow. Our L.A. trips have been so busy, and we've had basically zero downtime. Just photo shoot after photo shoot after interview. I haven't even been alone with him for thirty seconds, let alone the time it would take to have the conversation we need to have. We've e-mailed, but he mostly tells me about filming, a family trip he went on to Italy, and how good the coffee is in London. He doesn't ask about us, and I know he won't. I kept thinking that maybe he had moved on, maybe he had already fallen for someone else. The thought of it made me feel totally panicked, but I also knew it wasn't unreasonable. He's Rainer, and he's been all over the world—without me. But then I got this e-mail: "I miss you. Nothing seems to be the same without you anymore." I felt wildly, epically relieved. And that's wrong. I shouldn't feel relieved. Not yet. Not when there is still so much in front of us all.

I haven't taken off his necklace, though. Not once, except when I had to shoot. And even then I kept it in my pocket—a reminder of something I'm only beginning to understand.

I look at Laurie. "Thanks. I will."

She pulls me into a hug. I remember recoiling in the past at her embrace. Not because I haven't always liked Laurie, I have, but because her smell is so intense you could get hives from just breathing close to her. But this time, I let her. I don't even hold my breath. Something about the intensity of rose water and incense and something else—ginger?—is strangely comforting. Like nothing has changed even though everything has. It's funny—I spent my whole life wanting everything to be different, and now that it is I miss the way it was.

I wave over my shoulder and open the door, the familiar twinkle of bells and chimes going off as I do.

It's a Thursday, which means everyone is in school. I decide to forgo wandering by my old high school—too depressing—and instead head somewhere I know I can curl up in a corner and disappear.

I push past the double doors of Powell's and walk up the stairs to the second floor. On the left side, in the back, is where the scripts are kept. They're alphabetized by title, and I run my hand over the stacks and stop at *S*. They have the original shooting script of *Singin' in the Rain*. I've read it probably a dozen times, but not since I've been gone, and the last time I listened to it was at the audition. I pull it off the shelf and settle with my back against the stacks, my knees pulled up to my chest.

I read for a while. It's comforting being back here.

How many afternoons have I spent doing the exact same thing? The only difference is that this time Cassandra and Jake don't show up, and my head isn't plagued by math homework—instead it's the same question, scrolled across my mind like a proposal in the sky. *Are you ready?* it asks. *Is this what you want?*

And I think, I know, what my answer is. I've known all along. I've just been afraid of what I'll lose by making this choice. We're going to be together soon, and I need to tell Rainer I can't do this. Maybe if we were just average people, if this weren't going to be something we had to do in front of the world, it would be different. But I don't think I can make that choice for myself yet. I don't think I'm ready to take the other one away.

When I get home, Annabelle and my sister are gone, but my mom's car is parked in the driveway. Strange. She never takes a day off from school, or even leaves early. I think she's been absent exactly twice in her entire career. Once was when all four of us got the chicken pox, back when I was still a baby; the day is legendary in our family. The second is the day Annabelle was born.

"Mom?" I set my bag down on the counter and take the stairs two at a time.

I find her in her room, sitting on the edge of the bed, a sweater in her hands.

"Mom?"

"Hi, honey." She looks up like she's not at all surprised to see me, like maybe she's even been waiting.

"Um, hi. No school?"

She shrugs. "I took the afternoon off. I thought maybe we could spend some time together."

"I'm sorry," I say. I look down at my sweater. "I didn't know."

She nods. "Come here," she says.

I walk slowly over to the edge of the bed and sit down beside her.

"We haven't really talked too much lately, you and me." She sighs, shakes her head. "I'm not sure we ever have, really."

"What do you mean?"

She looks over at me. Her eyes look sad. Tired. "By the time you came along, we had a busy household. I always thought this acting thing was maybe my fault, that we didn't give you enough attention as a kid."

I feel my pulse quicken. Anger spikes. "Acting isn't a *thing*," I say. "It's my life now."

"I know, honey," she says. "That's what I'm trying to tell you. This dream—"

"It's not going to just be a moment," I say. "I'm not going to give it up the way you did."

My mom looks at me, her eyes hurt. "Is that what you think?"

"I've seen your stack of theater tickets and playbills," I tell her. "I know what you wanted."

She squints at me and then stands. She goes to her jewelry box and removes the top layer. She takes out the envelope, the one I've run my fingers over dozens of times before. The same one that's yellowed on the top and frayed on the side.

She comes back to sit next to me on the bed and opens it. She takes out a ticket for *Hair* and hands it to me. "The first play I saw," she says. "My girlfriends and I snuck in the back and stood the entire performance. I found this ticket on the floor and kept it."

She takes out another. *West Side Story*. She smiles. "The first play your father took me to. It was our third date. Our first kiss, too."

A third. "This is the play I saw the night I had Tom. When my water broke, your father wanted to walk out before the second act, but I insisted that the baby would wait."

She hands me ticket after ticket. Birthdays and anniversaries, and once, just a free summer afternoon. "I hired a babysitter and went," she says, a twinkle of mischief in her eyes.

When she's handed me the last ticket, she looks at me. "Do you understand now?"

I don't say anything. I'm not sure the lump in my throat would let me.

"I don't keep these things as mementos of what I don't have. I keep them as mementos of what I do."

I swallow. I can feel the tears starting to well up. Tears of shame and sadness and guilt. Love, too.

"I wasn't like you," she continues. "I didn't have the talent for it. And I realized once I had children that I had a lot of love to give. I wanted to be where I was most needed. That wasn't on the stage, sweetheart. For me, it was in the classroom. Sometimes you give things up because it's the right thing to do. And doing the right thing feels good. It feels better than the dream. Because the dream isn't real."

"Do you think my dream is real?"

She sighs. "Sometimes I worry about you. It's a tough business, and I try not to focus on it too much or talk about it, because more than anything, honey, I want you to know that it's not everything. There are things much, much more important than success."

"Like what?"

She looks at me and smiles, almost laughs. "You're smarter than that."

I sniff. "Sometimes it's like you don't even care. I have a big blockbuster movie coming out, and you act like it's a school play."

She takes her hand and runs it down my back, then up to smooth my hair. "I may not understand the film world, and selfishly, I want you home, but I never want you to doubt for a minute how proud of you I am. You were always different," she says, her voice catching. "I guess I ignored it because I hoped maybe if I did, it would mean you'd stay here and be my daughter."

"I'm still your daughter," I say.

"My daughter the movie star." She smiles, straightens up. "What do you say you take your mother to dinner, huh? Just us."

"I'd like that." I move to hand her back the tickets, but she shakes her head.

"Keep them," she tells me.

"But, Mom—"

She puts her hand over mine. "I'd like you to have them. Maybe they'll remind you of what's really important."

She touches her forefinger to my nose. "Now let your mother get dressed. We're going someplace nice."

I stand up, the tickets pressed into my palm.

"I'll take good care of them," I say.

My mother may not have jewelry, but these pieces of paper are her heirlooms. Because there's something in my hand you can't buy. Something sacred.

CHAPTER 23

We're all gathered at our dining room table for brunch on Sunday. Everyone except for Annabelle, who snoozes in her playpen a few feet away, and my brother Tom, who is with his wife visiting her family today. Even Bill is there, sitting next to my sister. "He's been on his best behavior lately," my mother whispers next to me.

"What is everyone doing today?" my father asks.

Bill and Joanna giggle, and my mom raises her eyebrows. "Anything you'd like to share with the group?"

My sister clears her throat. "Actually, we have an announcement."

My heart stops. I'm pretty sure my mom's does, too. I hear her fork rattle to the floor. *Please don't be pregnant,* I pray. I mean, Annabelle is great and all, but I think that should be a one-time thing. At least for the next decade.

"Bill?" Joanna looks at her boyfriend.

"Tell them."

"Well." She pauses, looking around at each of us.

"Spit it out," my brother Jeff hollers.

"We're engaged," she says.

"We're getting married," Bill says.

She slips something onto her finger—a gold ring with an amethyst stone. It's pretty—good quality, too. My time at Trinkets n' Things has made me kind of an expert on gems.

I glance at my mom. She's turned a very funny shade of yellow, and I worry she's not going to take this well, but then her face breaks into a big smile, and she leaps up, clasping my sister and Bill into a big hug. "This is fantastic news," she says. "Absolutely wonderful. We need to celebrate!"

"Awesome," my brother says, going back to his eggs.

"Today," my father says. "Paige leaves tomorrow."

My mother isn't listening. She's already in the kitchen, uncoiling the phone. I hear her chatter into it, to one friend after the other, as my father pours Bill more orange juice and my brother asks if Joanna's knocked up again.

No baby. Just love.

"We're having a party!" my mother calls.

"When?" Joanna asks. I can hear the glee in her voice,

see the joy on her face. In the way she beams at Bill. She's even being nice to me.

"Tonight," my mother says. "Your father's right. Paige should be here." She's talking with her hands now, moving closer to the door. "I'm going grocery shopping. You"—she snaps her fingers at my brother—"clean this up." She gestures toward the table and then grabs her bag, swinging it over her shoulder. The door slams a moment later.

Annabelle wakes up, screaming.

"I'll go," I say.

I walk over to her playpen, and she's standing, her little arms reaching up to the ceiling.

"Paige!" she calls, her sweet voice thick with sleep and sniffles.

"Hey, Annabelle Lee." I pick her up, propping her on my hip. She lays her little head down on my shoulder, and one of her tears falls on my chest. "Guess what?" I tell her, my voice light. "Your mommy and daddy are going to get married."

"Mary," she echoes, hiccuping.

I sit down on the floor cross-legged and place her into my lap. In the other room, I can hear my sister talking about the wedding, how they want to get married next spring, maybe even at our house. My brother makes comments, my sister raises her voice, and my dad intervenes. It gets loud and then quiet and then loud again as Annabelle and I play on the carpet.

I used to only think about how different my sister's life would have been if she hadn't had Annabelle. How she would have gone to a proper college, maybe even done something she wanted to do like be a designer or an architect. When we were younger she was always sketching things. I rarely think about that anymore, though. It's hard, with Annabelle here, to ever imagine she wasn't.

That's life. It just happens, and with it a lot of stuff you can't take back. But the wonderful part is that often, the things that challenge you, that require you to use your whole self, are exactly those that are really worth it.

"Paige," Annabelle coos again. "Book." She points to a copy of *Ducks Drive*, her favorite picture book. I think it's crazy, a bunch of baby ducks who also have cars, but she loves it. She laughs and squeals at the pictures like she's never seen anything so spectacular in her life.

We read together until my sister comes in.

"Hey," she says. "What are you doing?" She squats down on the floor next to us, and Annabelle puts her arms out to her. My sister scoops her up. "Hey, baby," she says. "You having fun with Aunt Paige?"

"Congratulations," I tell her.

My sister looks startled, like she hasn't heard me right.

"I'm really happy for you," I continue.

She smiles. "It's not a movie. But it's something."

"Yeah," I say. "It is."

I don't think we've ever had so many people in my house, and that's counting the time my brother won the high school basketball championship and we had three teams and their friends over. I guess I never realized how many friends my sister had. There are people from high school, middle school, and kids who I remember teasing me in my backyard when I was just a kid. People she's known forever.

Her friends shriek when they see her. My mother's friends hover over the ring.

And then I see her. The mess of curls greets me first, the purple polka-dot sweater second. There's only one person I know who could pull that off with red-and-blue-striped jeans. Cassandra.

She tucks her hands into her pockets as she reaches me. "Hey," she says.

"Hey," I say. My heart is beating frantically.

"How are you?" she asks.

"Fine," I say. It's like we're walking on ice, afraid to let anything crack. But I want it to crack. I want it to be real— not like this—not so light it's like we're not even really here.

I think about the last time I saw her, all those months ago, at the airport. About how I sped off without looking back.

"I'm glad you came tonight," I say.

I see her face break into a smile and feel relief flood my veins. "Yeah?" she says. "I wasn't sure. I wasn't sure you'd want to see me. I didn't even know you were home." She looks at her shoes. "Your mom called."

My stomach stirs, a giant waking up from sleep. I feel my face get hot with embarrassment. I suddenly feel really stupid. The kind of stupid you feel when a belief you've held on to turns out to be completely ludicrous. There isn't anything to argue. No defense, just *I was wrong*. I didn't call. I didn't let her know. It's been my fault we haven't kept in touch, not hers.

"I figured maybe you didn't want to talk to me," she continues, her voice small.

I shake my head. I feel my eyes fill up with tears. "I'm sorry," I say. "You were right. I didn't make enough of an effort after I left. I should have called more. I should have told you both how much you mean to me." I feel a lump in my throat. It rises, hovers, like a body in a magician's trick.

"I'm sorry I didn't tell you about Jake and me sooner," she says.

"No, you guys are good together. It should have been you two all along."

Cassandra looks at me, her blue eyes brimming with tears. "I've missed you," she says.

"Me too."

She pulls me into a hug, and I hold on tight. I can smell her LUSH perfume, same as always, and I close my eyes, wanting to capture this moment forever.

When she pulls back, we're both teary-eyed. "How's Jake?" I ask, swiping the back of my hand across my cheeks.

She links her arm through mine and leads me over to the buffet table. "Same. Crazy. He made me picket a pig farm last weekend. I had to take, like, twelve showers when we left. And then he complained about how much water I was wasting." She sighs, looks at me. "He's good."

We spend the rest of the night holed up in my room, a plate of snacks between us on the bed. She tells me about Denise Albert's nose job. About how Evelyn Membane got kicked out for smoking pot in the guys' bathroom after school.

"I mean, it was after school," Cassandra says, exasperated. "Why wouldn't you just go *home*?"

I want to tell her all about Rainer and Jordan, but it would take too long to fill her in on the details. I don't want it to be all about them. I want it to be all about *us*. And, actually, not talking about them feels good. Really good. It's just Cassandra and me in Portland now. Normal. When it gets to be eleven o'clock and the noise downstairs has quieted, Cassandra stretches and says she has to go home. "School night," she reminds me. "Some of us still have to climb the ranks before we are deemed stars."

She smiles. "Oh, I almost forgot." She opens her bag and pulls out the book. The final volume in the Locked trilogy. The one I sent. "Here." She holds it out and bounces it in the air, like, *take it*.

"I was starting to think you never got it," I say.

"Oh, I got it. I read it in one sitting."

"Well?"

"Well." She smiles, the corners of her mouth turning up into a mischievous grin.

"Are you going to tell me how it ends?" I cross my arms, raise my eyebrows. "That was my only copy, you know."

She frowns at me. "You mean to tell me you still have not read this book? Is there something wrong with you?"

I roll my eyes. It feels good to make fun of each other. It means we're back to being sure of each other. "I wanted you to tell me what happens," I say. "Just like last time."

"Paige," she says. "You know I love you. And I'd do anything for you."

"Yes, so."

"But." She places the book in my hands. "There are some things you have to find out for yourself." She pulls me into a hug then, the hardcover between us. "You're my best friend," she says, and there is something thick in her voice, something heavy.

"The best of the best," I say.

She pulls back, her hair sticking out every which way.

"Oh, hey," I say. "I have something for you, too."

I go to my nightstand, and take out an envelope with tickets in it. This one isn't my mom's, though. No reminders here. Just things to come. I take two out. "I'd love it if you guys came," I say. "I can get you airline tickets, too, if you'd like."

She looks down at the tickets in my hands. "We'll be there," she says. "I would not miss it for one single thing in the world."

She turns to go when I remember something. Something I've been meaning to ask her since I first landed on Maui.

"Cass," I say, stopping her. "When you first filled me in on Rainer, why did you never mention Britney?"

She smiles, her eyes crinkling around the corners in little lines of mischief. "My argument stands," she says. "There are some things you have to find out for yourself." With that, she leans over and plants a kiss on my cheek. "Later, Hollywood," she says, and disappears out the door.

"We'll see you in a few days," my mom says when they drop me off at the airport. She hugs me quickly, and when she lets go, my dad hands me my suitcase.

"Cassandra and Jake are coming, too," I say.

My mom smiles. "Fantastic. It will be a family affair."

I give my dad a hug and then head toward the gate. A

few people turn around and point. I leave my sunglasses on. It's a strange feeling. I keep wanting to make sure my shirt is on the right way, that there's no toilet paper stuck to the bottom of my shoe.

It's better when we're on the plane. I settle into my window seat and take out the final book. I open it and start reading. And I don't stop until we're in L.A.

A greeter meets me at the airport and leads me to a town car, and we head straight to the hotel. It's late. The air smells fresh, clean, expansive somehow. I know it's not possible—LAX is too far from the ocean—but it feels almost like sea air. But I barely register any of it. I'm still reading.

I check into the hotel with my nose still deep in the book. We're staying at the Beverly Wilshire, in the heart of Beverly Hills. I remember my agent telling me it was conveniently located and where all the press for the movie is going to take place. "That way you don't have to leave," she told me.

It's three AM by the time I close the book, and when I do, I'm shaking. I didn't see this coming. I've purposely been avoiding the Internet so that the ending wouldn't be spoiled. I probably wouldn't have believed this, anyway, though.

One thing is certain: August has made her choice.

CHAPTER 24

The next few days are press boot camp. My agent has hired me a media coach, Tawny Banks, who sweeps into my hotel suite like a hurricane. For four days all we do is go over how to speak into a microphone, how to answer this question, that question, what to do with my hair, how to talk about Wyatt, Rainer, Jordan. She doesn't even ask me what is going on with Rainer. She simply reiterates the sound bite I've already been given: "He's a great guy. Love working with him. *Blah blah blah.*"

Never open your mouth really wide, never yawn, never roll your eyes. If you don't understand a question, ask for it to be repeated. Never put down a coworker. Never speak negatively about anyone. Never congratulate yourself.

My head is spinning by the time the night of the premiere arrives.

I haven't been able to see Rainer or Jordan. Rainer has been holed up at his dad's. Apparently Greg wants to reserve all the buzz surrounding our reunion for the night of the opening and didn't want to risk anyone seeing Rainer and me together. We've spoken on the phone a few times but not about anything important. He's said he's excited, but that's all. We both know the decision that awaits us when we see each other. We don't have to bring it up.

Jordan is home in L.A., too, but I haven't spoken to him. Just knowing he's close makes me feel crazy. I want to call him, but I'm constantly surrounded by people. I couldn't get away even if I tried.

At six AM on the day of the premiere, there is a knock at my door. I open it, bleary-eyed, expecting to see Tawny's wiry, tense frame, but instead I'm met with round, familiar curves. Lillianna has arrived to do my hair and makeup. I'm so relieved to see her, I practically weep into her chest.

"Hey, hon," she says. "Remember me?"

She sits me in the chair, and when Tawny shows up, clipboard in hand, Lillianna somehow manages to shush her out of the room.

"It's just you and me this morning," she says. "So now tell me—what is up with those boys?"

By three o'clock, we're ready to head to TCL Chinese Theatre. I've already done one round of solo interviews, and they went pretty well. I managed not to spill my guts to anyone. So far, so good.

I'm wearing a black racer-back dress and tan heels with tiny orange buckles. My hair is blown out straight, and my makeup is all brown tones—neutral, but grown-up. I feel sleek and sophisticated. At least on the outside.

Tawny leads me out into the hall, down the corridor, and into an elevator. We take it to the first floor, and I follow her to the conference room.

My heart is beating a steady rhythm with my stilettos on the marble: *thump-thump, thump-thump*.

Acting is one thing, but having to answer all these questions in front of hundreds of people is petrifying. I think my face has turned green. I haven't been able to consume anything but an apple all day, and my stomach is simultaneously in knots and growling. Not a great combination, but at least now I know how Hollywood stars stay so damn thin. It's not diets. It's fear.

Rainer is standing by the double doors to a suite. He's wearing black pants and a crisp button-down, and his hair is shorter than the last time I saw him, trimmed expertly on the sides. He smiles when he sees me, his dimple winking.

"Hey, beautiful," he says. My pulse hammers. I can't tell if it's excitement at seeing him or terror at what I have to do, and for a moment I wonder if I'm making the right decision. I want to fall into Rainer's wide smile and welcoming arms.

I go over to him and give him a hug. He smells exactly like I remember, and I close my eyes against him. Warm. Safe. I take a deep breath. I will myself to focus on what I have to do.

Tawny clucks next to me.

"Rainer," he says, keeping one hand on my waist and extending the other to Tawny. "Do you think you could grab me a soda?"

Her forehead and mouth pinch up at exactly the same time, but she takes off down the hallway, leaving us more or less alone. He smiles down at me. "Alone at last," he says, but it's not exactly flirtatious. I think he might be as nervous as I am.

"Hey," I say. I disentangle us so we're facing each other.

"How are you?" he asks.

"Good," I say. "I think. How are you?"

Rainer smiles. "About the same. How was home?"

I nod. "Home was really nice, actually. My sister is getting married."

His face breaks into a wide, open grin. His dimples dance. "Yeah?" he says. "That's awesome."

"It is."

He looks at me for a beat. Neither one of us blinks, and all of a sudden the question is there, right between us. "I missed you," he says.

"I know," I say. I suck my bottom lip in. "I missed you, too." It's true, I did. I missed him so much. The way he makes me feel like this is all going to be okay. That as long as he's here I can do this. I can get through all of it.

He puts a finger under my chin and tilts my face up to his. His eyes search mine. They're bright, so hopeful they make my heart hurt. "Is this what you want?" he asks.

But I don't have time to answer because just as I'm about to, voices erupt through the door next to us. So loud it makes us both jump back.

"Don't you dare bring her into this," a voice bellows. It's Jordan.

"Keep it down. This is business."

"Bullshit," Jordan says.

Rainer and I look at each other. I can tell from the way his eyes dart to the door and then get wide that I'm right. The other person in that room is his father, Greg Devon.

"This doesn't concern you."

"She concerns me," Jordan says.

"Oh, I know that."

Who are they talking about? Britney? But then I hear it. We both do.

Greg: "Who Rainer dates is his business. I'd stay out of it this time."

I can see Rainer's fists clench up. He makes a move for the door, and I put my hand on his arm.

"Like you did? Like you *are*? Don't tell me you wouldn't be thrilled to have them holding hands on the cover of every magazine. You disgust me."

I hear Greg laugh. It makes the vertebrae of my spine feel like ice cubes. "Oh, we're back here, aren't we? You think I always have ulterior motives."

Jordan: "I know you do."

"And you don't? You took the part, Jordan. No one forced you to. You knew everything that happened with Britney, you hated me for it, but you took a job from me, anyway." There is silence. Then, "We all play the same game, Wilder."

There is some shuffling, an opening and closing of a drawer. I watch Rainer's face, a mixture of anger and confusion.

"So is that it? You just handed me this role to keep me quiet?"

"You're a good actor," Greg says. "You'd be wise to stop asking so many questions."

I can feel Rainer's body go limp, and in the next moment, the door opens. Greg comes strolling out, looking calm and collected. Until he sees Rainer. Instantly his face drops, like a diver over a cliff. "What are you doing here?" he demands. "You guys are supposed to be running questions."

Rainer inhales. "What did you mean about Britney," he says. It's not a question, though. Not even close.

Greg laughs. "What are you talking about?"

"She was telling the truth, wasn't she?" Rainer's voice is loud, angry. "She was right about you." Jordan comes into the doorway. I try to keep my eyes trained on Rainer. I can't look at Jordan, not now. I'm too afraid of what I'll do.

Greg's cheek quivers, and I see his eye twitch slightly. "Let's talk about this in private," he says.

I notice, out of the corner of my eye, a stray reporter. Rainer notices, too, but he doesn't flinch. He pushes on.

"No, Dad. I want to talk about it now. You told me she was crazy." His voice is coarse, dry. "I believed you. I believed everything you said to me, and it was all a lie."

I can feel Jordan's gaze on me, then on Rainer. Rainer looks at Jordan. "Say it," Rainer says to him. His eyes are wild. They look almost feral. "Say that my dad tried to sleep with Britney, my eighteen-year-old girlfriend."

Jordan nods slowly. "It's true," he says.

The reporter starts scribbling wildly. Greg's eyes are so on fire, I think they might combust.

I'm sure Rainer is going to lose it. That he's going to

start screaming at his father. But instead I feel him take my hand. "We have to go," he tells me. He starts pulling me forward, away, toward the conference room. I look back at Jordan.

Our eyes lock, for just a moment, but it's enough. Enough for me to see that whatever is going on inside me is going on inside him, too. That we're both there, right where the other one is. I think about Wyatt's warning over those pictures with Rainer. Jordan's words: "Have them holding hands on the cover of every magazine." Then Sandy appears, and we're all being shuffled in the same direction, toward the press junket, toward all the waiting journalists ready to hear our answers. Rainer is still holding on tightly to my hand when the doors open, and Tawny comes by and yanks us apart right before we enter the room. "Don't do that unless you mean it," she cautions.

We're greeted by an ocean of faces, stretching all the way back to the doors leading to the lobby, like the horizon.

We take our seats. Rainer on one side of me, and Jordan on the other. Too close—my hands are shaking.

The questions start. About the movie and working with Wyatt.

Jordan answers that Wyatt's the best in the business, and we're all proud of this movie because he was at the helm.

Then, finally, someone asks it. The question we've all

been waiting for. It's for me, and I'm glad. I want to get it over with.

"There have been a lot of rumors about a possible romance between you and Rainer. Some are even saying he's been after you since you got to Hawaii." Laughter throughout the room. My insides feel numb. "Can you confirm whether you're together?"

I take a deep breath, ready to answer, to finally say what is in my heart, but my gaze slips and lands on Rainer. His eyes are wide, hopeful. He's looking at me the way Annabelle does when she wakes up. Like his whole survival, his whole existence, is dependent on what I do next.

And then I think about it again. Jordan's words the day he saved my life on the beach: "Some things are sacred." The protection of love is sacred, but something else is sacred, too.

Our word. Rainer told me that day on the cliffs in Paia that whatever was waiting, whatever was going to come our way, he'd stand by me. He meant it. It didn't have anything to do with Greg Devon. It was just between us, me and him. And now, it's my turn.

I know what I have to do. Rainer needs me now, and I want to be there for him. To be *with* him. His world has just been shattered. His dad isn't who he thought he was. This journalist will write a story; the whole truth will come out. His family's reputation will be ruined. I know what that feels like. I remember those years with my sister, how people whispered about us. How they would point at the grocery store, the post office. I don't know what I would have done without Jake, how I would have coped if he hadn't put both his hands on my cheeks that night and kissed me. If he hadn't said he'd be there.

But knowing it's right doesn't make it easier. It's a choice. And the second you make one, you let go of the other.

I touch my hand to the small metal charm around my neck. I take a deep breath. It's easier than I think, to get out those three words. "Yes, it's true."

Then they start—a blinding, brilliant flash—so bright that for a second I think maybe the stars have fallen out of the sky straight through the ceiling. They keep going as Rainer pulls me close to him and then kisses me, right there in front of hundreds of journalists, cameras, television screens—uniting us for good. But I don't feel anything. Not his lips on mine. Not his hands at my waist. Nothing. When he pulls back, he looks at me. "Thank you," he mouths. Someone asks another question, and Rainer answers— explaining how we fell for each other on the set. I sit back in my chair, a smile plastered to my face like Tawny taught me.

I can feel him next to me. Jordan. But when I look at him, he doesn't look sad or angry. His eyes are lit up, like the flashbulbs that are pointed toward us. And all of a sudden, I understand why. I've been wrong. About everything. Because the thing I didn't understand about love—the biggest thing, the thing that makes it worthy of books and movies—is that epic, epic love is not about having someone. It's about being willing to give them up. It's sacrifice. It's my mom's theater tickets stuffed down at the bottom of her jewelry box. It's Noah and August. It's my sister and Annabelle. It's Jordan and his mom, the truth he reserves to protect her. And see, that's the thing I didn't understand. The thing no one tells you. That just because you find love doesn't mean it's yours to keep. Love never belongs to you. It belongs to the universe. To the same wind that blows the surfers across the waves and the current that carries you back to shore. You can't hold on to it because it's bigger than anything you could possibly grasp with your own bare hands. It's bigger than me or Rainer or Jordan. It's bigger than everything.

And then the announcement comes: The studio wants to green-light the other two movies. They got results back from test screenings and every audience loved *Locked*. They're thrilled with the film; they want to make two more with the same cast.

Rainer says he's sure we all have to talk to our agents, but that we all work well together and that he knows he speaks for all of us when he says we'd love to play out our roles. "They're a part of us now," he says.

And that feud between him and Jordan Wilder?

"I was wrong," Rainer says, staring straight ahead. "Jordan has been nothing but a good friend and a stand-up guy. I'd be honored to continue working with him."

Then we're separately ushered into waiting town cars. Tawny is sitting beside me, prattling on about what good press this relationship with Rainer is, how smart I was to save the announcement for the first official press junket. Why didn't I tell her! I think about how many more of these we have. How many more times he's going to kiss me onstage, with Jordan watching. How many more questions people are going to ask us about how we fell in love. It feels endless, almost too much to bear.

And then we are there. At the premiere. The three of us arrive at the same time, and when we step onto the carpet, the crowds go crazy. Screaming and chanting. They have signs and pictures and posters. All with our faces on them. Our names.

Just before we step up to take our first picture, I feel Jordan's pinkie loop through mine. I curl my finger around his, and we stay that way for a moment that feels impossibly long and tragically short all at once, like the sunrise, the beginning of one thing and the end of another. Then I turn to Rainer, to the crowds, and let myself be pulled into the sea of light, his hand at my waist.

I don't look back.

FIND OUT WHERE IT ALL BEGAN –

LOCKED

BY PARKER WHITTER

IS AVAILABLE AS AN E-NOVELLA

FIND OUT MORE AT
WWW.MYKINDABOOK.COM/FAMOUSINLOVE

ACKNOWLEDGMENTS

A giant thanks...

To Farrin Jacobs, my insanely talented, brilliant editor. I will always be so unbelievably lucky (and beyond grateful) that you chose me. Thank you for challenging me, for being way smarter than I am, and for never giving me a compliment I don't deserve. I promise to continue to do my best to make you proud.

To my fierce agent, Mollie Glick, who patiently listened to my one-track ramblings for well over two years when the only thing I could ask was "Is it time yet?" Thank you for agreeing to take this shot. And for being my partner, every single day, in all these books.

To Dan Farah, my manager, whose eyes lit up the moment I told him this was on deck. Thank you for loving this world, and fighting for it in all its various forms and incarnations.

To Leila Sales, who listened to the Lilith Fair Pandora station for a solid year while I wrote this—I don't want to wait. I'm so glad we don't have to anymore.

To my wonderful UK editor, Rachel Petty, for her incredible enthusiasm and vision.

To Pam Garfinkel, for her great, thoughtful notes, and to Liz Casal, for the world's best YA cover.

To Jess Regel, my foreign agent, for sending (and supporting) Paige, Rainer, and Jordan out in the great, big world.

To Wendy Dopkin, copy editor extraordinaire, who made me think very, very hard about using the word *stet* (and who knew far more about my hometown of Maui than I did).

To my girls, who don't always understand the ins and outs of what I do, but who are proud beyond measure even still. You fill all my worlds, fictional and otherwise, with joy.

To Katie Hanson, for saying, "Hey, you should write that book."

To Lexa Hillyer, for continuing to challenge me with the greatest of kindness.

To Brad, Yfat, Guy, India, and Foxy Gendell, for their boundless support and love.

To Carina MacKenzie, for telling me I wasn't too far off base, and for the vampires, always.

To everyone on Twitter, for obsessing as much as I do over behind-the-scenes young Hollywood.

To my parents, who continue to remind me that joy alone, apart from accomplishment or prize, has the greatest value.

And finally, to Katie and Josh—for falling in love all those years ago, and first making me wonder.